D0818853

CASSIE EDWARDS

THE *SAVAGE* SERIES

Winner of the *Romantic Times* Lifetime Achievement Award for Best Indian Series!

"Cassie Edwards writes action-packed, sexy reads! Romance fans will be more than satisfied!"
—*Romantic Times*

MIDNIGHT RENDEZVOUS

He held her close. His lips lowered to hers.

Mary Beth did not turn away from him this time. Their lips met in a sweet, tremulous kiss.

Mary Beth regretted now having ever denied herself the pleasure that came with his kiss and the warm sweetness of his arms. In his kiss and embrace, everything else disappeared from her mind!

There was only the two of them, their love breaking through all the barriers that had kept them apart.

When they stepped away from each other, Brave Wolf gently touched her cheek. "My body aches for more than a kiss," he said huskily.

"Mine too," Mary Beth said in a voice that did not sound like her own. "Tonight, Brave Wolf. After the celebration . . . tonight . . . ?"

He swept her into his arms again and kissed her. Their bodies strained hungrily together.

"Ah, yes, tonight . . ." he whispered against her parted lips.

Other books by Cassie Edwards:

TOUCH THE WILD WIND
ROSES AFTER RAIN
WHEN PASSION CALLS
EDEN'S PROMISE
ISLAND RAPTURE
SECRETS OF MY HEART

The *Savage* Series:

SAVAGE DESTINY
SAVAGE LOVE
SAVAGE MOON
SAVAGE HONOR
SAVAGE THUNDER
SAVAGE DEVOTION
SAVAGE GRACE
SAVAGE FIRES
SAVAGE JOY
SAVAGE WONDER
SAVAGE HEAT
SAVAGE DANCE
SAVAGE TEARS
SAVAGE LONGINGS
SAVAGE DREAM
SAVAGE BLISS
SAVAGE WHISPERS
SAVAGE SHADOWS
SAVAGE SPLENDOR
SAVAGE EDEN
SAVAGE SURRENDER
SAVAGE PASSIONS
SAVAGE SECRETS
SAVAGE PRIDE
SAVAGE SPIRIT
SAVAGE EMBERS
SAVAGE ILLUSION
SAVAGE SUNRISE
SAVAGE MISTS
SAVAGE PROMISE
SAVAGE PERSUASION

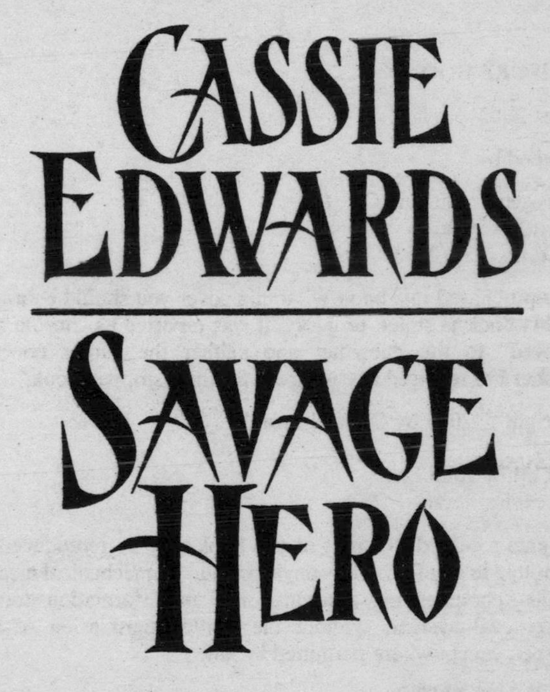

LEISURE BOOKS  NEW YORK CITY

A LEISURE BOOK®

August 2003

Published by

Dorchester Publishing Co., Inc.
276 Fifth Avenue
New York, NY 10001

Cover art by John Ennis.
www.ennisart.com

ISBN 0-8439-5052-8

Printed in the United States of America.

Visit us on the web at www.dorchesterpub.com.

In appreciation and admiration, I dedicate Savage Hero *to two special people at Dorchester Publishing:*

My editor, Alicia Condon, who has been there for me for so many years with her guidance and her support of my Savage *series. It means so much to me.*

And also to George Sosson, the President and Publisher of Dorchester, whose heart is in all that he does for Dorchester and its authors.

SAVAGE
HERO

The brave sits alert atop his spirited steed,
Both being the very best of their breed.
He sits perfectly silent, no sound at all,
Fearless, prowess, sitting so flawless and tall.
A slight breeze approaches, barely moving his braid.
Cautiously alert, his hand moves to his blade.
Instantly ready, an arrow awaits in his bow;
If accurate, there's little hope for a foe.
His horse remains quiet, trained as a colt.
No matter the danger, he will not bolt.
Suddenly Brave Wolf hears a noise to his right,
So thankful the day has turned into night.
He was taught to use his senses,
Taught many a skill, to use any defenses.
Thanks to his teaching, he knows who is there.
Why would she come, how could she dare?
Out of the shadows, she steps into sight,
Skin white as snow, hair just as bright.
She had to come, to keep her word;
She escaped her prison like a caged bird.
She traveled all day, until night finally came.
She would have searched forever, feeling no shame.
God led her there, so she would know
Brave Wolf was there, her full-blooded Crow.
He smiles at her, calling out "My Sunshine."
She runs to him, her smile so sweet.
He gently lifts her; she grabs without haste.
He loves feeling her arms encircling his waist.
So very thankful, for here come the rains,
Erasing their tracks, from across the plains.

Soon on the horizon, they're only a dot,
Heading for home at a very fast trot.
Brave Wolf's woman is going home at last,
Dreaming of a future, and forgetting the past.
Living as a Crow is all she's desired,
With Brave Wolf's people, respected and admired.
As they ride, the sun starts to awaken,
Their lives entwined, their futures for the taking.
A doe crosses her path with her fawn,
Watching the lovers disappear along with the dawn.
A song is on the breeze, whispering of their love.
Hear it whispering, "Brave Wolf loves his Sunshine!"

—Darcie L. Wright
Cassie Edwards Fan Club member

Chapter One

> She spoke and loosened from her
> bosom the embroidered girdle of
> many colors into which her
> allurement was fashioned.
> —Homer, *The Iliad*

June 1876

The Battle of the Little Big Horn was now over.

The battlefield was eerily quiet. Bodies lay everywhere.

General George Armstrong Custer lay amid those who had battled alongside him . . . red-skinned and white alike.

Among them lay Night Horse, one of Custer's head scouts. He was pretending to be dead as the victors moved through the bloody field, taking valuables from some whites, scalping others.

Night Horse, who had chosen the road of the white man instead of traveling that of his Crow brothers, scarcely breathed as his people prepared many travois upon which to carry their fallen warriors back to their families for mourning and burial rites.

Night Horse hoped no one would realize that he was still alive. His life would be gone in an instant if he was spotted, for he was hated now by both the red man and the white eyes. The Crow, who resented his companionship with the white pony soldiers, would relish the pleasure of seeing him dead.

The white pony soldiers might also wish to see him dead. They might feel that Night Horse had betrayed the cavalry and was somehow responsible for the deadly attack.

It would be especially bad for Night Horse now, for among the dead was the revered leader General George Armstrong Custer who was called Yellow Hair by some red men and Long Hair by others.

To the white eyes, Yellow Hair was a hero. To the Indians, he was a cowardly murderer who killed not only warriors, but also their innocent women and children.

With someone else's blood spattered all over his buckskin clothes, yet no mortal wounds on himself, Night Horse breathlessly waited for that moment when he could leave this place of death.

And then finally he heard the horses' hoofbeats

as they were guided from the battlefield, dragging behind them the travois piled with fallen warriors.

Night Horse still lay quiet on his belly until the hoofbeats faded away and he knew that it was finally safe to rise. Slowly he crept up from the ground. He flinched with alarm and cowered as a brown and white spotted eagle descended from the sky, talons out, its hooked beak open, then swept as quickly away.

Night Horse stood and stared at the death all around him. He had known to expect the worst, but nothing could have prepared him for what he was seeing, or just how horrifying it would be to see the outcome of the battle.

Over and over again he vomited until nothing was left inside him.

Wiping his mouth with the sleeve of his shirt, dashing away the tears spilling from his eyes, Night Horse at first stumbled along the bloody ground, wincing when he had to step over one body and then another.

Then he broke into a mad run.

Even when he reached the fresh green grass waving gently in the breeze, he ran. He continued until his legs would hardly carry him any farther, until he found himself safely hidden in a blue-black pine forest of spruce, where sunlight scarcely penetrated the dark tangle of interwoven branches and overgrown needles.

Breathing harshly, his side aching, Night Horse fell to his knees.

He held his face in his hands and cried again.

He had cheated death today, but he now wondered if he was really so fortunate to still be breathing.

He was now a man without a people. As such, was he not, in a sense, dead, himself?

He had lost the right to live among people, either white or Crow. He would now live the life of a lost man who belonged nowhere, a man whose pride was gone.

In his heart he had longed to gain celebrity as a Custer scout, yet that would never be. He was now alone—totally, totally alone.

He could never return to his home, to his mother, or his brother, because when he left to ally himself with Custer, he was told by his Crow people never to return.

Even then, he had been dead to them.

Dispirited, filled with remorse and a deep, gnawing regret and shame, Night Horse rose to his feet and walked onward, his steps listless, his heart heavy.

Feeling empty inside, plagued by recurring visions of the battlefield, he walked awhile, and then he made himself remember that he had been a proud warrior before he had become a scout for the white eyes. His *ahte*, his father, had instilled within him much courage.

He reached deep inside himself now for what remained of that courage.

He had been taught the art of survival, as well, by his *ahte*, and Night Horse vowed he would survive even this . . . the worst day of his life.

He would make a new life for himself, even if he must live it alone.

The first thing he must do was steal a horse, and then find a place where he could be hidden from any who might realize he had not died and come looking for him.

He smiled as he thought of the perfect place where he could be safe, where he could make a world for himself as he learned to live alone.

It was a place that he and his brother Brave Wolf had found when he was a young brave trying to pretend he was a great, valiant warrior.

Yes, Night Horse would go there. He was a survivor, a man who had just cheated death.

Now he must find a way to tolerate his empty life, and he would, for this place where he would make his new life was a place of beauty where he would live among animals, and where eagles made their nests and taught their children how to soar among the clouds.

But even those things, which had always before filled his heart with joy, would not keep him from remembering, over and over again, what he had experienced today.

It was *sheetsha-sheetsha,* bad, bad!

Chapter Two

The American Indian once
grew as naturally as the wild
sunflowers; he belongs just
as the buffalo belonged.
—Luther Standing Bear,
Oglala Sioux Chief

Three months later—Montana

The fire burned soft and low in the tepee. Shadows thrown by the flames leapt on the inside buffalo-hide walls of the lodge, where there were no painted designs, for this was the home of an elderly widow.

The tepee that she had shared with her chieftain husband had been taken down, hide by hide, pole by pole, and removed from the village, for it was not good to live in a tepee where someone had died . . . not even a powerful chief.

Only the exploits and victories of a husband were painted on the inside walls of a lodge, a woman's victories did not compare with a man's since she mainly bore the children and cared for the family.

Although women considered their accomplishments just as important, still it was only the man's doings that were painted inside their lodges.

Pure Heart, aging and ill, sat with her son of twenty-five winters, Chief Brave Wolf. They were of the Whistling Water Clan of the Crow tribe. Brave Wolf had been given the title of chief upon the death of his beloved chieftain father.

Her moon-white hair was braided and coiled atop her head, her cheeks and eyes sunken by age, Pure Heart sat with a blanket wrapped warmly around her frail shoulders. It was the time of the Moon of the Falling Leaves, when the days became cool and the nights cold.

"*Micinksi,* my son, you must do this one thing for me before I die," Pure Heart said as she gazed over the low flames of the fire at Brave Wolf.

In him she saw a replica of her late husband. His face was sculpted and handsome, and his bare, copper shoulders were as muscular as his father's had once been. He wore only a breechcloth and moccasins.

In his midnight-black eyes she saw wisdom, much of which he had learned from his father.

There was also warmth and caring in his gaze as he looked back at her.

She also saw how her words had brought trouble into those eyes.

She had two sons. She realized that one was good, and one bad.

One had chosen the good road of life, the other wandered far from it.

It was for the son who had gone astray that she was so concerned today, a son whom she had not seen for too many moons.

"*Ina*, my mother, you know that I always try to do all that you ask of me, but *this*?" Brave Wolf responded, his voice drawn.

He lifted a piece of wood and placed it with the other burning logs in the fire pit, watching as the flames caught hold.

"*Micinksi*, I understand your hesitation, but remember that we are not talking about just any warrior who chose to ally himself with whites," Pure Heart said, her voice breaking. "Son, this is your brother. This is Night Horse, the brother who was born only one winter after you took your own first breaths of life. Think of the good times you had with your brother, how you each defended the other when anyone offered too many challenges for only one young brave to deal with. Brave Wolf, it was you who protected your brother that time when you were hunting and a bear threatened Night Horse. You even now carry that bear's claw in your medicine bundle. Do you not realize the meaning of that? It is a reminder, always, of a brother who loved a brother."

"I did love him with all my heart, *Ina,* but he went away from us and chose to be someone I no longer know," Brave Wolf said thickly.

In frustration, he wove his powerful fingers through his long black hair, which hung loose and flowing to his waist.

He brushed a strand back from his face, then sighed heavily and nodded. "But, *hecitu-yelo,* yes, I do understand your enduring love for your youngest. I also see that he has brought sadness into eyes that were at one time always filled with sunshine and laughter."

He leaned forward, his eyes now peering intently into hers. "*Ina,* he does not deserve such love and devotion," he said tightly. "He deserves no loyalty from me."

"But, Brave Wolf, he is still my son, just as you are my son," she said, then swallowed back a sob. "He . . . is . . . your brother. He is and he always will be. Brothers, no matter what shame one might have brought into a family, are . . . still . . . brothers."

Brave Wolf sighed heavily, lowered his eyes, then rose to his feet and walked around the fire to sit down beside his mother.

He drew her into his arms. "Does this truly mean so much to you?" he asked, as she clung to him and he slowly caressed her back through the soft blanket. "Is it this important to you?"

"I would not ask it of you if it were not," she

said, this time unable to hold back the tears. She sobbed and clung, then inched away from Brave Wolf so that she could again peer deeply into his midnight-dark eyes. "As long as Night Horse holds breath within his lungs, he is my son and he is your brother. How can you not want to know whether he is alive or dead? He was not found among the dead on the battlefield where yellow-haired Custer died."

She swallowed hard, then said, "As far as we know, Night Horse did not die," she said softly. She reached a hand to Brave Wolf's cheek. "When we received word of this battle, and that it was over, a battle where none of our own Whistling Water Clan fought, I sent you to look for Night Horse. You did not find him among the dead, and we both know that he was one of Yellow Hair's favored scouts and would have gone into battle with him. He was so enthralled by the evil white leader, he would have died alongside Yellow Hair."

"Night Horse is probably alive and well and planning to join another group of white pony soldiers riding against his own people," Brave Wolf said, his voice a low growl. "When he chose the life of a scout, he ceased to be my brother."

"But by blood, he is and he always will be," Pure Heart said, lowering her hand away from his face. She wiped tears from her eyes with hands so bony, Brave Wolf shivered and knew that she was surely not long for this earth.

He made himself look away from her hands.

Such reminders of his mother's condition caused great pain inside his heart.

"You know that when Night Horse left our village to ally himself with the cavalry, I did not ever want to see him again, whether or not he was my brother by blood," he said.

He gazed deep into his mother's eyes and took her hands in his. "Yet still I went to claim his body for your sake, for proper burial. I did not find him anywhere among the dead on the battlefield," he said. "I cannot help concluding that Night Horse did not die, but instead had sneaked away like a coward, who must now be hiding. That was many sleeps ago, Mother. If he wanted to be with his people again, with *you*, he would have found his way home by now."

"He might be terribly injured and . . . and . . . slowly dying," Pure Heart said, her voice catching. Tears streamed from her old and faded eyes. "Does it truly matter who he was with when it happened? The fact that he might be dying should be all that matters. He should be with family for his last moments on this earth."

"*Ina*, what he did with his life goes against everything *Ahte* ever taught his two sons," Brave Wolf replied. "You know that I walk in my father's shadow and, like him, I am known as a peace chief who deals wisely with the United States Government. I have tried to win every advantage for our people, whereas my brother joined the whites and worked against our people for what he could gain personally. My father, your chieftain husband, represented our tribe at the Fort Laramie Treaty of 1868. What would he have thought of a son who plotted and planned with whites to try to wipe from the face of the earth red men and women . . . even innocent children."

He framed her face between his hands. "Remembering this, can you still want to see and hold your youngest son in your arms again?" he asked, searching her eyes. "*Ina,* he should be as dead in your heart as he is in mine."

"I am so proud of everything that my husband did, and of what you are doing for our people," Pure Heart said softly. "So is your father proud as he gazes down at you from the stars in the sky where he now makes his home."

She lowered her eyes, then again looked into Brave Wolf's. "Although I am not as proud of Night Horse as I am of you, nothing can take away the fact that I gave birth to him and that I shall love him, no matter what he has done, until the last breath leaves his lungs . . . or mine," she murmured. "Knowing this, will you not do as I ask? Will you not at least go and search for him one more time? If you do, and you cannot find him, then I shall never ask such a thing of you again. I shall know that you at least made an attempt to bring him home to me so that I can make some sort of peace with him."

"You know that the search could carry me across a vast area, and even then I might not find him," Brave Wolf said. "The search will take me from our people for many sunrises and sunsets. Knowing that, and also knowing that it is my place to stay with our people, to keep ugliness from our village, you still wish for me to go? If I choose others to go on the search, would that satisfy you?"

"I trust our warriors when a request is made of them that does not go against everything they believe in, but now? When I ask something they will frown upon . . . to search for someone who has betrayed the Crow . . . I cannot wholly trust that they would bring him home alive to me."

Brave Wolf was disturbed to hear that his mother did not fully trust those who were under Brave Wolf's command, but he could not dispute her words.

He was beginning to see that he had no choice but to do this for his mother. He saw how distraught she was, and had been since she had become aware of Night Horse's disappearance. He feared her anxiety might hurry along her death. He would do anything to keep her with him longer on this earth.

If he had to come face to face with Night Horse again, so be it.

"Yes, Mother, I hear you well and I feel your pain when you speak of your youngest son, so I will do as you ask of me," Brave Wolf said tightly. "If I find Night Horse, I will bring him home to you. If I do not find my brother, you must realize that it is time to put aside your grieving and work at becoming stronger."

Pure Heart smiled through her tears. She placed a gentle hand on Brave Wolf's cheek. "You just called Night Horse your brother," she murmured. "That must mean that inside your heart, you do still see him as such."

"Although I do not wish to claim him as blood kin, he is my brother, for did we not come from the same womb and seed?" Brave Wolf said, then drew her gently into his arms. "Mother, I love you so much. Please rest while I am gone. I shall search until I feel it is time to return home. You must accept Night Horse's fate then. Will you?"

"Yes, I will openly accept it, but inside my heart, if Night Horse is not with you, I will be crying," Pure Heart murmured. "Go now, son. Prepare those warriors who will ride with you, and those who will remain home to provide protection to those who need it in your absence. I will pray for your return, as well as for your brother's and those who ride with you."

He hugged her tenderly, kissed her softly on the cheek, then left her lodge.

Reluctantly he brought his warriors into the council house and told them his plan, that they would search for Night Horse, and if they found him, would bring him home.

Hardly any of his warriors wanted to accompany Brave Wolf on this particular mission, even if it was their chief asking them, and even if it was his mother who needed this son at her side during her illness.

As they saw it, Night Horse was no longer one of them. He was a disgrace, someone who deserved not even one more thought.

Brave Wolf had said that he understood their feelings, for they matched his own, but it was a mother's plea that had reached inside his heart.

After he had asked them to think of her, his warriors finally agreed to go with him.

Not long before, Brave Wolf had captured a prized dark sorrel from those he had seen picketed close to an enemy camp. He rode that horse now through Crow country, his warriors dutifully accompanying him.

They carried a varied assortment of weapons, some even carrying rifles. Some time ago, his people had believed that those whose skin was white were people of magic. When they had arrived in this land, they had carried "firesticks" that barked like thunder. At first, the Crow had truly thought the "firesticks" made lightning, capable of killing them from afar.

But the Crow no longer feared this fiery weapon. Sun Father watched over them and Mother Earth guided them as the warriors rode proudly across lush meadows and wooded hills that abounded with game.

The Crow saw their country as a gift to them from the First Maker, who created the world. Their land had snowy mountains and sunny plains, different climates and good things for every season.

When the summer heat scorched the prairies, the Crow could draw up under the mountains where the air was sweet and cool, the grass fresh, and where the bright streams tumbled out of the snow banks.

There with his powerful bow made of mountain-sheep horn and covered with the skin of a rattle-snake, Brave Wolf had proudly hunted the elk, the deer, and the antelope.

There one could always see plenty of white bears and mountain sheep.

There, a warrior could find many places to hide. But Brave Wolf knew of one special place. It was where he was leading his men.

He was almost certain that his brother would be hiding there.

Chapter Three

Dull sublunary lovers' love
(whose soul is sense) cannot admit
absence, because it doth remove
those things which elemented it.
—John Donne

A procession of wagons, accompanied by a contingent of cavalry, rolled through tall, waving grass and sage meadows. Soldiers rode at the front, the sides, and at the rear, their eyes constantly sweeping the land as they watched for Indians.

Mary Beth Wilson, twenty-three, and her son David, five, rode in one of the wagons. As she held the reins, Mary Beth's long auburn hair blew back from her oval face in the gentle breeze. The bonnet she had worn only moments ago was now in the back of the wagon. Since the air was so sweet and warm on this mid-September day, she wanted to revel in it.

She wore a pretty lace-trimmed cotton dress, the design of flowers against a backdrop of white almost as delicate as the woman who wore it. Mary Beth was tiny, yet she was strong inside and out. She had learned strength as a child, living on a farm in Kentucky where she worked alongside her parents raising crops that kept them fed throughout the long winter months.

She worked even harder now at her own farm, since her husband was no longer there to see to the chores. She had not hired helping hands because she saw that as a waste of money. She loved the outdoors enough to do everything herself.

And her garden was not all that big. It was only large enough to keep her and David in food.

Her son was old enough now to help till the beans and to plant rows of corn, and then harvest everything alongside his mother.

But that garden and her home were far removed from her now. She was in a distant land, her fingers aching from holding the reins so tightly in her fear of the unknown.

She had not wanted to be the last wagon of the train that was carrying the wives and children of the men who had died in the Battle of the Little Big Horn. They were traveling to a different fort, a safer one farther from hostile activity.

No one had imagined that the Indians had such strength and determination, or that there were so many who were willing to put their lives at stake by fighting the cavalry. Mary Beth had put her faith in General Custer, who had been so victorious in his battles with the Indians.

But she had been proved wrong. They all had been.

Custer had died alongside his men that day beneath the bright sun when Indians not only outnumbered the white pony soldiers, but also outwitted them.

Yes, it had been three months since the battle, and Mary Beth had been living a life of dread at Fort Kitt where her husband had been stationed.

Since the massacre on that damnable battlefield, the widows and children had stayed at Fort Kitt while they waited for the colonel in command there to say that he thought it was safe enough to travel to another fort. From that point, the widows could continue onward, returning to their homes far from Montana and its dangers.

Tears fell from Mary Beth's violet eyes as she fought off the remembrance of the moment when word had reached her that her husband, Major Lloyd Wilson, had died alongside Custer.

She and her son had only been at the fort for one day before he died.

The reason Mary Beth had traveled west made her heart ache even more. She had come from her home in Kentucky to tell Lloyd that she wanted a divorce. She had felt that she could not import such news by way of an impersonal letter or wire.

Her reason for wanting the divorce was not because she had found another man. It was just that she had never truly loved Lloyd. She had married him because she was lonely after her parents died at the hands of highway robbers, and because she had known him since childhood.

She had been married to him for six years, but no matter how hard she had tried to love Lloyd the way a woman should love a man, she just never got those special feelings that she had heard women speak of.

She had cared for Lloyd, but only in a sisterly, perhaps even motherly, way.

While he had been away from her and his son, she had had more time to think about things and had finally concluded that it was time to make a break. By doing so, Lloyd could eventually find true love, as could she.

But now?

All that Mary Beth felt was guilt.

She had told Lloyd her decision just before he'd left to fight alongside Custer in the battle that would claim not only Custer's life, but also Lloyd's.

She could not get past the feeling that she had sent her husband to his death. Surely he had been too distracted by her revelation to fight or even protect himself.

She was tormented by the knowledge that Lloyd had not been part of General Custer's usual troops. Because of Custer's plans to hurry along his campaign against the Indians, he had needed additional soldiers. He had gone to Fort Kitt and asked for volunteers.

Because Lloyd had heard so much about Custer's illustrious reputation as a leader, he had deemed it an honor to be a part of any battle that would be led by the general. He had been the very first man at Fort Kitt to step forth and sign up with General Custer.

That decision had made her husband a marked man even before she gave him her news about the divorce . . . news that she now knew had torn his world apart.

Mary Beth and her son David had attended Lloyd's funeral three months ago. Although she hated leaving his grave behind, knowing that she would never see it again, she could hardly wait to reach the fort that stood on the banks of the Missouri River. From there she would travel by riverboat to her farm in Kentucky.

She would be so glad to be away from this place where death might be lurking around every bend or behind every tree.

Ah, fate. Who could ever know what fate had in store?

Home.

Oh, Lord, she could hardly wait to get back home to her own little world!

She wished that she had never left Kentucky. Now she understood what the word "loneliness" truly meant, for she had never felt so empty or so alone.

Knowing that she would never hear Lloyd's laughter again, or be able to look into his beautiful blue eyes, filled her with a despair she had never thought possible.

"Lloyd. . . . Lloyd . . ." she whispered as hot tears rolled across her lips.

"Mama, what did you just say?" David asked, drawing Mary Beth's eyes quickly to him. "Mama, you have tears in your eyes again. Is it because of Papa? Is it?"

She almost choked on a sob when she turned to look at her son. He had Lloyd's blue eyes, the same golden hair, the same long, straight nose.

And she could already see that David's shoulders were going to be as wide and powerful as his father's.

Yes, her David was Lloyd all over again, and at least in him, she would have her husband with her forever.

She reached over and tousled David's thick, golden hair. "Yes, it's because of your daddy," she murmured. "His death is too fresh in my heart for me not to cry occasionally at the thought of him."

"I miss him too," David said, wiping tears from his own eyes. "Why did it have to happen, Mama? Why do Indians hate us so much?"

"I've thought about that, David, and I think I can see why they would," Mary Beth said, sighing.

She looked away from him and swept her eyes over the vastness of the land, on to the mountains, and then closer, to the deer that could be seen browsing in the brush.

It was a lovely land. The grass was green and thick, fed by the bright streams that came tumbling out of the snow banks of the mountains. There were lush meadows and plentiful game.

It was a paradise, a paradise that the red men saw as being spoiled by white people.

"Why would Indians want to kill Papa?" David asked, wiping more tears from his eyes.

"They see all white people as takers of their land, interfering in their lives," Mary Beth said.

She found it strange to be defending the very people who were responsible for her Lloyd lying in a grave.

Yet she had heard about so many atrocities against the Indians.

She supposed that even Lloyd had participated in such horrendous action against the Indians, because he was a man who followed orders.

"But the Indians are murderers, Mama," David said stiffly. "They murdered all . . . all . . . of the men who fought with Papa and General Custer."

"It was a battle and everyone fought for survival, both red-skinned and white, David," Mary Beth said, her voice breaking. "It just happened that during that battle, the red man was the strongest."

"But I thought General Custer was supposed to be the best soldier ever," David said, gazing intently at his mother. "Papa, too. He was a good soldier."

"Even good soldiers die, David," Mary Beth murmured.

She looked quickly past David when she caught a movement along the ridge of a hill. But it was gone as quickly as it had come.

"Mama, what are you looking at?" David asked when he saw her peering past him.

He turned and flinched when he, too, saw what looked like an Indian that suddenly appeared on the ridge, and then was gone again.

"Are we going to die today, Mama?" David asked, again gazing at his mother. "Are those Indians going to come and kill us like they killed Papa and General Custer?"

Mary Beth reached over and gently touched David's cheek. "No, they're not," she said. She tried to sound convincing enough that David would believe her. "That's why there are so many soldiers with us. They won't allow anything to happen."

"But you saw him too, Mama," David said. "You saw the Indian. I know you did. I saw fear in your eyes."

"Yes, David, from time to time I've seen Indians appearing along the ridges, but they disappear as quickly as they appear," Mary Beth said softly. "I guess they are playing some sort of game."

"What sort?" David asked, raising a golden eyebrow.

Mary Beth returned her hand to the reins and again clung tightly to them. "Cat and mouse," she said, catching a glimpse of three Indians on the same ridge.

"Cat and mouse?" David asked.

"They only want to frighten us, that's all," Mary Beth said, hoping it was true. She had seen the soldiers repositioning themselves, bringing themselves more tightly together in one group alongside the wagon train.

"I wish we were at Fort Henry already. I wish we

had already left it and were at the other fort where we will board that boat that's going to take us home," David said. "I wish we were already on the boat." He swallowed back a sob. "I wish we were home, Mama!"

"Me too, son. But we're not, so work on your whittling awhile, David," Mary Beth encouraged.

She, too, wished that they had reached the Missouri. The sight of the river would give her some confidence they might return to Kentucky alive.

"Get your mind on something besides Indians. You've got a pretty horse started on that big chunk of wood that Colonel Jamieson gave to you."

"Papa would like it," David said. He reached behind himself for the chunk of wood that was already taking the shape of the head of a horse.

"Yes, Papa would like it," Mary Beth said.

She glanced again at the ridge.

This time she felt faint. There was not one, two, or three Indians, but a whole mass of them.

From this vantage point she could guess there might be a hundred warriors moving along the ridge, their eyes following the progress of the wagon train.

Suddenly a bugle blew and soldiers began to shout, ordering everyone to drive their wagons into a wide, protective circle.

Everything became a frenzy of horses and wagons and screaming women and children as the soldiers leapt from their horses and positioned themselves for firing just as the war whoops rang out and the sound of horses' hooves upon the land came to Mary Beth's ears like huge claps of thunder and the Indians came in a mad rush toward the wagon train.

Terrified, her heart thumping wildly in her chest, Mary Beth struggled to get her horse and wagon into the circle.

But somehow there was not enough room for her wagon.

She found herself and David stranded outside the circle, the soldiers oblivious to her plight as they began firing their weapons at the approaching Indians.

"Mama, I'm afraid!" David cried as he stared at the Indians growing closer and closer. He screamed when some fell from their horses, blood streaming from wounds in their chests.

"Be brave, David," Mary Beth cried.

She scrambled to the back of the wagon and desperately searched for her own rifle. How she wished she had kept it near at hand.

"Mama!" David screamed again.

As Mary Beth turned to him, she went cold inside. An Indian was yanking her son from the seat, then before she knew it, riding away with him.

"Oh, Lord, no!" Mary Beth cried.

Filled with a deep, cold panic, Mary Beth breathed hard as she grabbed up the rifle she had just uncovered.

She rushed to the front of the wagon, her eyes on her son as he fought the Indian who held him in his arms as he continued riding away from the fight.

"David. . . . David . . ." she whispered as she took aim at the Indian's broad, copper back.

But before she could fire the rifle, her breath was stolen away as she caught sight of an Indian coming up alongside her wagon. He swept an arm out and grabbed her, causing her to drop her rifle.

"Help me!" she cried as the Indian slammed her across the horse in front of him, his strong hand holding her there on her belly as he rode away from the wagon train. "Oh, please, someone, help . . . Help!"

She could hear bullets whizzing past and knew that someone *was* trying to save her, but to no avail. The Indian rode at a furious pace and soon had her far from the wagons and riding along that same ridge where she had watched the warriors appear and disappear for most of the day.

She was so terrified, she could scarcely breathe. She was so afraid, she could not even find the strength to fight back.

She just lay there at the mercy of the scarcely clothed man. His face was streaked with red and black paint, his eyes filled with an anger she could feel deep within her soul.

She thought of David.

Some hope came into her heart that she might be reunited with him when she arrived wherever she was being taken, for surely the two who'd abducted them were from the same tribe.

Unless they were renegades, she thought quickly to herself.

She had heard that renegades came from all different tribes.

If David was taken to one renegade's hideout and she to another, then she might never see her son again.

"Please take me back!" she screamed. "My son! I must find my son!"

When the Indian spoke back to her, it was in his language, but she did not have to understand the words to know that he was a man who would not listen to reason.

His words were forceful and angry.

Tears filled her eyes and her body flinched when in the distance she still heard gunfire, and then a strange, even morbid . . . silence.

She could only assume who was the victor again.

The Indians, for they had far outnumbered the soldiers.

Mary Beth began repeating scripture from her Bible, murmuring a prayer she had been taught as a child . . . one that she had taught her little son.

"Yea, though I shall walk through the valley of the shadow of death, I will fear no evil."

•

Chapter Four

Terminate torment of love unsatisfied,
The greater torment of love satisfied.
—Eliot

Sharp stars burned in the heavens. Coyotes howled in the distance and an owl called from a smooth-skinned aspen tree. Frogs serenaded the night along the creek beds, and the lonesome song of a loon came to Brave Wolf as he continued onward on his mother's behalf.

The moon was full, and the night was filled with its milky light, making a path of white along the ground as Brave Wolf and his warriors rode forward on their muscled steeds. Most carried sinew-backed bows of mountain ash, their arrows carried in quivers of otter skin, embroidered in a quill pattern.

In order to conclude this chore as quickly as possible, he and his men stopped only long enough to take brief rests. They slept for only short periods of time, making no exception whether it was day or night.

Brave Wolf hated to waste even another minute searching for the brother who had fought alongside Yellow Hair. As a scout for the white cavalrymen, Night Horse must have led the pony soldiers to where his people had their villages, where the women and children awakened every morning with fear in their hearts, knowing that the pony soldiers might come any day and slaughter them.

Brave Wolf looked from side to side at the expressions on the faces of his men. He saw hate and resentment in their eyes.

And he understood why they carried these emotions in their hearts. Even though Night Horse was his brother, Brave Wolf now felt nothing but loathing for him.

He gazed straight ahead past stunted pines and oaks. He wondered, even if Night Horse *was* found, could he truly go to him as a brother with news of their mother?

Or would he be more apt to kill Night Horse for betraying their people?

Each mile they traveled, bringing him closer and closer to Night Horse, the dread of actually finding him grew within Brave Wolf's heart.

For he did expect to find his brother up high in the mountains, where a cave was hidden behind a waterfall, a place they had found while exploring one day, oh, so long ago.

They had claimed it as their own private place, a place they called their own. They had vowed to one another never to tell anyone else about it.

But now things were different.

Brave Wolf felt no allegiance now to a brother who had gone against everything Brave Wolf had always stood for.

He had thought that Night Horse held the same convictions . . . the same honor.

But he had been proven wrong.

Now it was time for Brave Wolf to decide how his brother would pay for his crimes against his people.

"Brave Wolf, how much farther must we go before we give up and return to our people?" Two Tails asked as he brought his horse close. "You do intend to travel only a while longer, do you not? You do not truly plan to find him, do you?"

Brave Wolf gave his warrior a slow gaze. "Do you truly believe that I am planning to go back on my word to my mother?" he said thickly. "Do you believe that I am playing a game by pretending to search, when all along I do not really intend to find Night Horse?"

"No, I have never known you to play games, especially with a mother's emotions, yet this quest is wrong, my chief, oh, so wrong," Two Tails said dryly. "I had hoped you would have reconsidered by now. You do know that none of us want to see that traitor's face again, do you not?"

"Nor do I," Brave Wolf said. "But I do plan to find him and take him back to our village."

"And then what?" Two Tails asked, his gaze intent as he stared into his chief's midnight-dark eyes.

"And then fate will have its way," Brave Wolf said. "That is all I can say now. Let us continue onward. I have a good idea where he is. We shall see if he is there; if he is not, we shall return home. Mother will believe me when I tell her that I went where I thought Night Horse would be."

"We will go only there, nowhere else?" Two Tails asked softly.

"Nowhere else but home," Brave Wolf said. He reached out a hand to his warrior's shoulder. "My friend, I understand your feelings. They match my own."

"Where does the trail take us?" Two Tails asked as Brave Wolf lowered his hand away from him. "How much farther?"

"It is not far," Brave Wolf said, swallowing hard. "It is not far."

He gazed ahead, where out there in the darkness his brother was hiding from life itself.

Each mile that took Brave Wolf closer to that beautiful place where he and his brother had played as children, his heart ached more.

The ache was for the camaraderie that would never be again with a brother he had adored.

The ache was for a mother whose shame for her

son had to be tearing at her very being!

The latter made Brave Wolf feel a contempt for Night Horse that was like a sour bitterness in his mouth.

Chapter Five

> The life of a man is a circle,
> From childhood to childhood
> And so it is in everything
> Where power moves.
> —Black Elk,
> Oglala Sioux Holy Man

A fire burned low as juices from a rabbit dripped into the flames. Night Horse sat inside a cave beside the fire and smiled when an owl hooted from a tree outside. He remembered a time when he was a small child and sat on his mother's lap in their lodge, listening to his first owl somewhere outside his family tepee. His mother had told him that owls see all . . . that they are the feathered cat of the night. She had said that the mother owl lived with her brood in a nest full of moon-splashed shadows.

He had felt safe in his mother's arms, and he felt safe now in the cave behind the waterfall, hidden by groves of yellow aspen and frosted leafed cottonwood.

But he knew that down in the dry runs and ravines, he would be easy quarry for those who sought him out.

He had learned long ago to suffer fear and conquer it, but now there was a strange coldness in the pit of his belly when he thought of what the future might hold for him . . . death at the hands of those who hated him!

He listened to the peaceful sound of water falling over rocks. He was carried away to another time when his life was uncomplicated, to a time when he loved his older brother more than life itself.

He had idolized Brave Wolf, for his brother seemed to know everything about everything, especially the goodness of life.

Night Horse gazed into the flames of the fire as he thought about the times when he and his brother had played in this very place.

It was their very own.

They shared it with no one.

As it was Night Horse's hideout now.

He hunted at night, scaring up rabbits and deer from their sleeping places. He killed them silently with arrows.

So far no one had found him.

But he knew that if his brother decided to search for him, to make him pay for betraying his people, Brave Wolf could find him.

"But you will not do this, will you, big brother?" Night Horse whispered.

He gathered a blanket more securely around his shoulders, thankful that when he had found a horse to steal, it still had its owner's travel bag on it, in which were supplies that had made Night Horse's hiding more comfortable.

Yes, his brother would know where to look for him, but surely he would see no reason to. Brave Wolf had disowned Night Horse when his younger brother joined Custer.

Although Night Horse knew that Brave Wolf despised him now, because of the love they had shared as children he would surely not send anyone up into these mountains to take him captive, or to kill him.

"I feel safe enough," Night Horse said, shivering as the cold air crept beneath his blanket.

Night Horse had had a lot of time to think about things since he had come to this place of his childhood.

He ached to see his mother.

He ached to see Dancing Butterfly, the only woman he had ever, or ever would, love. He knew that she must hate him now and surely would even turn her back to him if he could ever go home again. He would not blame her. It had been he who had left her behind, choosing instead to be a scout for whites. Oh, how foolish he had been. He loved her. He would always love her!

He had also thought often of his *ahte,* Chief Sharp Arrow, about what a valiant, courageous leader he had been. His father had died at the hands of Ute renegades four moons ago, leaving the road clear for Brave Wolf to be chief.

Night Horse was proud of his chieftain brother and missed him with every beat of his heart.

He now knew that he had been wrong to align himself with whites.

By having done so he had lost everything that was truly valuable and precious to him . . . his family's love . . . his people!

Only now did he realize the greatness of those losses.

He was so ashamed of what he had done, he felt the bitterness of vomit even now in the depths of his throat.

He coughed, but not from the bitterness of vomit. It was his lungs. They pained him so.

He realized that he was not as well as he should be in order to survive the cold nights high in these mountains.

He heard the screech of a mountain lion and shivered. He knew that he was vulnerable, all alone and without a firearm.

And he had only a few arrows left of those he had stolen when he had found the horse hobbled as several renegades crouched beside a night fire, laughing and boasting about what they had achieved that day.

Yes, he had been lucky to have gotten away with stealing a renegade's horse and supplies. Had they caught him, they would have enjoyed killing him slowly, then scalping him and leaving him for the wolves to feast upon.

He had been so relieved when he reached his childhood hideout in the mountain.

But now?

He was afraid that he might die where he had at one time been so happy.

He hated the thought of dying alone.

Chapter Six

> There was never any yet that
> wholly could escape love,
> and never shall there be any,
> never so long as beauty shall be,
> never so long as eyes can see.
> —Longus

The smell of food cooking on an open fire came to Brave Wolf in the soft breeze. He looked cautiously around him, and then up ahead, for he knew that where there was food cooking, there were those who were waiting to eat it.

When he saw the flames of a campfire through a break in the trees, he drew a tight rein, his warriors following his lead as they stopped, as well.

Two Tails brought his horse closer to Brave Wolf's. "Perhaps we have found him," he said, his voice only loud enough for Brave Wolf to hear.

Brave Wolf gazed intently at the fire, and then shook his head. "No, the man I know as my brother would not be so careless," he said stiffly. "If he is still alive, he knows that there are those who wish that he was not. He is where no one can see or smell food cooking over his fire."

Two Tails gazed at the fire again, now making out shadowed figures crouched around it. In the night breeze came laughter and voices . . . voices that did not speak the language of the Crow.

"Renegades?" he said, his voice suddenly filled with hate. "Would they be this reckless? Or do they place themselves out in the open because they wish for a confrontation?"

"They believe they are invincible," Brave Wolf growled. "So, yes, I do believe we have found a renegade camp, but no, I do not think they wish for a confrontation. It is late in the night. They would not expect anyone to be riding past, especially this far from all villages and forts."

"Could these be the Ute?" Two Tails asked, frowning at Brave Wolf. "The same renegades who spilled the blood of our people on our land? Who took our chief, your *ahte*, from us?"

"*Ka*, no, I do not believe it is they, or that they are anywhere near, for they know that if they show their faces again where we can see them, they will have no more time on this earth," Brave Wolf said tightly. "When they took my *ahte* from his people and family, they knew they had crossed the line. They scattered far and wide, knowing that was the only way they could keep from dying a slow, painful death for the crimes they committed."

Brave Wolf dismounted and tethered his horse to a low tree limb. He motioned for his warriors to do the same.

After they were all on foot, the warriors gathered around Brave Wolf.

"We shall go see whose camp this is," Brave Wolf said. "Bring your bows and quivers of arrows. We must be ready to fight if there is reason."

Each man positioned his quiver of arrows on his back, and carrying their powerful bows, they crept stealthily closer to the campsite.

When they got close enough to see more clearly, they halted in surprise.

"A woman," Brave Wolf gasped as he gazed with troubled eyes at a white woman who was tied to a tree behind the campfire. Gathered around the flames, the renegades were laughing, talking, and eating. "A . . . *white* woman."

Brave Wolf felt great hatred for the shameful men who took whites captive, especially women. To him such men were the worst of cowards.

He himself had worked hard at keeping a peaceful relationship with the *washechu*, white eyes, for he saw that it was necessary in a world where whites now outnumbered his own people.

Brave Wolf had learned from his peace-loving *ahte* how to make things work with the white eyes. So many people of other clans, who had fought against the whites, had lost their freedom, confined on plots of land called reservations.

Brave Wolf had hoped that if he proved to be a strong and peaceful leader, he could keep his people on their own land at least for a while longer. He did not want to see them forced onto land where the deer were not as plentiful, and where the soil might not be fertile enough for growing food.

Tonight as he gazed at the white woman being held captive, he knew there was only one thing to do: release her and reunite her with her people.

"The woman must be saved from a fate worse than death," Brave Wolf said, his gaze moving from renegade to renegade. "I hope that she has not yet suffered the disgrace and shame of being raped by those who took her."

Brave Wolf nodded at his warriors. "We shall make a wide circle around the camp, and then I shall shout at them and tell them how it must be if they wish to live to see another sunrise," he growled out. "We must try our best to settle this peacefully. It is not best that we enter into a fight with these renegades. I am on a quest. I do not want it hampered by more spilled blood, even if it is not our own."

His jaw tightened. "But have an arrow notched to your bowstring in case they do not listen to reason," he said, his eyes narrowed.

Their bows notched with feathered death, they circled the camp. Brave Wolf positioned himself somewhat closer than his warriors, with his friend Two Tails only a short distance behind him.

"Renegades, you are surrounded!" he then

shouted. "But there need be no fight tonight. Just hand over the white woman and then you can be on your way, unharmed. If you do not comply with my demands, you will all die. There is an arrow readied for each of you renegades. So which shall it be? Life? Or death?"

Mary Beth's heart skipped a nervous beat as the voice in the dark came to her. She couldn't help believing that things were getting worse for her by the minute, for surely the presence of other Indians meant still more men who would want to take their pleasure of her.

After the renegade had abducted her, he was soon joined by others. But her heart had sunk when she had seen that none of them had David with them. She could only conclude that the renegade who took him had gone on elsewhere, or . . . he had killed her son and left him somewhere for animals to feast upon.

The possibility of her son dying such a death made her heartsick and ill.

And now?

What was going to happen to *her*? Would she become a pawn between two factions?

She was even more afraid than before. Whichever group won her, she would more than likely end up being raped, perhaps by many, then surely slaughtered.

She waited breathlessly to see what the response of the renegades would be to this new threat.

She watched, then flinched and screamed when one of the renegades raised a rifle and shot it. A cry of pain from the hidden Indians was proof that although the renegades could not see whom they were shooting at, a man had been hit.

Brave Wolf turned and gazed in disbelief at Two Tails as he crumpled to the ground, a bloody wound gaping in his chest. By the stare of Two Tails's eyes, Brave Wolf knew that he had been killed instantly.

A rage he had not known since the death of his father swept through him. He shouted at his men to release their arrows.

Mary Beth gasped as she heard the whine of flying arrows. The deadly missiles sped from the darkness and showered onto the renegades until they had all fallen.

She felt a bitter taste rise from her throat at the sight of all that blood . . . even though those who had died were her ardent enemies.

Everything was now eerily quiet. All that could be heard was the crackling of the campfire.

Mary Beth watched, wide-eyed, as the killers stepped from the darkness and entered the camp, their bows now resting over their shoulders, their eyes moving from one fallen renegade to another.

"They are silenced forever," Brave Wolf said quietly.

His gaze moved to Mary Beth; then he looked over his shoulder at one of his warriors. "Big Hawk, take our valiant fallen warrior home for burial," he said, his voice hoarse with sadness. "Tell his mother, *ahte,* and wife that a piece of my heart died with him, and that he will be honored in death, as he was in life. Take his children into your arms and tell them they will be cared for and loved, forever and ever."

The warrior silently nodded and went to Two Tails.

Mary Beth soon heard hoofbeats and knew that the one who had been given the order was now on his way home with a warrior who had died at the hand of the renegades.

Then she swallowed hard when she saw the warrior who seemed to be in charge coming toward her.

The flames of the campfire gave off enough light for her to look deeply into his midnight-black eyes and she felt a moment of relief when she saw something in his eyes that said he did not plan to kill her.

She saw kindness.

Or . . . was it a ploy to gain her trust?

No.

She would never trust a red man. Was it not Indians who had killed poor Lloyd and stolen David?

She had no choice, though, but to wait and see what this redskin's intentions were for her. She was at his mercy, as David had been at the mercy of the renegade who had taken him.

She truly doubted now that she would ever see her son again. Perhaps she would never even see a new sunrise.

There was one thing that she could not help noticing about this man. Not only did she see gentleness in this warrior's eyes, but also how handsome he was. There was a clean, noble quality about him that she had not seen in the renegades.

She would have to watch herself. She could not allow herself to be fooled by his handsomeness . . . by his attitude.

She must remember to be on guard at all times. She had to find a way to survive . . . to escape. Above all, she needed to be able to search for her son.

Brave Wolf saw the fear in the woman's eyes and how she cowered from him as he took another step closer to her. "Do not be afraid," he said, speaking English surprisingly well. "I am a *wicasa-iyutanyapi*, a man of honor. I am from a friendly clan of Indians. I am Chief Brave Wolf of the Whistling Waters Clan of *Absarokee*, Crow."

Mary Beth was stunned that this young warrior was a chief. His face was so handsomely set, so perfectly formed, and he was tall and very muscled, not at all how she envisioned an Indian chief to be. She had always imagined chiefs to be old, gray, their faces lined with wrinkles.

She wasn't sure if it was a good thing that he was so young and vital, his dark eyes so mesmerizing.

What danger was she in now? Would he assist or rape her?

Brave Wolf went behind her and cut the ropes that held her captive, then stepped quickly in front of her as she crumpled to the ground, her legs seeming to have lost their ability to hold her up.

He bent to his knees before her and gazed into her eyes. "What is your name?" he asked, seeing now just how beautiful she was.

Her hair was the color of autumn leaves, and hung down past her waist. And her oval face had such soft, pretty features. And she was so tiny! He could not see how any man could want to harm her.

He was so glad that he had come this way tonight and found her. A night with the renegades would have probably been her last.

And her eyes! The fire's glow revealed to him a color like that of the tiny flowers he saw growing in clusters along the mountain slopes—violets.

Mary Beth used every bit of strength that she could muster to stand again. She pushed herself up from the ground, then leaned against the tree for support as the Indian rose and stood before her.

"You want my name?" she said, her voice filled with disgust. "Here is all that I will give to you."

She spat angrily at his feet, then shot him a defiant stare.

Brave Wolf was not at all surprised by her attitude toward him. He knew that she was right not to trust him, for she surely knew the horror stories that had spread about what some redskins did to white women . . . what was probably even planned for her tonight had he not come along and rescued her.

So he was not insulted by her behavior.

In fact, he saw it as valiant. This lone woman

might pose more of a challenge than the renegades he had surprised tonight. They were all dead. This woman was very much alive.

He thought of Two Tails's death, and an ache crept into his heart. He and Two Tails had been friends since they were young braves learning the ways of warriors. It did not seem possible that he was gone from him so quickly, and so needlessly.

He wondered how he might have approached the confrontation without placing his best friend in danger. Shaking his head, he left off such fruitless speculation. He had to decide what he was going to do with the white woman.

He couldn't take the time to escort her to Fort Hope, where he had friendly relations with the colonel. And he did not dare send her away with just one of his warriors, especially since there were still renegades out there who would enjoy getting their hands on a white woman.

She was best kept where there were many warriors to protect her from the threat of any other renegades who might wish to claim a white woman as a prize. Yes, he had to keep her with him and his warriors, at least until he could return her to people of her own skin color.

"White woman, I have no choice but to take you with me for now," Brave Wolf said, making certain that his voice was friendly and reassuring.

"I am on a quest for my mother," he said. "I am looking for my brother and I have traveled far in my search. I cannot turn back for your sake. You must travel with me, but I assure you that when I succeed with my quest, I will return you safely to your people."

He was not surprised when he saw no look of relief upon her face. He guessed that she truly did not expect to come out of this alive. But there was no way to reassure her other than what he had already said. She would learn to trust him in time.

"Please, oh, please take me to Fort Henry," she begged, overwhelmed by a horrendous sense of powerlessness. "That was where I was headed before . . . before the renegades attacked our wagon train." She hung her head, then slowly looked at Brave Wolf. "I am so weary . . . so tired."

"I have promised to return you to your people at my first opportunity," Brave Wolf softly explained, yet even then he would not take her to Fort Henry. The colonel there was not his ally.

He gazed into her eyes and saw a renewal of defiance. She looked guardedly around her, as though she had it in her mind to attempt an escape.

He sighed heavily. "Seeing that you just might try to escape, I have no choice but to tie your wrists as we travel," he said.

He nodded to a warrior and told him to bring leather thongs from their travel bag.

"No, please don't," Mary Beth pleaded. "I promise not to try to run away. I will cooperate."

"I do not know you well enough to know whether or not promises mean anything to you, so I must secure your wrists," he said regretfully. "I am doing this for your own benefit, to assure that you won't suddenly break free and ride away from me and my warriors. I fear for your safety should you find a way to escape. There are other renegades besides those who abducted you. You are treated as a captive by me now only to keep you safe from harm. In my heart you are anything but a captive."

Mary Beth's eyebrows rose at what he had just said.

She had no idea how to feel about her situation now. How should she regard this handsome chief who had come in the middle of the night to save her from the hands of those hideous, murdering renegades?

She was quiet as he tied her wrists, then led her to a horse and lifted her into the saddle. She winced when he tied her ankles to the stirrups.

"You will be riding my best friend's steed. Two Tails was slain as we rescued you," Brave Wolf said.

Mary Beth could see torment in his eyes when he mentioned Two Tails. She almost felt as though she should say she was sorry for being the cause of his friend's death. But no, she was the one who was owed an apology, not him.

She set her jaw firmly and looked straight ahead, ignoring anything else this redskin savage might say to her.

When Brave Wolf mounted his own steed, he rode close to Mary Beth. He took the reins of her horse, then held them as he rode onward without another word to her. He noticed that as she rode beside him she was giving him occasional angry glances. He ignored them.

Once again he focused on the true reason he was riding so far from his home in the middle of the night: the guest he had undertaken for his mother.

Seeing that giving him angry glances did not seem to move the young chief, Mary Beth looked straight ahead. Her thoughts returned to David. She was far more worried about him than herself.

Where could he be?

And was she being taken farther and farther away from him?

She wished she could tell this Indian about her son's plight and seek his help. But she couldn't because she wasn't even sure what his true plans were for her.

And why would he care about her child? Did he not have his own worries? Was not he searching for his own brother?

She had no choice but to keep her fears to herself and pray that the good Lord above would keep her son safe from harm. She prayed that she would see him again one day, and that they would be reunited.

For now both she and her son were at the mercy of Indians, but not the same ones. If only they could at least be together in their captivity, she might find some peace.

As it was, she felt only hurtful despair deep inside her soul!

Chapter Seven

> There was never any yet that wholly
> could escape love, and never shall there
> be any, never so long as beauty shall
> be, never so long as eyes can see.
>
> —Longus

Lightning lit the sky in lurid flashes. Thunder boomed, shaking the ground beneath the horses' hooves. When rain began falling, Mary Beth shivered, the wetness seeming to go clean into her very soul.

She struggled to hold onto the pommel, but the binding around her wrists made it hard.

She gazed questioningly at Brave Wolf, who continued to lead his warriors onward in the rain. Why didn't he stop?

She looked quickly around when the lightning

flashed and realized why. They were riding across a straight stretch of land, toward the base of a mountain. There was nothing to offer protection from the elements. There was only blowing grass, bending double with the wind.

The wind whipped incessantly around Mary Beth. The rain blinded her. Then just as suddenly as it had begun, the storm was over.

Mary Beth coughed and sputtered as the last of the rain ran down her face and across her lips.

Brave Wolf drew rein, his warriors following his lead. He turned to Mary Beth. His gaze moved slowly over her.

Her dress was so wet, it clung to her body, defining the curves beneath it. He had not thought that such a tiny woman could have such large, beautiful breasts. But she did, and the sight aroused an ache in his loins that he tried to fight off.

He had not yet taken a woman as his wife. He had not found a woman who made his heart sing. But he had felt a hungering for a body next to him at night, and for the soft laughter of children in his lodge.

He had never thought he would be aroused by a woman whose skin was white, whose tongue was spiteful, and who looked at him as though he were the devil.

But he understood all of her emotions. She thought of him as her captor. He had hoped that she would begin to trust him so that he would not have to keep her bound like a captive. But so far, she still wore a mask of hate on her lovely face.

Her hair was wet and hung in tight, rusty ringlets over her shoulders and down her back. Some loose curls lay across her brow, almost across her eyes.

But they did not keep him from seeing her glare. It seemed to go clear through him, making him uncomfortable.

He had been around many women in his time, and none had ever looked at him in this way. Instead, the looks had been filled with admiration.

But this woman? She seemed to hate the very sight of him.

"We will stop here, make a fire, and dry off before we venture onward," Brave Wolf said, dismounting.

He went to Mary Beth and undid the thongs at her ankles, where she had been tied to the stirrups. Then he reached up, placed his hands at her waist, and lifted her from the saddle.

He noticed that she scarcely breathed as he untied the thongs at her wrists. He could almost see her mind working. No doubt she was making plans to escape the moment she was freed of her bonds.

Yet she must know that she could hardly get an inch away from him if she turned and tried to run. All he would have to do was reach his arms out for her and she would again have no choice but to accept her fate.

He only wished there was some way to convince her that she had nothing to fear from him.

But surely, as each hour passed, she would begin to realize that he meant her no harm.

"Come with me," Brave Wolf said. He gently placed a hand at her elbow and ushered her away from the horses. He took her to where his warriors were already preparing a fire.

"Soon there will be a fire," Brave Wolf said. "You can warm yourself by it. Your clothes can dry so that the night air will not harm you."

"I need nothing from you except my freedom," Mary Beth said. She yanked her elbow away from him.

Turning to face him, she placed her fists on her hips. "If you truly mean me no harm, take me to Fort Henry," she said tightly. "I must see if anyone survived the terrible wagon train attack. I . . . I . . . want to . . ."

She started to mention David, then thought better of it. There might be a danger in alerting another warrior that she had a son, and that she sorely feared for his life.

Wasn't one Indian as bad as the next? How was she to know what any of them might have in mind for a child David's age?

And . . . was David even still alive?

She hung her head so that the tears she was fighting couldn't be seen by Brave Wolf. She wanted to look courageous and strong.

"I promised you fire—you have fire," Brave Wolf said, motioning toward it. "Go. Stand beside it. Warm yourself."

She did not have to be asked twice. Longing for the warmth against her trembling flesh, Mary Beth hurried to the fire and stretched her hands to the heat.

Never in her life had the warmth of a fire felt as delicious as now. Every part of her was cold.

Brave Wolf was glad to see that she had followed at least one of his orders.

He went to his horse and removed his travel bag and saddle, then hobbled his horse with the others as his warriors made themselves comfortable around the fire opposite from where Mary Beth stood.

Brave Wolf turned and gazed at length at the woman, again taken by her loveliness. Even wet and shivering from the cold, she was beautiful.

He hoped to gain her trust soon, for he would like to talk with her and hear why she was in this area, and about her family.

Was she married? Did she have children somewhere? Had she heard about what had happened at the Battle of the Little Big Horn?

Was that why she hated him so much? Did she believe that he had had a role in the killings?

He gazed down at his bag, then back at Mary Beth. There was usually one way to break through a barrier of silence. Food.

Surely she was hungry. She might not have eaten for many hours now.

He carried only pemmican on jaunts like this. When someone was hungry, pemmican was very welcome.

He bent down and got a stick of pemmican from his bag, then went to Mary Beth and held it out for her. "If you are hungry, this pemmican will fill at least some of the empty space in your belly," he said. He flinched when she turned quickly and glared at him again.

Instead of accepting his offer of food, she spat at his feet as she had before.

"I don't want that disgusting-looking mess," she said, but in truth she badly wanted to eat it. She was so hungry she felt weak, yet she could not accept anything from this Indian . . . except her freedom! "Take it away. Do you hear? Take . . . it . . . away!"

Finding her insulting, Brave Wolf gazed at her for a moment, then slowly turned and walked away from her.

Yes, she was insulting, yet beautiful and spirited. He smiled, for he enjoyed seeing spirit in a woman.

Hating to behave like a spoiled child, Mary Beth almost regretted her words as Brave Wolf walked away from her.

But how could she behave any other way than angry and spiteful? She was cold, wet, miserable, and she missed her David so much she could no longer keep from crying.

Ignoring the warriors who sat opposite her on blankets, Mary Beth crumpled to the wet ground and held her face in her hands, sobbing.

Brave Wolf stopped and turned to gaze at Mary Beth. He was now seeing her soft side. His heart went out to her, for surely she felt lost and alone without any of her family . . . without any of her people anywhere near for her to flee to. He felt much for her at this moment, mostly compassion.

He opened one of his travel bags and took a blanket from it. Hurrying back to Mary Beth, he bent to his knees beside her.

He gently wrapped the blanket around her shoulders, surprised when she flinched as though she had been shot and grabbed the blanket away from herself. She gave him a cold, defiant look as she tossed it into his face.

Mary Beth badly wished to keep the blanket, but she wasn't sure what it represented. Had he offered it to her because he planned to use it with her?

Did he plan to take her into this blanket with him, forcing her to sleep with him?

Not giving up so easily, Brave Wolf placed the blanket around her shoulders again. "This blanket is for your comfort," he said softly. "Do not be too stubborn to take it. I mean you only good."

Again she grabbed it away from herself and shoved it into his arms.

"I want nothing from you but my freedom," she said, furious when her voice broke and her eyes wavered.

Then she blurted out, "I am afraid of you and your warriors! Please, oh, please let me go!"

He was stunned that she was still so afraid of him when he had done nothing to deserve such fear.

"You are wrong not to trust me," Brave Wolf said softly. "I offer you friendship. I will eventually return you to your people, but I have explained to you that I am on a mission. I must succeed with this mission first."

"What sort of mission are you on?" she cried. "More raids and destruction against whites, especially the cavalry?"

Understanding her wrath, her mistrust, he ignored the coldness in her voice . . . the accusation. "The mission is for my mother. I have promised to find my brother, Night Horse," he said. "Can you not understand that my mother's wishes come before yours . . . a woman I never knew until tonight?"

"You still don't know me at all," Mary Beth said, her voice softer now. "I . . . I . . . have never been with Indians before. Can't you see why I'm so afraid? Why I want to return to my people as quickly as possible?"

"Yes, I understand, but you must understand a son's feelings for his mother," Brave Wolf said tightly.

His words made her break down and cry again. Yes, she did understand a son's feelings for his mother. If her David was still alive, he surely cried for her even now.

"I wish I could make you understand things that I know are causing you to mistrust me and my warriors," he said.

"How can I ever understand what is happening, when so many of my people have needlessly died?" Mary Beth said, wiping tears from her eyes. "Only recently there has been a terrible battle that claimed so many soldiers' lives. How do I know that you were not there, sending arrows into the hearts of the men? Perhaps you even killed my . . ."

No.

She must not let him know that her own husband had died that day. She would not give him the chance to gloat over something that tore at the very core of her being.

"I have told you that I am a peaceful Crow chief who does not enter into warring with whites," Brave Wolf said, again attempting to place the blanket around her shoulders.

This time she allowed it. He moved to his haunches beside her, soaking up the warmth of the fire himself, as he attempted to tell her some more about himself. He hoped that more information would help her to trust him.

"I told you before that I am *wicasa-okinihan,* an honorable and respected individual and that I am a *bachay-chay,* a good man, a chief, concerned with helping people, not harming," he began. "Under first my father's and then my leadership, my Whistling Water Clan of Crow has never entered into confrontations with your white people. It is my role in life to help my Crow people learn to live in the way of the white man. Like my chieftain father, I have even gone and met with the Great White Father in Washington on behalf of my people. This recent battle was not of my doing, nor my people's."

He went quiet, for there was one warrior of the Whistling Water Clan who *had* participated. His brother. But he felt it was best not to mention that to this white woman, not yet anyhow.

When Night Horse was found, it would be soon enough to confide in Mary Beth.

But first, Night Horse had to be found!

Mary Beth was stunned by what he had just said . . . that he had actually been to Washington to speak with President Grant. Oh, surely he was lying. It was just a ploy to make her trust him.

But as he had been talking to her, he had sounded so convincing, she could not help gazing at him. She wished that he was, indeed, the way he represented himself . . . a caring, truthful man, who *did* fight for peace.

He was such a handsome man with such a soft, kind voice. His midnight eyes could entrance her if she allowed them to.

He was a man of athletic build, lean and tall, and his skin was fairer than most Indians she had seen. It was a lovely copper color and looked soft to the touch.

His sculpted face had a noble expression, and she admired his long, thick, black hair which hung down his back to his waist, held back from his face with a beaded band. One lone eagle feather was woven into a lock of his hair at the back.

He wore only a breechcloth which revealed much of his muscled body to her, she had to keep herself from gazing where she knew that he surely was so very gifted, for he was very virile. He was all man.

Suddenly she realized that he had noticed her

studying him. He was gazing back at her with a curious look, for surely he was wondering what she was thinking as her eyes took in so much of him.

She was angry at herself for letting down her guard for even one minute. She saw danger in allowing him to think that she was softening in her feelings toward him.

She could not, she would not, give in to him and his soft voice and alluring eyes.

If he thought that he was winning her over, might he not then go further and try to seduce her?

The thought did not altogether sicken her, for he was not a man who would make a woman feel disgusted at the thought of his taking her into his arms and kissing her.

Suddenly she realized where her thoughts had now gone. She was angry that he had this effect on her.

"All that you have said is a lie," she declared venomously. "Please take yourself and your lies elsewhere. I tire of hearing you."

Absolutely stunned by her attitude, after he had opened himself up so much to her, Brave Wolf rose quickly to his feet.

"You choose not to believe me, and that is alright," he said softly. "At the moment you are not my concern. It is my mother whose face I see in my mind's eye and inside my heart. It is for her that I travel far from my village. Not you. Only by chance did I find you . . . and save your life. It is up to you whether or not you ever believe that."

He gave her another lengthy gaze, glanced over the fire at his warriors, who had heard her insulting him again, then walked away. He went to his horse and rubbed it down with his hands.

This woman. Surely she was talking out of anger and hurt.

He just could not believe that such a lovely person normally had such a spiteful, hurtful tongue.

Mary Beth gazed at Brave Wolf as he tended to his horse. What he had said about his mother did seem true enough, for he had mentioned her more than once.

Despite her best efforts, she was beginning to see him in a different light. A man who put his mother before other things, even his own best interests and health, was surely a good man with a good heart.

Yet . . . he was an Indian. She knew too much about them, and the hate they felt for whites, ever to allow herself to trust one.

Even a man who made her pulse race when his eyes met hers, stirring flames within her that no other man had ever caused.

It was that sort of feeling that she had never known with Lloyd. Strange that it was a red-skinned man who aroused such feelings now.

She had to fight those feelings with every fiber of her being! She did not want to feel anything but loathing for this man and those who rode with him!

She was still too afraid to trust Brave Wolf.

"Brave Wolf," she whispered to herself.

Even his name made her feel something she had never felt before for a man: desire.

Chapter Eight

For man, as for flower and beast,
and bird, the supreme triumph is to
be most vividly, most perfectly, alive.
—D. H. Lawrence

The blowing night winds in the pines moaned low outside the cave. The campfire gave off a strange whistling sound.

Chilled to the bone, Night Horse trembled beneath his blanket as he sat as close to the fire as he could get. Although he had been in the cave during the rain, it had not kept out the cold dampness that blew through the entrance.

The fire and the lone blanket were just not enough to warm Night Horse any longer. His skin was clammy cold, yet he knew by the stars that seemed to be exploding inside his skull, and by the pounding of his temples, that he had a fever.

His cough was deep. He could even hear a rattling in his lungs with each breath he took.

He was very, very ill, and he had begun to think of death. He was afraid of dying.

For the past three months, the faces of the dead on the battlefield had haunted him day and night. The blood, the stench of it, seemed to cling to him even though he had washed himself repeatedly in a nearby creek, defying the cold air and water just to get himself clean.

Those baths, the cold nights, the dampness of the cave, were taking their toll on Night Horse. He knew that it wasn't wise to stay in the cave any longer, but he had nowhere else to go.

"I do not want to die alone!" he suddenly cried, tears falling from his eyes as he again thought of his beloved mother and how it would feel to have her comforting arms around him.

In his mind's eye he saw his mother sitting contentedly beside her lodge fire on a cold, blustery winter night. It was during the winter months that his mother softened the autumn elk hides by chewing the tough skins, wetting them with her mouth.

In the summertime, he and Brave Wolf always took their mother hives of succulent honey.

When he and Brave Wolf had gotten old enough to hunt, they had proudly brought home meat for their mother, some of which she roasted, while the rest was hung on the lodge poles.

If he was with his mother and brother when he took his last breath, oh, surely he would leave this earth with a happier heart. If his mother and brother were there loving him, it could only mean that they both had forgiven him of all that he had done against his Crow people.

"Yes, I must find my way home," he whispered as he shakily pushed himself up from the rocky floor.

He had made a decision. He *did* want to go home. He wanted to die among his people. He wanted their forgiveness before he died, especially his mother's and brother's.

He was filled with such shame at his decision to leave his village to ally himself with whites.

But he had felt so important while working as a white man's scout, especially when he had become one of General Custer's most trusted scouts.

Now he wondered why he had felt that way, when deep down inside he knew even then that it was wrong to be with the white soldiers, leading them where he knew they would take advantage of his own people. He had known of the pony soldiers' atrocities against many tribes, even that women and children had died.

He had forced those facts from his mind and had ridden proud and tall in the saddle alongside Yellow Hair, pointing the way here and there, expecting many rewards for his alliance with such an important man.

"Brave Heart. . . ." he said as he went to the cave entrance. There was still a fine mist hanging in the air.

He stepped out into it and pulled the blanket

over his head as he stared up at the moon that was just coming into view as clouds slid away from it.

He had badly wanted the special title of Brave Heart for being one of Custer's main scouts.

Had Custer lived through the battle, had he been victorious over those he fought, Night Horse *would* have been honored with such a title, for he was one of those scouts who advised Custer and rode with him into the center of the battle.

"But now he is dead," he choked out. "All of those who rode with me and General Custer are dead. I . . . alone . . . survived."

He gazed into the heavens. "Why?" he cried. "What is the purpose of my survival? Is it only because You want me to suffer these memories that weigh down my heart? Take me, First Maker. Let me die. But please, first let me reach my home. I do want to see my mother's face one last time. I do want to hear my brother tell me that he can find it in his heart to forgive me."

Sobbing, he prayed again . . . asking that he be accepted among his people again, so that he would have a proper burial among them.

Then, hanging his head, with barely any life left in his step, he saddled his stolen horse, managed to pull himself into the saddle, and started making his way down the steep incline of the mountain.

He reached deep inside himself for the strength to get to his home.

"*Ina* . . . brother . . . I am coming," he whispered.

He clung tightly to the reins as he coughed so hard he felt something tearing at his lungs.

"*A-i-i-i,* I . . . am . . . dying," he whispered. "I know I am!"

Chapter Nine

> O for life of Sensations
> rather than thoughts!
> —Keats

The smell of something cooking over the campfire and the bickering of bluejays from somewhere close by in the trees awakened Mary Beth. The growling of her stomach reminded her of how long it had been since she had eaten. She could not imagine anything smelling as good as what she was now smelling.

She raised herself up on an elbow and looked slowly around. The blanket which had covered her fell down to rest around her waist.

It was a crisp dawn. Mary Beth saw the deep shadows of early morning and a hint of pink along the horizon which meant that the sun was ready to rise and warm the world.

She could hardly believe that Brave Wolf had stayed in their makeshift camp the rest of the night instead of pushing onward.

When she had fallen asleep, oh, so bone weary from the long ride, and dispirited from her horrible experiences, she had expected to be awakened as quickly as she had fallen asleep and made to mount the horse again.

Her eyes met now with Brave Wolf's as he stood over the campfire, his muscled body seeming to tense when he saw that she was awake. She was not sure why seeing her awake should make him tense.

A part of her was afraid of his reaction. What if he had plans for her today that were worse than those experiences she had already survived?

She firmed her jaw and rose quickly to her feet, gazing all the while into Brave Wolf's midnight-dark eyes.

She ran her fingers down the front of her dress, trying to smooth out the wrinkles. Although it was now dry, the dress still clung to her body.

Brave Wolf returned her gaze steadily. Even with her hair in such disarray and with her dress wrinkled, she was still beautiful.

Because she was such a lovely woman, and white, it would not be wise to travel openly with her during daylight hours. Renegades would want her for themselves, and white pony soldiers would conclude that she was a captive. He doubted that they would ask questions first. They would shoot to kill his men and rescue the woman.

If she was wearing something besides her dress, perhaps she would not be so noticeable.

Without much further thought, he went to his travel bag and took one of his buckskin outfits from it.

Of course he knew that his clothes were much too big for this tiny woman; some adjustments would have to be made.

Mary Beth inhaled the scent of food again, and she noticed that the warriors were preparing their animals for travel. That had to mean they had already eaten. Was she not to be offered food for herself?

She was so hungry, she longed to take whatever was left of the food, but she waited to be told that she could. She didn't want to do anything hasty which might cause Brave Wolf to tie her up again as they traveled onward. Since he'd left her untied through the night, surely he would trust her during the day when he would be awake and could see her every movement.

Her gaze turned to Brave Wolf as he came back toward her carrying what looked like buckskin attire. When he held the clothing out to her, she raised her eyebrows quizzically.

"Go and change into these clothes," Brave Wolf said. "Bring your dress back to me. I shall place it in my travel bag. I will return it to you when we arrive at my village."

"When *we* arrive at your village?" Mary Beth

gasped out. "Are you saying I will have to go with you? I thought you were going to escort me to Fort Henry. Why would I have to go with you to your village?"

"When I find my brother, I must return him to my village as quickly as possible so that my mother will know that he is alive and well," Brave Wolf said. "Then I will escort you to a fort. Only then."

"That could take days," Mary Beth said, tears springing up in her eyes. "I so badly want to be among my own people."

She still had not told him about David. She was wondering if that had been a good decision. If she did tell him about her lost son, surely he would sympathize with her and listen to reason.

Yet, no. She saw his determination to continue onward to find his brother. She would wait for another time to tell him about her son.

Again she admired him for being so dutiful to his mother, yet Mary Beth had her own rights. Brave Wolf's decision to keep her with him was wrong. If he would let her go today, while it was daylight, she could travel far before it got dark.

Perhaps she could even reach the fort. She knew it was not far from where the wagon train had been attacked.

But could she truly find her way to the fort alone? Something told her that wasn't a wise move to make, for this was not safe country for a lone female traveler.

"I have wasted much valuable time by allowing you to sleep," Brave Wolf said, his jaw tight. "I am wasting time even now as I wait for you to do as you are told. Go. Change into these clothes. I will put some of the food in a bag for you to eat as we travel. I do not have time for you to sit and have a leisurely meal."

"Ha! Leisurely?" Mary Beth said, yanking the clothes from him. "Nothing about this experience with you is leisurely."

Then she recalled that she had been allowed to sleep and regretted being sarcastic when she saw the hurt in his eyes.

It seemed strange that this man could have any feelings for her, yet she knew that he did.

When she said something hurtful to him, he did not react angrily. Instead, he looked as though he was stung by her anger and sarcasm.

Was it possible that he cared for her? The fact that he had allowed her to sleep was proof he did.

"Why must I change?" she asked. She gazed at the clothes, then unrolled the breeches and grimaced when she saw how large they were. She gave Brave Wolf a perplexed look. "Why, I shall be swallowed whole by these clothes."

"I will help you adjust them to a smaller size," he said, relieved that at least she had seemed to accept the necessity of changing her clothes.

"Oh, alright," Mary Beth said, then turned and stomped away toward a thick stand of trees, where she could have some privacy to change her clothes, and attend to other matters that needed to be done out of sight of the warriors.

She had found it embarrassing to seek ways to

relieve herself while in the company of these men. But thus far, she had managed it.

She hurried out of her dress, then worked herself into the other clothes. She sighed heavily when she saw just how big they were on her.

She shook her head slowly as she rolled the sleeves up so that at least her hands were visible. She then bent over and rolled up the pants legs until she felt she could at least walk in them without tripping.

But when she stood up and the breeches fell instantly to the ground, she again sighed heavily. This wasn't going to work. But she had to give it a try, for she understood that it wasn't safe to be seen with these Indians during the daylight hours in her own clothes.

She gathered the waist of the breeches up into a tight bunch at her left side and walked dispiritedly back to where Brave Wolf waited for her.

She saw a look of quiet amusement enter his eyes when he caught sight of her.

He went to his travel bag and removed a long buckskin thong, then tied it around her waist so that she would no longer have to hold the pants up.

"That should do it," Brave Wolf said. He stepped back and eyed her again. A slow smile curved his lips. "You look like a starved wolf pup."

"Thanks for the compliment," Mary Beth said, then raked her fingers through her long auburn hair in an effort to remove the witches' knots.

When she had combed out the tangles, she dropped her hands to her sides.

She eyed Brave Wolf in wonder when he took another thong from where he had stuffed it inside his waistband, then stepped closer to her.

"Turn around," he said softly.

"Why?" Mary Beth gasped, her gaze locked with his. "Oh, no. Don't tell me you are going to tie my wrists again. How on earth do you expect me to eat while we travel? I only have two hands."

"The thong is not to tie your wrists, but your hair," Brave Wolf said. He had decided not to tie her again, not unless she attempted an escape. Then he would keep her tied both day and night!

"My hair?" she asked, reaching back to lift its heaviness from her shoulders.

"If left to hang long, the sun will reflect off its brightness, and prove to any passersby that you are not Indian, whose hair is black like mine," he said softly. "If your hair is tied and held back from your face, then less of it will be seen."

Mary Beth understood his logic. She nodded and turned to wait for him to place her hair in a ponytail.

When she turned back to him, she saw such gentleness in his eyes, such genuine caring, she felt guilty for having doubted his goodness.

Yet . . . might not that look be forced, as well, to fool her?

She would not trust him totally just yet. He had to prove himself first.

The growling of her stomach was a reminder to

both herself and Brave Wolf that she hadn't eaten. She smiled awkwardly at him, and then he turned, reached down for a buckskin bag, and handed it to her.

"Inside you will find food, but it is best that we go to our steeds now and resume our travel," he said. He took her by the elbow and escorted her to the same horse she'd ridden before. He lifted her onto the saddle. "Wait until we are on our way, and then eat."

Mary Beth nodded.

She clung to the bag with one hand and lifted her reins with the other.

She was glad that he hadn't tied her wrists or ankles. He was trusting her to have more freedom.

His trust, his long looks, his concern, told her he did care for her. Perhaps she had been wrong to mistrust him. Perhaps his intentions were good, and he would return her to her own world as soon as he could.

She looked over her shoulder at the warriors, who were now on their steeds, then glanced down at where the fire had been burning through the night. The cooking food had dripped grease into the flames, emitting tantalizing aromas that even now made her mouth water.

The fire was out. Dirt had been kicked over the fire pit to make it look as though no fire had burned there. The blankets were rolled up and tied on the horses. They were ready to set out again.

They rode across level land and hollow hills.

White antelope lifted their heads above the grass as they rode past. The mountain slope was now not far away.

Finally able to eat, Mary Beth nibbled the meat from the bones of what she surmised was a roasted rabbit. At last her belly seemed comfortably full again. She hoped this meal would last her until Brave Wolf saw the need to stop and eat again.

She was sure he would not stop again for hours. She dreaded the long day which lay ahead of her.

The sun was now up and getting warmer by the minute. Back in Kentucky, this season would be called Indian summer.

She gazed heavenward and sighed when she saw golden eagles soaring above her, their wings spread wide. When they were lost to sight, she looked back at the ground. The remains of the rain lay in puddles where there was no grass.

The horses splashed through them and loped onward.

Suddenly Mary Beth stiffened. Fear raced through her as she heard the loud, distinctive roar of a bear.

Brave Wolf grabbed an arrow from his quiver and quickly notched it to his bowstring.

They traveled onward at a much slower gait until the bear came into sight a short distance away, straight ahead of them. Mary Beth froze with fear as Brave Wolf raised a hand in a silent command to stop.

As everyone held still, the large bear lumbered

past them, oblivious to the fact that it was being observed.

Mary Beth waited for Brave Wolf to shoot, and was surprised when he didn't.

"Aren't you going to kill it?" she whispered to him, hoping the bear would not hear her.

"I never kill needlessly," Brave Wolf replied softly. "The bear has not seen us. It is minding its business. So shall we mind ours."

"But when it sees us, we will be his business," Mary Beth argued. "We will be his meal, especially if you have this strange notion that you shouldn't kill it."

"If it becomes a threat, I will not hesitate to send an arrow into its heart," Brave Wolf said, frowning at her. "But until he is a threat, be still and just watch."

"But he doesn't have to *see* us," Mary Beth said. "Surely he can smell us."

"Not while the wind takes our smell away from him," Brave Wolf said. "Relax. It is best that you let me do what must be done, *if* it is required."

Mary Beth nodded and swallowed hard, still gazing anxiously at the bear.

Brave Wolf brought his horse closer to Mary Beth's. "Do you see how the bear's head is down?" he asked, having decided that if he explained things to her, she might understand better.

Mary Beth nodded.

"That is an indication that he is looking for rodents and insects," Brave Wolf said, again watching the bear. "See how he occasionally flips over a slab of rock? I imagine he is looking for ants to lick up."

"Ants?" Mary Beth said, shuddering. "How horrible."

She stiffened when the bear began walking toward them on all fours in a strange swaying motion, not looking forward but from side to side.

Then the creature suddenly stopped.

Mary Beth saw why. There were some remains of a dead deer partially hidden amid the tall grass.

The bear rolled the carcass over, sniffed it, then began to dig a hole with its sharp claws and large paws. To Mary Beth's surprise, it soon buried it find.

The bear then used its large paws to scrape the dirt over the deer, totally covering it.

"The bear has buried his find to let it spoil for a while before coming back to feast upon it," Brave Wolf explained.

"Truly? It prefers spoiled meat over fresh?" Mary Beth said.

Then she sighed with relief as the bear made a wide turn and sauntered away, soon hidden from view in the thickness of the trees.

"We must wait for the bear to get ahead of us before resuming our journey," Brave Wolf said, watching intently for a possible return of the animal.

Then, finally, they were able to move onward. After some miles they came to a wide, treeless plain, the last straight stretch of land they would traverse before starting the climb into the mountains.

Mary Beth now guessed that Brave Wolf had a set destination, for he seemed to know where he was going.

She hoped he would reach it before too much longer. Only then could she see light at the end of her tunnel, for until Brave Wolf found his brother, she would be forced to travel with him, instead of being able to search for her son.

"David," she whispered, and his name caused that terrible ache to begin inside her heart anew.

She was so afraid that she might never see him again. If only he had been fortunate enough to have been seen by a contingent of roaming cavalry and saved by them! She would continue thinking that, for only in doing so could she keep her sanity.

She slumped in the saddle as they rode onward toward the mountain slope. Again she was feeling dispirited and as though nothing in her world would ever be the same again.

She had lost her husband. She had lost her son.

She only wished now to be back on her farm in Kentucky with David safe beside her. There she would find solace.

She regretted that she had had to bury Lloyd so far away from his beloved Kentucky. At least if his grave was in Kentucky, she could have gone and talked to him from time to time. She could have placed flowers on the grave every day.

Now she had no grave to speak over, nor to take flowers to. . . .

"A man!" one of the warriors suddenly shouted. "I see a man on horseback in the distance. He seems ill. See how his head is hanging and how he barely holds onto the steed?"

"Oh, my Lord, he's fallen," Mary Beth cried when she caught sight of the man just as he slipped and fell from the horse.

The stranger was dressed in buckskin, with long, thick black hair and a face that shone copper colored beneath the brightness of the early afternoon sun.

She glanced over at Brave Wolf, whose eyes were wide with surprise just before he sank his heels into his horse's flanks and rode off at a hard gallop. She was left behind with the other warriors except for one who rode with Brave Wolf.

Mary Beth strained her neck in order to see when Brave Wolf leapt from his horse and sank to his knees on the ground beside the fallen warrior.

When she heard him cry out the name Night Horse, she realized that he had found his brother, and that his brother might have just died in his arms.

The warriors rode in a hard gallop toward Brave Wolf and the fallen warrior.

Mary Beth suddenly realized that she was alone. Her heart skipped a beat, for she knew that she had just been given the opportunity to ride in the opposite direction.

No one would even notice. She could find Fort Henry!

The cavalry could send out a search party for David.

But then she recalled the bear, the cries of mountain lions in the night, the baying of wolves, and yelping of coyotes. All of those wild creatures were a threat to her, perhaps more of a threat than being with Indians who so far, had treated her with only kindness. Instead of fleeing, she hurried forward, stopping when she came a few feet from where Brave Wolf was cradling the fallen warrior's head on his lap.

Yes, surely he had just found his lost brother, and by the looks of things, he might be at death's door.

She slid from the saddle just as Brave Wolf lifted Night Horse into his arms and carried him to a nearby stream. Its banks were shaded by willows, their leaves looking silver as they fanned in the gentle breeze.

Mary Beth watched as Brave Wolf laid his brother on a bank of purple primrose, then reached his hands into the water and brought some out to bathe his brother's fevered brow.

Mary Beth tied her horse with the others, which had been tethered to the limb of a lone tree that stood beside the stream.

She continued watching Brave Wolf, touched by his gentleness and caring toward his brother.

She could not help thinking of David and wondering if her son was being treated kindly by his captors, or being mistreated, possibly abused. . . .

That last thought filled her with such dread, she turned and ran away from Brave Wolf. Her face in her hands, she stopped and let the tears flood from her eyes. She sobbed.

And then she felt strong arms surround her.

"Why are you crying? Have I treated you so terribly?"

She recognized the voice and knew who was holding her so tenderly.

Brave Wolf.

He had left his brother to see to her welfare. At that moment, she knew that he would never do anything to harm her.

He did care for her.

Touched deeply by his tenderness, she made a snap decision to trust him. She turned quickly and gazed up into his eyes.

"No, it is not you," she sobbed out. She wiped the tears with the palms of her hands. "It is my son. I am so afraid for my son! Seeing your brother lying there so ill reminds me of how things might be for my little boy."

"Your son?" Brave Wolf said. "You have not spoken of a son before."

He was seized by jealousy, for if there was a son, surely there was a husband.

Then where was the husband?

Why had he not protected her better? If she were Brave Wolf's woman, he would have guarded her with his life.

"I didn't tell you because . . . because . . . I

wasn't sure if I could trust you with such information," she murmured. She wiped her eyes dry.

"And now you can?" Brave Wolf asked softly. He placed his hands at her cheeks, causing her to gaze into his eyes again. "Why do you trust me now when you would not before?"

"Because, oh, because . . ." she began, then sighed heavily. "Just because."

She looked past him at his brother, then looked into Brave Wolf's eyes again. "Because you left your brother and came to me when you heard me crying," she blurted out. "That proves that you care, truly care for me."

"I handed my brother over to a friend so I could come to you, and, yes, it was because I care for you that I momentarily put you first over my brother," he said thickly. "Now tell me about your son. Where is he?"

She explained as quickly as she could, for she knew by the way he kept glancing at his brother that he wished to be there with him.

When she was through, she saw a strange sort of relief in his eyes.

"Your husband died in the battle that killed Yellow Hair," Brave Wolf said thickly. "I am sorry for your loss."

But he was also glad, for he knew now that he would do anything to win this woman for his own.

She was free to love. And he would make sure that she loved him.

"Yes, he died," Mary Beth said, lowering her eyes.

Then she looked quickly up at him again. "But when I last saw my son, he was very much alive," she said. "I need to find him. Can . . . you . . . help me?"

He placed his hands gently on her shoulders. "I will get my brother home as quickly as possible, and then my warriors and I will search for your son."

"Why would you do this?" she asked, searching his eyes and finding emotion there that told her the answer to her question without his even saying it.

She knew that he would do this because he cared as deeply for her as she now allowed herself to feel for him.

"Why?" he said, knowing that it was not time to tell her the true reason . . . that he was in love with her and wanted her forever as his. "Because I am a just man who will not tolerate injustice toward others, especially toward small, innocent children."

She didn't believe that he was telling her everything about his feelings, and she understood.

This was not the time. . . .

Suddenly Night Horse emitted a cry of pain.

Brave Wolf hurried to his brother and knelt, lifting his head onto his lap again. "Night Horse, it is I. It is your brother who holds you," he said gently. "Night Horse, I have found you and will take you home to *Ina.* Do not die, my brother. Do not die."

Night Horse's eyes opened only momentarily.

He smiled up at Brave Wolf, then fell into another deep sleep.

Mary Beth went to Brave Wolf. Wanting to repay him for his kindness, she decided to rip a portion of her dress off so that she could use it as a cloth for bathing the warrior's face, but then remembered that she wasn't wearing her dress.

She was in the clothes of a man.

She suddenly realized that she had forgotten her dress where she had taken it off. Now what was she to do?

If she ever did have the chance to return to the white world, she would not want to arrive in Indian attire, especially a man's.

When Night Horse groaned in pain, Mary Beth cupped her hands and reached into the stream where the water was so clear she could see the white pebbles on the bottom. She filled her hands with water and brought them close to Night Wolf's face. Slowly she let the water trickle over his brow. Mary Beth turned to Brave Wolf, smiled, then suddenly realized she had never even told him her name. "I know you are called Brave Wolf," she said. "I am Mary Beth Wilson."

Brave Wolf smiled, for it was good to know that this woman no longer saw him as a man she could not trust. Instead he heard in her voice a note that told him she cared as much for him as he had grown to care for her.

He was touched by what she was doing for Night Horse. He saw her gentleness, her kindness, her beauty.

He was suddenly overwhelmed by deep, wondrous feelings for this woman. Yes, he now knew that destiny had brought them together, and destiny would not allow them to part. Somehow he would find a way to convince her that she should never return to the world of the white people again. Even her son, if he was found, would be accepted as a part of the Crow.

Mary Beth felt something mystically sweet flowing between herself and Brave Wolf and did not fight it. She was beginning to realize that events had unfurled as they had in order for them to meet.

Could it be that she'd had to travel this far to find true love?

Yes, it did seem so!

Chapter Ten

I feel again a spark of
that ancient flame.
—Virgil

Mary Beth was exhausted by the time they reached the Indian village that was Brave Wolf's home. But despite her exhaustion she was alert and somewhat fearful as she rode beside him into the village.

Mary Beth brought her horse closer to Brave Wolf's as she looked cautiously around her. She saw women busy cutting meat into thin strips and laying them on racks, as others cleaned skins that were stretched out on the ground.

She saw big-eyed children run over to Brave Wolf's horse and reach up to touch their chief as he continued to thread his way through the settlement.

Mary Beth stiffened when she saw the women stop their work and stare at her, then hurry to their children and lead them away.

She noted how all of the people's eyes went to the man who was being brought into their village on a travois behind Brave Wolf's steed. Mary Beth was glad that the attention was focused on Night Wolf now, rather than herself.

And she knew why. This man was someone they had never expected to see again. He had walked away from them and allied himself with whites.

She knew this because she had heard a warrior discussing it with Brave Wolf during their journey. She had heard the warrior tell Brave Wolf that he still was not certain Night Horse should be taken home, where so many would resent his presence.

Brave Wolf had told the warrior that it no longer mattered who thought what, for it was his decision to bring Night Wolf home.

And Brave Wolf's word was final.

Mary Beth had not asked Brave Wolf why one of his warriors would not want Night Horse taken home. He had suddenly volunteered that information after his warrior had fallen back to ride with the others.

As he had told her about a brother who had allied himself with white cavalrymen, she had been more aware than ever of Brave Wolf's true goodness.

Seeing the bitterness in so many of the Crow people's eyes, she knew that most did not forgive Night Horse. But she guessed they would tolerate him for the sake of one person: Brave Wolf's mother. Everyone understood the importance of his mother making peace with Night Horse, before she, or he, died.

Yes, Mary Beth knew the depths of love a mother felt for her son. Hers was so deep, she again felt a tearing at her heart when she thought of David and what he might be going through at the hands of his captors.

She brushed that fear from her mind as best she could and focused on the present. She gazed past the people and saw how large the village was. It was so large a settlement, she could not see where it began or ended.

Mary Beth again gazed into the crowd, noting especially the appearance of the women. Most were very attractive. She admired the porcupine-quill embroidery work on the women's doeskin dresses, and their black hair which hung in long braids down their backs. Their skin was as light as Brave Wolf's, and as smooth.

At that moment a warrior approached Brave Wolf to tell him that Two Tails's parents were in mourning and would not be among those who welcomed him home. His friend had been buried yesterday on top of a rocky bluff and covered with poles and rocks, with all the rites of a favored warrior.

Mary Beth could see the pain in Brave Wolf's eyes as he was told about the mourning and burial. She felt a pang of guilt, for if Brave Wolf had not taken the time to save her, putting himself and his warriors in danger while doing so, Two Tails would now be alive.

She shook off her guilt and sad memories and looked over at Brave Wolf. She knew he mourned his friend's passing, but for now his first priority must be getting his brother help.

Night Horse was terribly ill. When she had heard the rattling in his lungs, she remembered another time when she had heard that same sound just prior to someone's death. Her grandmother. Yes, shortly after Mary Beth had heard those strange rattling sounds in her grandmother's lungs, she had died.

She glanced over at Brave Wolf. She knew there was a problem between him and his brother. Though she had seen him gather his brother in his arms when he first found him, she knew that was because of the childhood they'd shared.

The man on the travois was vastly different from that young brave who grew up with his brother Brave Wolf.

She knew that Brave Wolf's concern for his mother was the main reason he had searched for Night Horse and reunited him with those he had turned his back on. Yet she could tell by the way he gazed at his brother when no one else but she caught him looking, there was much feeling left in his heart for his brother.

But could he ever truly forgive him? She did not think that he would have time to decide, for she believed Night Horse would be dead before another sun rose in the heavens.

"Mary Beth, we are almost at my mother's lodge," Brave Wolf said, interrupting her thoughts. "I believe it is best that you stay with me, since my people do not yet understand your presence among them."

Fear overwhelmed her at his words, for she understood that she might not be safe until his people knew more about her.

She swallowed hard, looked over her shoulder at the women, and then the men, and was glad that they no longer seemed to notice her, but instead focused their attention on the travois and the man lying upon it.

"Yes, Brave Wolf, I would be much more comfortable if I could stay with you," Mary Beth blurted out.

Then she hurriedly said, "I hope your mother is alright."

"My mother's will to live is strong, especially since she has peace to make with her younger son," Brave Wolf said stiffly. "If not for her, I . . ."

Mary Beth understood why he didn't finish what he was about to say. She saw a thin, very frail elderly woman being led from the tepee, flanked by two warriors who helped her, their muscled arms around her waist.

Mary Beth was reminded again of her grandmother. This woman, too, was at the end of her life. That truth was evident in her dark eyes and the thinness of her face and arms, and how she seemed to struggle with each step because of her weakness.

The sight made tears come to Mary Beth's eyes, for her grandmother had withered away almost to nothingness and had been buried only two years ago.

"*Ina*," Brave Wolf said, suddenly stopping and leaping from his saddle. He went to Pure Heart and swept her into his arms as the two warriors stepped away from her.

He hugged her, then held her at arm's length as he explained things to her. Then he led her onward until they came to the travois.

Mary Beth scarcely breathed as she awaited the reaction of the elderly Crow woman.

She grimaced as she watched the woman struggle and groan as she bent to her knees beside the travois.

And then the strength of a mother's love was obvious as she swept Night Horse into her arms, her voice awakening him.

His arms twined around her.

They both cried and clung, and then Pure Heart gazed up at Brave Wolf and nodded for him to help her to her feet.

When she was standing, she reached a gentle hand to Brave Wolf's cheek. "*Micinksi*, my son, please carry Night Horse to my lodge," she murmured. "There he will be made well."

"*Ina*, he is very ill," Brave Wolf cautioned, his eyes searching hers. "Do not expect too much."

"I have prayed for my second born from the moment you left until now," Pure Heart said, her jaw tightening. "He *will* be well again."

"Faith does mean a lot, *Ina.* I will take Night Horse to your lodge," Brave Wolf said, holding her hand and kissing its palm. He saw how his mother glanced quickly up at Mary Beth.

"The woman," Pure Heart said. "Is this the white woman I was told about when Two Tails's body was brought home to his parents?"

"Yes, this is the woman that my warriors and I saved from a band of renegades," Brave Wolf explained, looking past his mother and gazing into Mary Beth's eyes. "I made certain that everyone knew of her before her arrival, because I knew they would question how and why Two Tails died."

"Yes, I see, and you were right to prepare everyone before she arrived," Pure Heart said.

Mary Beth was so relieved when she didn't hear any resentment in Brave Wolf's mother's voice, nor did she see it in her eyes. This woman's heart was filled with more pressing concerns than curiosity about a white woman.

Pure Heart turned her eyes back to Night Horse and stepped away as Brave Wolf swept Night Horse into his arms. With the assistance of the same two warriors, Pure Heart followed Brave Wolf into her lodge, where he laid his brother on blankets and pelts beside the lodge fire.

"I have already sent for the shaman," Pure Heart said as she settled down on the mats beside Night Horse. She gazed up at Brave Wolf. "I know that you have the woman to see to. I will send word about Night Horse whenever there is a change in his condition."

Brave Wolf knew his mother was very aware that he was still torn about his brother. That was the only reason she had dismissed him so quickly. He knew that she hoped things would change and Brave Wolf would forgive Night Horse.

Brave Wolf nodded, leaned down and gave his mother a hug, then glanced again at Night Horse, whose eyes met his in a quiet plea of forgiveness.

Without another word, Brave Wolf walked away. He was glad that his mother seemed better than when he had last seen her.

Brave Wolf now believed that his mother's ailment had been exacerbated by a broken heart over a son she feared she would never see again.

And he understood. She was the best of mothers, who dearly loved both her sons.

He, on the other hand, was feeling far from brotherly toward Night Horse. He did not see how he could ever truly forgive him, yet so much inside his heart wanted to.

For now Brave Wolf would center his attention on Mary Beth. There was still too much left unsaid between them. When he had promised her that he would reunite her with her people, he believed he had seen feelings other than mere gratitude in her eyes.

He knew that what he felt for her was more than just admiration of her beauty.

He had wanted to find a woman to make a home with, and he had found her. Now to convince her that she wanted the same with *him.*

He found her waiting beside her horse.

His warriors had dismounted and had joined the others mingling outside his mother's lodge.

Just as Brave Wolf stepped up to Mary Beth, he saw the shaman, Many Clouds, enter his mother's lodge. He knew his brother's life lay in the shaman's hands now, and the First Maker's.

"Come with me to my lodge, where we can talk in private," Brave Wolf said. He took Mary Beth's horse's reins and handed them to a young brave who held his own horse's reins. "Little Fox, take the horses to the corral and remove the travois from mine."

The young brave nodded and hurried away with the animals.

Mary Beth realized now that Brave Wolf's tepee was not far from his mother's. Just before he raised the flap for her, she noticed a pole stuck in the ground on one side of the entranceway, a pole that she had heard described as a scalp pole.

She turned to him. "Is this your scalp pole?" she asked uncertainly, for on it were colorful pennant-like streamers of red cloth waving in the wind, not scalps.

"*Hecitu-yelo,* yes, this is my scalp pole," he said, seeing her grimace. "But notice that there are no scalps. With us Crow, taking scalps is not a thing of pride. We take no coup during warring."

"Warring?" Mary Beth gulped out. "I thought you said you are a peaceful people, that you are a peace-loving chief."

"The only time we take up arms against anyone is when a threat is made against our people by enemy tribes, and that is rare. It is known that if our warriors are forced into a fight, they are always victorious over their foes," Brave Wolf said proudly. "It is my place to ensure that no warring is brought into my camp. Thus far, we have been left untouched by both our brothers and whites."

He took her gently by the hand. "Come inside and sit with me beside my lodge fire," he said. "I know how tired you are. The weariness shows in your eyes."

"Yes, I am sorely tired," she said softly, trying not to let him see her reaction to his holding her hand.

The touch of his flesh against hers made her heart soar in a way that was new to her. She had never truly loved before.

She only wished it were possible for them to be free to love. But surely it was as taboo among his people for him to love a white woman as it was among hers for her to love a red man.

And . . . she had just lost a husband. She felt ashamed to have fallen in love when Lloyd was in his grave for such a short time.

And her thoughts should be on her son.

Yes, she did feel ashamed, but also more alive than ever before in her life. And it was all because of one man. Brave Wolf.

She went inside with him and he gently pulled her down onto a thick pallet of pelts beside the smoldering fire. She watched as he added wood to the slow-burning flames, then sat down beside the fire opposite her.

She again wondered whether he might have a wife. She looked quickly around and saw no signs of a woman living with him. Surely that meant he wasn't married.

If he was, and she had fallen in love with a married man, she would want to die, for surely feelings such as she had for Brave Wolf could not come twice in one's lifetime.

She made herself stop thinking such things. She would find out in time whether he was married, or had children.

"So many of your people seemed unhappy to see your brother brought home," Mary Beth said as she tried to find a way to make small talk with him before she asked him whether he was married, and when he was going to search for her son as he had promised to do.

She felt that he would have a better chance of finding David than the soldiers at Fort Henry, for surely an Indian could find other Indian camps much better than whites.

This was Indian land. Surely Indians could find a lost boy on it much more quickly than soldiers who were new to the area.

"His return troubles me also," Brave Wolf said, slowly nodding. "It was so wrong for my brother to ride with *washechu,* white pony soldiers, especially the one all red men called Yellow Hair. Custer was hated by us all. He is known far and wide for his atrocities against our people."

A warrior's voice outside the tepee drew both

Mary Beth and Brave Wolf's eyes to the entranceway.

"Chief Brave Wolf, there are some of us who need to speak with you about Night Horse's presence in our village," the warrior said.

Brave Wolf rose to his feet.

He went to the entrance flap and swung it aside. Outside, he found several of his warriors waiting.

"What is it you wish to say?" Brave Wolf asked, slowly moving his eyes from man to man.

Mary Beth sat stiffly beside the fire, listening.

"We have had a quick council and have concluded that it is not good to have Night Horse at our village for very long," the first warrior said, speaking for the others. "He turned his back on us once before by going to the pony soldiers. If he recovers, what is to stop him from betraying us again?"

"I believe you are wrong. I understand your feelings, but my brother will stay until he is well. Only then will I ask him to leave again," Brave Wolf said tightly. "At first I sought him at my mother's request. But now he is here to recuperate. Brothers are brothers, and for now, no matter what Night Horse is guilty of, I will stand by him."

Mary Beth became very aware of the sudden silence that fell among those who stood outside. Chief Brave Wolf had denied their request.

She hoped that Brave Wolf had made the right decision.

Chapter Eleven

Love looks not with the eyes, but with
the mind, and, therefore, is wing'd
cupid painted blind.

—Shakespeare

Mary Beth was just working up the nerve to ask Brave Wolf how soon he could send warriors out to look for her son when he began to speak himself.

"I had not known that my warriors so adamantly opposed my brother being here in the village," he said in a worried tone. "Now that I do, I must go into council and explain further my decision to allow Night Horse to stay, at least until he can fend for himself. Otherwise, I will most surely be sending my brother to his death."

"But those who rode with you did not question

your decision or your authority." Mary Beth said, wanting to direct his attention elsewhere . . . to David.

And she still didn't know if he was married or not. She wasn't sure how to ask, for she didn't want to appear brazen. Anyone who knew her well knew she was anything but that.

But she had never before met anyone like Brave Wolf; nor had she found any other man who made her want him so much.

"Those who are questioning my brother's presence are the warriors who stayed behind, hoping that Night Horse would not be found. Now that he is among our people, they find it hard to accept. And I understand. My brother turned his back on our people. He betrayed the Crow by riding with Custer.

But my brother must not be judged by us. The First Maker, who made the world, and who presides over it even now, will hand down his final sentencing. Until then, I will stand behind my promise to my mother. I will see that Night Horse is well enough to fend for himself again, and then I will ask him to leave."

"I'm sorry things have to be so difficult," she murmured. She watched as he turned and moved slowly toward the entrance flap. "I admire your dedication to your brother despite the wrong he has done. A brother's love must be special."

Brave Wolf turned and gazed at her. "It was . . . it *is*," he said thickly. "Surely no two other brothers have ever grown up so close. Thoughts came to us at the same time. Often we had no need even to speak, for our thoughts . . . our feelings . . . were shared. I had always thought that nothing could separate us from each other. When we rode our steeds, our shadows merged in the moonlight. Our hearts beat to the same drum."

He raked his fingers through his long, thick hair in frustration. "I never knew when, or why, my brother's shadow separated from mine, or when our heartbeats changed their rhythm," he said tightly. "Suddenly one day he was a stranger to me and to our people. Why? I am not certain I will ever know the true cause."

He sighed. "I must hurry now to those who wait for me," he said softly.

"Will you be long in council?" Mary Beth asked, knowing now that she had no choice but to wait.

When Brave Wolf heard the softness in Mary Beth's voice, he knew that they had arrived at a different level of friendship. She was no longer a woman of defiance. She was a woman who trusted . . . who possibly even cared more than she was saying.

It was in her eyes that she saw him as a desirable man.

But now was not the time to consider what could be between them. For now, he must concentrate on making things right in his village.

His people came first. That was why he was chief.

But one day soon he must make room for a woman in his life. If at all possible, it would be the white woman with the caring heart and pretty eyes!

"I will be gone for as long as it takes to calm my warriors' anger. And then I will also take time to go speak with the parents of Two Tails, the one who died as we were rescuing you," Brave Wolf said, wishing he could take Mary Beth into his arms and tell her that he cared for her and that he still planned to hunt for her child. But he did not dare to be so openly affectionate with her just yet.

He hoped that soon he would feel free to do so . . . when she showed that she wanted it from him.

His gaze swept slowly over her, noting that she still wore the clothes that were far too big for her, and yet she had not complained.

That, too, he liked about her. With one more smile for her, he left his lodge.

Again Mary Beth realized she'd been left alone. How easy it would be to flee if she wished to.

But the very thought of being out there on wild land, where wild savages roamed, made her tremble with fear. Instead of leaving, she sat down on the wondrously soft pelts beside the fire and waited for Brave Wolf to return.

Then she would beg Brave Wolf to send a search party out for her son. Surely his men knew all the local hiding places, since they had lived in the area all their lives.

Yes, back in Kentucky, she knew every nook and cranny on the land that surrounded her home. She smiled as she recalled a monstrous cave that she and Lloyd had found when she was ten and he was twelve. It was a mammoth place of caverns and stalagmites. It had been like entering another world . . . a place of fantasy.

Again shame filled her as she recalled what had brought her to this land in the first place. A divorce from a man she had been best friends with since his parents had bought the farm adjoining her parents' land, when she was five and he was seven. Now . . . he . . . was dead!

Mary Beth brushed tears from her eyes just as she heard a movement behind her.

Thinking that Brave Wolf had returned, she turned her head quickly. She was surprised to see Brave Wolf's elderly mother coming into the tepee, a dress draped over her arms.

Mary Beth hurried to her feet and smiled weakly at Pure Heart. She could guess why the kind old woman had come. No doubt she had seen how hideously Mary Beth was dressed and wanted to turn her back into a lady.

"On his way to the council house, my son Brave Wolf came and asked a favor of me," Pure Heart said in just as perfect English as Brave Wolf spoke. She held the heavily beaded dress out to Mary Beth. "He asked that I bring you a dress." Her face crinkled into a smile. "At one time I was more your size than I am now. Now I am so thin my son says that I am no heavier than a feather and if a strong wind should come along, it would sweep me into the air and carry me away."

She gazed at her dress, then smiled again at Mary Beth. "I took this dress from those I wore when I was young and pretty like you," she murmured. "The dress is now yours."

"Mine?" Mary Beth asked, amazed that Pure Heart should be so generous to her, a stranger . . . and a white one at that.

"It would please me if you would accept the dress," Pure Heart said. "My son Brave Wolf has never taken a wife, so he cannot ask any other woman to lend you her clothes."

Mary Beth's heart skipped a beat at those words. Now she knew Brave Wolf wasn't married and the knowledge filled her with sudden joy.

She could hardly wait to see him again, yet when she did, how would she behave now that she knew he was free to be loved?

And, ah, yes, she did love him. She wasn't sure of the moment it had happened, but nonetheless, it *had* happened!

Pure Heart stepped closer to Mary Beth and placed the dress in her arms. "Brave Wolf told me of your kindness to Night Horse when he was found," she murmured. "I, too, would show kindness. This dress is only a small way of thanking you."

"Night Horse looked so ill, how could I not have helped in whatever way I could?" Mary Beth said softly, pulling the dress up against her. She was truly glad to accept it, even though she might look more Indian than white when she wore it.

Then she gazed into the old woman's faded eyes. "How is Night Horse now?" she blurted out.

"The fever is less," Pure Heart said. "And soon

it will disappear altogether. Our people's shaman, Many Clouds, is with Night Horse now. That is the only reason I could leave my son's side during his time of illness. Night Horse and Many Clouds are in the sweat lodge, where my son's illness will be sweated out of him as Many Clouds brushes smoke across his eyes with feathers. Thus the evil spirits that are responsible for making my son foreign even to himself will be gone. When Night Horse is wet with sweat, he will be taken to the river where the cold, cleansing water will heal him. Women are not allowed in the sweat lodge or I would have accompanied my son and Many Clouds there."

"I hope that Night Horse will get well soon," Mary Beth murmured.

Pure Heart placed a gentle hand on Mary Beth's face. "Brave Wolf sees something in you that is special," she murmured. "So does his mother, even though I never thought I could see goodness in any white eyes. They are takers. They are selfish. Thanks only to the efforts of my husband and Brave Wolf, thus far the white eyes have not taken from our Whistling Water Clan of Crow."

"I understand your feelings, even though it was people of your color who took my husband's life," Mary Beth said, swallowing hard. "I know that there is good and bad in whites, *and* Indians. I'm glad to know that I am among a good people. I do so appreciate your kindness toward me."

"I must go now," Pure Heart said. "My son's time at the sweat lodge should be almost over. I want to be in my tepee when he is brought back."

"Thank you so much for the dress," Mary Beth said. "And . . . for not seeing me as the enemy."

"Anyone with such a beautiful smile and such softness in her voice could surely be no one's enemy," Pure Heart said. She patted Mary Beth's cheek, turned, then stopped and looked back at Mary Beth. "I am called Pure Heart."

"I am called Mary Beth," Mary Beth said, delighted that she had made such a friend in Brave Wolf's mother!

Pure Heart nodded, smiled, then turned again and left the tepee.

Still marveling over what had just transpired, Mary Beth held the dress out before her. She sighed at its loveliness and at the generosity of its giver. She had two special allies . . . Brave Wolf and his mother!

Yes, she was happy about how things were and she was glad to have the beautiful dress. She threw off the ugly breeches and shirt and replaced them with the pretty white doeskin dress.

She ran her hands down the front, around the beautiful beaded designs, and sighed at the softness of the doeskin. Feeling how prettily it hung on her body, she smiled. She wondered how Brave Wolf would see her.

She didn't have any longer to wonder about it. Her pulse raced when Brave Wolf came into the tepee, stopped, and gazed admiringly at her.

Oh, Lord, the longer she was with this man, the more she cared for him.

Now that she trusted him and knew that he was not married, she could allow herself to feel things for him that she had never felt for any other man.

When he stepped up to her and gently drew her into his arms, she allowed it.

"*Mitawin*, woman, I cannot help having feelings for you," he said huskily. "There is so much goodness in you . . . so much love."

He placed a finger beneath her chin and lifted her face so that their eyes met and held. "My heart tells me to kiss you," he said thickly. "Will you allow it?"

The way he asked her, and the passion in his eyes, made her want him to kiss her so badly, yet she knew that it was wrong. Her husband had been dead for only a short while. And David. She should be concerned only about David, not her own selfish needs.

Afraid of where even one kiss might lead them, Mary Beth felt that she had no choice but to step away from him. She fought the pounding of her heart, the longing she felt for him, and sat down on the pelts.

She forced her eyes to gaze into the fire, not at him. She knew that if she gazed up at him again, all thoughts but those of being with him would be swept away.

She would go to him.

She would melt into his arms.

There would be such magic in his kiss.

She knew she must fight against this need,

against the wondrous feelings that being in his arms had stirred.

She knew, as well, that it was not right at this time to ask him to search for David. It would not be right to deny him one thing and then suddenly ask for another.

For several moments, there was only a strained silence between them.

Oh, surely he heard the throbbing of her heart.

Oh, surely he felt the passion that was flowing between them!

But surely he now also felt a deep rejection.

She scarcely breathed as she waited for him to speak . . . or to leave.

Understanding why a white woman might be afraid to show her true feelings for a red man, knowing that in her world it was forbidden, Brave Wolf gazed at Mary Beth for a moment longer, then left the lodge.

Mary Beth dropped her face into her hands and wept for a man she knew she shouldn't want; for a son captured by warriors she knew were nothing like Brave Wolf; and for herself. How she missed her husband, even though she had never loved him as a woman should love a husband.

At this moment, she ached for arms around her, to comfort her, and not just any man's. She ached for Brave Wolfs!

"What have I done?" she sobbed, for she feared her rejection might have turned Brave Wolf into her enemy.

She felt a chill race across her flesh. She looked

over her shoulder and saw a robe lying half unrolled on the floor. It looked inviting and warm.

Without much thought she reached for it. She turned it in her hands, recalling the bear that had frightened her earlier. This fur looked like it might have come from a bear.

She remembered how Brave Wolf had allowed the bear that crossed their paths to live. But surely bears *were* killed for their warm pelts. The winters were long and cold in Montana.

She ran her hand slowly over it, envisioning Brave Wolf wearing the robe. Smiling, she slipped into it, sighing at its warmth and softness.

She yawned sleepily, stretched her arms above her head, then curled up in the robe by the fire stones that circled the lodge fire. Within moments she had drifted off into the welcome void of sleep.

Chapter Twelve

> We were taught to believe
> that the Great Spirit sees and hears
> everything, and that he never forgets;
> that hereafter he will give every
> man a spirit-home.
>
> —Chicf Joseph

When Brave Wolf returned to his tepee, he found Mary Beth asleep by the fire. He smiled when he saw her asleep in his bear robe, so cozy and beautiful.

He stopped and gazed down at her.

He was touched anew by her loveliness.

And asleep there was such a quiet beauty about her . . . such a soft innocence.

Her hair lay around her head like a splash of sun's glow. Her long, thick lashes rested upon her cheeks like veils. And her lips, parted only slightly, made him long to kiss her.

Slowly he knelt beside her, so close he could feel her soft breath upon his bare knees. It was hard not to reach out and run a finger across those lips, harder still not to bend low and press his lips to hers.

But he recalled with much regret how she had denied him a kiss only a short while ago. Yet he was not hurt or angry. He understood her denial, without her even explaining it to him.

It was because he was of a different culture . . . a different color.

He was of the people who had taken her husband's life and stolen her son from her. Would she always see her husband's death and her son's abduction when she gazed into Brave Wolf's eyes, even though he'd had no role in either?

Or would she one day allow herself to realize that *he* was of a different breed from those who'd fought upon that battlefield where all white eyes had died, among them her husband?

Was he fooling himself to believe that a small part of her cared for him, no matter the color of his skin? How could he not believe that, when she gazed at him with the look of a woman who felt desire for a man?

When she began stirring, Brave Wolf rose quickly to his feet and sat opposite the fire from her. He did not want to alarm her by staying so close, observing her. He must be patient and hope that she would soon let down her guard and allow herself to feel . . . to love. . . .

Mary Beth yawned, licked her lips, then slowly opened her eyes.

Just as her eyes caught sight of the fire, and then the walls of the tepee, she was again reminded of where she was, and why.

David sprang quickly to her mind and just as quickly brought tears to her eyes.

She wiped away the tears as she slowly rose to a sitting position. And then she saw Brave Wolf sitting so quiet across the fire from her, his gaze upon her.

In a flash of memory she recalled their last moments together and how she had denied him a kiss. Even worse, she had denied *herself* the kiss.

She was filled with pangs of guilt. Surely he hated her now.

Yet as her eyes held his, she saw no hate, no resentment.

She saw something akin to adoration and knew without a doubt he had fallen in love with her, just as she had with him.

She hated this complication. He was Indian. She was white. She hated that word "forbidden."

How could something so beautiful be wrong?

Yet she still felt a twinge of guilt over falling in love with him so quickly and never loving Lloyd at all in that special way.

And Lloyd was dead for such a short time!

"Did you get some rest?" Brave Wolf asked, choosing to break the awkward silence.

He could read people well . . . even women, and knew that she was battling many conflicting emotions.

He hoped she would soon win the battle and allow herself to love him. Life was short. When one found a true love, one must act, or risk losing it forever.

"Yes, I feel very much rested," Mary Beth said, then laughed softly. "I do not even recall falling asleep. It . . . just happened."

"These past days have taken a toll on you," Brave Wolf said thickly. "It is only natural that you would seek the solace of sleep."

She ducked her head so that he would not see a resurgence of tears. "Yes, what I have gone through has been terrible," she murmured. "I do welcome those moments when sleep takes the memories away, if only for a short while."

"I have sent many of my warriors out to search for your son," Brave Wolf said, drawing her eyes quickly to him. "I explained to them that he is a young brave of five winters, and that his hair is how you described it to me . . . the color of wheat. I told them that his eyes are blue like the sky."

A slight frown creased his brow. "I must tell you that my warriors' reaction to that description was what I expected," he said. "When I told them of the golden hair and blue eyes, they thought of someone else whose hair and eyes were those colors."

"Custer," Mary Beth said, her eyes wavering.

"*Hecitu-yelo*, yes, Custer," he said, lifting a log and sliding it into the flames.

"Did that truly make a difference?" Mary Beth asked warily.

"Not after I reminded them that this was a child, not a man with a likeness to Custer," Brave Wolf said. He sighed. "My warriors are even now searching for your son."

"You did not include yourself in the search," Mary Beth said, searching his eyes. "Why?"

"I must stay close at hand for my brother in case he takes a turn for the worse," Brave Wolf said, his voice drawn.

"Then it is not because of me . . . because you thought I might flee if you were not around to stop me?" Mary Beth asked guardedly.

"No, it was not because of that," Brave Wolf said, his eyes now searching hers. "I was gone long enough during my council for you to leave . . . and you did not. You now understand the dangers of being alone, away from my protection. I am glad that you do."

"Yes, I do understand, but, Brave Wolf, I wanted to be with those who searched for David," she said, her voice breaking. "I wanted to be there when my son was rescued, if he *is* rescued. Surely he is terribly frightened without me. The sooner he sees me, the better it will be for him."

"It is not safe for you to accompany my men on this search," he explained softly. "You see, it might turn into a raiding party, as it was when you were rescued from the renegades. It may be necessary to fight to get your son."

"I hope they can get him without a fight," Mary Beth said, shivering at the thought of her David being put in still more danger.

"If your son is found, my warriors will do everything within their power to see that he is not harmed," Brave Wolf said. "Please do not worry. All is being done to save him."

"Thank you so much," Mary Beth said, stifling a sob behind a hand. "You have been so kind to me."

"You do not deserve what fate has handed you," he said. Then he looked toward the entrance flap when a soft voice spoke from outside it. The words spoken were in Crow, so Mary Beth had no idea what the woman was saying.

"At my request, food has been brought for us," Brave Wolf said. He rose and went to the entranceway. He held the flap aside as a beautiful young Indian maiden entered. She carried a wooden tray of food. From what Mary Beth could tell, it was a combination of meat, fruit, and bread.

Dancing Butterfly smiled up at Brave Wolf, then walked past him and without a nod or a hello to Mary Beth, acted as though she wasn't even there. She set the tray opposite the fire from Mary Beth, then smiled once more at Brave Wolf and left.

Brave Wolf had seen how Dancing Butterfly had behaved toward Mary Beth and was embarrassed, for both Mary Beth and Dancing Butterfly. His clan's women were normally kind. But he must remember that none of them had seen a white woman up close, especially one who sat in their chief's lodge.

He knew that a keen resentment toward Mary Beth was running rampant among his people. All knew that he would soon bring a woman into his lodge as a wife. He knew that none would want this wife to be white.

But if he, their chief, did choose a white woman, which he now hoped to do, his people would have no choice but to accept his decision. His word was final in all things.

"I apologize for Dancing Butterfly's rudeness," he said. He took the tray and placed it beside Mary Beth, then sat down with the tray between them.

"Never has Dancing Butterfly seen a white woman in her chief's lodge," he explained. "It is something she does not understand, or like. By not speaking to you or looking at you, she was pretending you are not here."

"I'm sorry for the resentments your people feel," Mary Beth murmured. "I wish things hadn't happened to cause it, but there are greedy white men who behave toward your people just the same as Dancing Butterfly acted toward me. They do not see your people when they look at them. What they see is what they can steal *from* them . . . the land, the animals, the streams and rivers."

"*Hecitu-yelo,* as it has been since that first bullet was fired upon my people," Brave Wolf said sadly.

"Yet you still seek the peaceful ways with the white community," Mary Beth marveled. She nodded a silent thank you when he gave her the wooden tray of food. She took a piece of meat from it, then handed the tray back to him. "Will you still be this peaceful if the cavalry comes and . . . and . . . attacks your village?"

"I seek peace, but I have been appointed as chief to protect my people," he said, taking a piece of cooked rabbit, then setting the tray between them. "I will do what I must to keep my people free of harm. Under normal circumstances, life for my people is such a simple one. You see, the Crow economy is based on the availability of game and edible foods. Both game and plant foods are abundant in the Crow country. Men are responsible for hunting game, women for curing it. Do you not see how easy it would be for my people to exist as they have for generations if whites would allow us the same existence as our ancestors?"

Mary Beth took a bite of meat, chewed and swallowed it, then turned her eyes back to Brave Wolf. "I understand what you are saying, but, Brave Wolf, you know that President Grant will be out for blood after what happened at the Battle of the Little Big Horn," she said guardedly. "Although your clan played no role in the terrible battle, you could be accused of it."

"I am friends with the Great White Father in Washington, so he will send an order to all forts here in Montana land *not* to include my people in his retaliation," Brave Wolf said.

Yet in his heart he knew that at a time like this, the President might forget their friendship and see him as no different from any other Indian.

Brave Wolf would keep sending his prayers to the First Maker that what he feared would not come to pass.

He bit off a piece of meat and looked again at Mary Beth as she spoke.

"How did the council go today?" she asked, wanting to change the subject.

"My warriors listened well to what I had to say about Night Horse, and agreed to what I have done," Brave Wolf said, looking sad as he gazed into the fire.

"Perhaps they agreed because he was once loved so much among your people," Mary Beth said softly. She smiled when that brought Brave Wolf's eyes back to her. "How could he not have been the sort of man who would be loved? Is he not your brother? Was he not like you in many ways before he chose the wrong life path? You have spoken of how it was between you when you were growing up. You had such devotion to one another. Surely everyone saw and admired the same goodness in Night Horse as in you, his brother."

"You are wise to see such a truth, because it was that way," Brave Wolf said. "Everyone did admire my brother as I admired and loved him."

"What happened to make him want a different life from yours when he grew into a man?" Mary Beth asked warily. She was afraid that she might be asking too many questions.

But it was so good to have this gentle time of camaraderie with Brave Wolf. It helped make her forget how much she wanted him to hold her . . . to kiss her.

She ached for his touch and was weakening in her defenses. If he came to her even now and held her and again asked her if he could kiss her, she knew that she would not deny him.

The longer she was with him, the more she doubted she could follow the rules that forbade her from loving him. She had lost so much in her life . . . oh, Lord, she did not want to give up this wonderful man, too.

"What happened?" Brave Wolf repeated, sighing. "Night Horse saw the power of the white man's guns. He saw their riches. He saw the chance to have what whites had. Greed, greed for what he should not have wanted—that was why my brother became my enemy, for he *is* my enemy."

Again he sighed. "My brother, the enemy," he repeated, drawing his fingers through his hair in frustration. "How can . . . that . . . be?"

"In life there are so many things that make no sense," Mary Beth said, her voice breaking. "My son. How can he have been taken from me? Where is he?"

Hearing her sorrow, her frustration, her sadness, Brave Wolf pushed the plate of meat away and moved to Mary Beth's side.

Without even considering being rejected again, he wrapped his arms around Mary Beth and brought her close to him.

Mary Beth melted in his arms. She nestled close.

"This feels so wonderful," she murmured. "So right."

Brave Wolf's heart soared at those words. His heart drummed inside him.

But he didn't dare spoil the moment by trying to kiss her again.

He would relish this moment, and hope to go further than a hug soon. For now, it was enough that she allowed his comforting arms around her. He was stunned, when a moment later, she pulled free of him again. Turning her back to him, she had her face in her hands and softly sobbed.

Believing that her reaction to their embrace had nothing to do with him, yet worrying about it and needing answers, he placed his hands on her shoulders and gently turned her. He framed her face between his hands and even more gently lifted it so that their eyes met.

He didn't question her with words. His eyes said it all.

"Please never think that my behavior is because of you," she said through a blur of tears. "What I said earlier about your embrace feeling so right is truly how I feel, but . . ."

"But?" he asked softly.

"I feel so much guilt," she gulped out.

"Guilt over having feelings for me, a red man?"

"No, oh no, please don't think that."

"Then what causes this guilt?"

"I cannot stop thinking that if I had not left Kentucky, which is my home, my husband would still be alive," she said, her voice breaking. "For certain my son would not be in the hands of murderous renegades. I . . . made . . . the wrong decision. I can't stop thinking about it."

"Do you believe, then, that you are making the wrong decision by allowing yourself to love Brave Wolf?" he asked, his eyes searching hers.

"No, *no,*" she said, a new guilt grabbing at her . . . guilt over making him feel all the wrong things. "I . . . I . . . do love you. Oh, truly I do. I . . . adore . . . you."

She was stunned that she had actually said it . . . that she had told him she loved him.

She was not a person to be so forward, especially with men.

She had truly known only one man . . . her husband.

But she felt such ease while with Brave Wolf, as though she could tell him everything.

His heart sang to realize his deepest hopes were true, that she did . . . she could . . . love him.

He had believed she did, but knew that those beliefs could have stemmed from wanting her to love him so badly.

"You say words that mean so much to me," Brave Wolf replied. "I love you. I knew that I did almost the moment I saw you."

"As did I, although I was afraid to admit it because I didn't dare trust you," she murmured.

"But now you trust enough," he said, drawing her closer, yet not fully into his arms.

"Yes, oh, yes," she said, her heart throbbing, her knees weak with passion.

"Yet you always pull away from me when we embrace . . . when we are about to kiss," he said, again searching her eyes.

"Only because I think I shouldn't be feeling these things for a man so soon after my husband's death . . . and when I don't even know the fate of my son," she said, swallowing hard. "Now do you understand? Do you?"

"Yes, now I understand," he said, then brushed kisses across her lips that made her feel faint with rapture.

He stepped away from her, yet still held her hands. "And because I do understand, I will wait for you to tell me when you are ready to follow your heart's desire. When you are ready, I shall give you such loving. . . ."

"I know," she said, grateful that she was in love with a man who was not only handsome and gentle, but also so sweetly understanding. "I know that what we will share will be so beautiful. You . . . you are such a special man. Thank you, oh, thank you for loving me and for giving me the time I need to get past my guilt . . . my sadness."

"Until then, we shall share in simple things, like talk, like teaching you the ways of the Crow, because I want you to be as one with my people when you become my wife."

Her eyes widened. Her heart was filled with sweet, wondrous joy as she gazed lovingly up at him.

His wife?

Could it truly be?

Knowing he loved her so much made her feel less guilty already. She finally could see the promise of a happy future. . . . a future with him!

Chapter Thirteen

> She's beautiful and therefore to be woo'd.
> She is a woman, therefore to be won.
> —Shakespeare

Several days had passed and still the warriors had not returned with word about David. Mary Beth feared the search had been unsuccessful.

But not all of the warriors were involved in the search for David. There were normal, everyday chores to be taken care of. Some men had gone hunting, returning with bucks slung across their horses' rumps.

Mary Beth was trying to prepare herself to accept the news Brave Wolf's men might bring back with them about David. Brave Wolf had told her this morning that he expected them to return either today or tomorrow.

"Do not give up hope that you will be reunited with your son, whether or not he is found by my warriors," Brave Wolf said as he sat with Mary Beth beside the fire in his tepee.

A soft rain had just begun to fall from the gray heavens, the dampness making the day cold and uncomfortable outside.

But inside Brave Wolf's lodge, Mary Beth felt cozy and strangely at peace, even knowing that more than likely she might not be seeing her son today, or perhaps ever. Brave Wolf had such a way about him, he had made Mary Beth's guilt and hurt lessen day by day.

They shared such a wonderful love, how could she not feel the bliss that came from being with him?

The fact that he had not pressed her or even mentioned making love, although she knew that he hungered for it, proved the sort of man he was.

He was honorable in every way. He showed such respect for a woman.

When they did make love, ah, how sweet it would be.

"I can never give up on finding David, not until . . . until . . . proof of his death is brought to me," Mary Beth murmured. She shuddered. "But I can't even think about that. I have to keep faith in the good Lord above that David is still alive, and that we will be reunited."

She scooted closer to Brave Wolf, but not so close that she would get in the way of his arrow making. She was learning new things every day from him.

Of course, as a woman she didn't really need to know how to make arrows. It was the man's job to keep his cache of weapons ready in case a threat came upon his people. But she wanted to learn everything she could about his way of life.

Since it was raining, the people were doing their chores inside their lodges now. If it wasn't raining, she would have sat with the women outside in the shade, learning either beading or how to decorate a cradleboard, which was used for carrying Indian babies.

She had even helped the women make pemmican. The women had dried a lot of thinly sliced meat strips. She had helped pound them into pemmican, which they mixed with buffalo-leg bone marrow and dried chokeberries. She had helped them roll this mixture into different-sized balls that they had then spread on a buckskin, and covered.

She was surprised that the women had accepted her among them so readily and she knew that Brave Wolf was responsible for their changed attitude. Surely he had met with them in private and explained his feelings toward Mary Beth, making it clear what he expected of them.

None showed resentment of her any longer, but she knew that surely many felt uncomfortable at her presence among them. She hoped that they would eventually care for her, for she was going to be a part of their lives forever.

She was going to marry their chief!

Yes! As unbelievable as it was to Mary Beth, she *was* going to have a future with Brave Wolf.

She was going to be his wife.

She thought further of the cradleboards. They were so lovely and sweet. Just thinking about having a child born of her and Brave Wolf's love made her insides glow. To give David a brother or sister would be something she knew her son would enjoy. He had often spoken of having a brother or sister.

Since Lloyd's army career had kept him away from her more than with her, it had been almost impossible for Mary Beth to provide David with a brother or sister.

And the problem wasn't only that Lloyd was gone for such long periods of time. Even when he was at home, she could almost count the times she and he had made love these past four years.

She had known long ago that Lloyd's love for her was more that of a brother than a husband, because even when he was home, he seemed more interested in reading books than making love.

That had came as a relief to Mary Beth, since she just enjoyed *being* with Lloyd, not making love to him.

Now she anxiously awaited the lovemaking with Brave Wolf, but she did hope he could be patient with her a while longer.

"I not only make my own arrows, but also my own bows," Brave Wolf said as he saw her interest in what he was doing. As her eyes followed his hands' movements, he explained, "My favorites are those made of two buffalo horns. I take a large horn and saw a slice off each side of it. These slices are then filed or rubbed down until the flat sides fit nicely together. They are then glued and wrapped at the ends."

"Glue?" Mary Beth asked. "Where do you get your glue?"

"Glue is made by boiling buffalo gristle or various other parts of the buffalo," he explained.

"And the arrows," Mary Beth said. "Tell me about them."

"The arrows I am making now are used for hunting standing or motionless animals," Brave Wolf said, trying hard to keep Mary Beth's mind occupied. Although she had said that she had not given up on finding her son, he knew that doubt was creeping into her heart.

Every once in a while she would lower her eyes, and he knew it was because she did not want him to see her pain. He knew that she was trying hard to be courageous, but that no matter how hard she tried, her hope was weakening.

"I am making a greasewood shaft for this arrow," he continued. "Do you see its hardened tip?"

Mary Beth nodded, trying to concentrate on his words so she would not think about David. But as each moment passed with no good word about her son, she felt more and more hopeless.

"Is this shaft more deadly than others?" she asked.

She had seen him make many types of shafts and

had learned that there were arrows with small points, so-called "bird points," and now arrows with no points at all.

He held the arrow out for Mary Beth to examine more closely. "All are deadly," he said. "Some bowmen can send such arrows clear through animals, including the big buffalo."

He laid the arrow aside and paused in his chore for a moment. "For moving animals, especially buffalo chased on horseback, arrows with standard-sized barbed heads are used," he said. "A hunter can send an arrow about six to eight inches into the soft flank just behind the ribs, and as the buffalo continues to run, the arrow cuts deeper and deeper into its vital organs. Before long the animal stops and soon dies."

He lifted another arrow and ran his fingers along the smooth finish of the shaft. "In warfare, the largest barbed points are preferred because of their incapacitating effects," he explained. "When a warrior is hit with such an arrow, it is less painful to extricate by pushing it through than by trying to pull it back out. A small-pointed arrow might go clear through a man and not mortally wound him if no vital organs or bones are hit."

He had not realized how telling her such details was affecting Mary Beth until he heard her gasp and saw how pale she had become. She rose quickly to her feet and turned her back to him.

He quickly laid the arrow aside and went to her, drawing her into his arms and turning her to face him. "Going into such detail about what arrows can do was wrong," he said huskily.

He lifted her chin with a finger so that their eyes met. "I apologize."

"*I* apologize for proving over and over how weak I am," she murmured. "It is so much unlike me. I . . . I . . . have always been proud of my strength. But you have seen me shed tears too often, and now today I let you see that hearing such details made me feel ill. How could you want someone like me as your wife? I'm afraid I would embarrass you."

"You prove over and over again that you are a woman with deep feelings," he said. "There is nothing wrong with that. And embarrass me? Never will you do that. I will be so proud to call you wife."

"Truly?" Mary Beth asked, her heart warmed by those words.

"Truly," he said. He was just lowering his lips to hers when the sound of horses arriving at the village drew them quickly apart.

Mary Beth's eyes grew anxiously wide. "The warriors," she said, her voice breaking. "They . . . they . . . have returned!"

She wheeled around and ran from the tepee just as the warriors came into view at the far end of the village.

Her heart immediately sank when she saw no child with them. No David.

Blinded by tears, she turned and ran in the opposite direction, then felt strong arms stopping her.

She flung herself into Brave Wolf's embrace. She clung to him.

"Again I am crying," she sobbed. "Again I am given cause to cry. Oh, my sweet David. They didn't find him."

"That does not mean the worst," Brave Wolf said. "Remember, my woman, never give up hope."

He continued to hold her as the warriors came and dismounted behind him. One approached him.

"The search was unsuccessful," the warrior said. "There is no trace of the child, or those who took him."

Brave Wolf nodded.

The warrior walked away, along with the rest, leaving Brave Wolf and Mary Beth alone.

Brave Wolf placed an arm around her waist and gently led her to his lodge, then helped her down to the pelts.

Mary Beth wiped her eyes.

"There is only one thing left for me to do," she said stiffly as Brave Wolf sat down beside her.

"And what is that?" he asked.

"I have thought long and hard about what I would do if the warriors returned without David," she said, her voice drawn. "I concluded that if they did not find my son, perhaps the cavalry *can*."

She saw how that made Brave Wolf's jaw tighten. She knew he did not want her to believe that the soldiers could succeed when his warriors had not.

She moved to her knees before him. She touched him gently on the cheek. "Please understand why I must do this," she murmured. "I cannot just give up on David without trying every means to find him. I can go on to Fort Henry, where the wagon train was headed before the ambush. I can explain to the colonel there what happened, and how I have been with you . . . how you rescued me from the renegades, and that I did not come immediately to the fort because I thought your warriors would have a better chance of finding David than the cavalry. But now? I must give them a chance. I have no other choice."

"This is what you truly feel you should do?" Brave Wolf asked.

"Yes," Mary Beth said, swallowing hard. She lowered her hand to her side. "Please understand?"

"I do, but I strongly urge you to go to another fort—Fort Hope," Brave Wolf said. "The colonel there is my friend. Let him do what can be done to find your son. The colonel at Fort Henry is my enemy."

"Please understand why I feel that I must go to Fort Henry," Mary Beth said. "That is where survivors of my wagon train would have gone, if there are survivors, because that fort was the wagon train's destination."

"Then go where you must," Brave Wolf said tightly. "But I need to know that you will come back to me."

He twined his arms around her waist and drew her next to him. Their eyes met and held.

"You were born to be my wife," he said huskily. "I was born to be your husband. It is meant for us to grow old together . . . to have children of our own."

"How could you think that I would not want the same as you?" she murmured. "I love you so much, Brave Wolf. I love you more than I ever knew was possible to love a man."

"As do I love you," he said, brushing soft kisses across her lips.

Then he held her face between his hands. "My woman, will you stay just one more night with me and my people?" he asked thickly. "Will you stay and be a part of a special celebration?"

"What sort of celebration?" Mary Beth asked, her eyes widening.

"It is a ceremony enjoyed by my people," Brave Wolf said. "It is the time of the Bear Song Dance, held in the autumn when the ripe berries cause the bears to dance in the mountains. The women have gathered chokeberries to provide food for the dance."

"I helped prepare food with chokeberries," Mary Beth said softly.

"What was prepared was made specifically for tonight's celebration," Brave Wolf said, smiling at her. "Will you stay? I feel it is important that you experience these special moments with me and my people so that once you are away from me, you will not forget me."

"I could never, ever forget you," she said, snuggling close in his arms. "You know that I will return to you. I do want to marry you."

"But still . . . will you stay one more night with me?" he persisted. "It is too close to dusk for you to leave. It is best to travel to Fort Henry in the daylight. A man with red skin arriving at a fort at night is taking a big risk, especially in the company of a white woman. The pony soldiers might think the wrong thing."

She gazed up at him and nodded. "Yes, I guess they would," she murmured. She smiled. "So, yes, I will stay."

He held her close. His lips lowered to hers.

Mary Beth did not turn away from him this time. Their lips met in a sweet, tremulous kiss.

Mary Beth regretted now having ever denied herself the pleasure that came with his kiss and the warm sweetness of his arms. In his kiss and embrace, everything else disappeared from her mind!

There was only the two of them, their love breaking through all the barriers that had kept them apart.

When they stepped away from each other, Brave Wolf gently touched her cheek. "My body aches for more than a kiss," he said huskily.

"Mine too," Mary Beth said in a voice that did not sound like her own. "Tonight, Brave Wolf. After the celebration . . . tonight . . . ?"

He swept her into his arms again and kissed her. Their bodies strained hungrily together.

"Ah, yes, tonight . . ." he whispered against her parted lips.

Chapter Fourteen

Things are always at their
best in their beginning.
—Pascal

Latc swallows swooped down through the lilac night. The sun was already being replaced in the sky by a bright full moon as the first stars pricked the darkening night.

A huge, roaring fire crackled and roared in the center of the Crow village where the entire Whistling Water Clan had gathered in a wide circle around a pole. A bearskin with red-painted claws was tied to the eastern side of the pole.

Mary Beth sat amid the women on one side of the circle, her thoughts on this afternoon's food preparation. She had enjoyed being a part of the group getting ready for the exciting night. She had gladly volunteered to prepare the corn, which even now gave off its wondrous scent from the great copper pots at the edges of the fire.

She had shucked a lot of corn in her day. She suddenly missed her garden in Kentucky, where the corn would be ready to be harvested. She had known that she wouldn't be home in time, so she had given her friend Maddie permission to take the corn and can it for her own family.

Maddie had said that when Mary Beth and David returned home, some of those home-canned jars of corn would be waiting to see them through the long Kentucky winter.

When she arrived home, the jars would already be in Mary Beth's fruit cellar along with other goodies that she knew Maddie would prepare for her. There would be canned green beans, pickles made of her cucumbers, stewed tomatoes as well as tomato juice, and even grape jam made from the luscious grapes that grew on an arbor behind her house.

It seemed so long ago now, that discussion of canning and taking care of Mary Beth's precious cat, who would by now have had a new litter of kittens that she would never hold and cuddle in her arms.

There had been tremendous change in Mary Beth's life, much of it sad. But one sweet thing had come with all this change . . . her feelings for Brave Wolf and his for her.

And now there was someone else sweet in her life. She smiled as she looked at the lovely woman who sat beside her. It was Dancing Butterfly, the young and vivacious maiden who had shunned Mary Beth when she'd brought food into her chief's lodge that day.

But as Mary Beth had diligently worked with the women most of this afternoon, preparing the various kinds of food for the Bear Song Dance celebration, her eagerness to help had drawn the admiration of many of the women, among them Dancing Butterfly.

Dancing Butterfly had sat beside Mary Beth, first offering to show her how to roll the special balls of pemmican so that the meat and fruit were more equally distributed in the ball. Mary Beth's answering smile and thank you had opened up a brand new world between two women who seemed destined to be special friends.

Mary Beth didn't even feel awkward sitting among the Crow people without Brave Wolf at her side. Strangely enough, she felt as though she actually belonged there.

She anxiously awaited the beginning of the dance, for Brave Wolf had told her that he, his people's chief, would have a role in it.

"Is it not a perfect night for dancing?" Dancing Butterfly asked as she clasped her hands together on her lap. "Mary Beth, look at the moon. The First Maker has given its silver sand to us tonight instead of clouds for our celebration."

"It is so very lovely," Mary Beth said as she turned her eyes up to the moon. She could not help wondering if her son might be gazing up at that same moon this very moment. She had held him on her lap many nights as they sat on their swing on the front porch, looking up at the moon.

As they had swung slowly back and forth, she had told him stories. She could even now hear his giggle.

"Mary Beth, the moon does many things for us," Dancing Butterfly said, drawing her away from thoughts of a son she missed with every fiber of her being. "It not only gives us light at night, but also shows children how to dream."

"Yes, to dream," Mary Beth said, swallowing hard as she again thought of her David and what sort of dreams he might be having at night. She hoped they weren't nightmares. She hoped he was alive to dream.

When Mary Beth noticed how Dancing Butterfly's voice trailed off to whisper, she thought the other woman must be responding to her distraction. She had not been all that attentive to what Dancing Butterfly was saying to her.

She turned to apologize, then realized she had not been the cause of Dancing Butterfly's sudden silence. The other woman was staring at Brave Wolf's mother's tepee. Mary Beth questioned Dancing Butterfly with her eyes.

"I wish Night Horse could sit among our people beneath tonight's moon," Dancing Butterfly blurted out. "I wish he could enjoy tonight's festivities as much as you and I will enjoy them."

Dancing Butterfly swallowed hard. "I wish he was not ill," she murmured. "But I mainly wish that he had never left our village to ally himself with Yellow Hair and his evil soldiers."

Mary Beth was stunned by Dancing Butterfly's attitude toward Night Horse, especially her openness, when everyone else avoided the mere mention of him. "Why would you care so much about Night Horse?" she asked, looking at Pure Heart's tepee. The glow of the lodge fire inside could be seen through the buffalo-hide cover, silhouetting Pure Heart as she sat vigil by her son's side.

Mary Beth had been told that Night Horse's health had improved, that the rattling in his lungs was gone. When he slept now, it was in quiet peace.

"Why?" Dancing Butterfly repeated, absently running her fingers over a long row of turquoise beads that were sewn up the front of her doeskin dress.

She wore a necklace made of the same turquoise beads, as well as a matching bracelet. Her voluminous black hair hung loose and flowing down her perfectly straight back. A headband with turquoise beads sewn onto it held her hair back from her lovely face.

"Yes, why," Mary Beth said, hoping she wasn't pressing too hard for answers. It was so nice to have a friend among Brave Wolf's people.

"Except for his mother, and perhaps his brother and me, Night Horse is disliked by everyone else in our village," Dancing Butterfly said softly. "I understand that, because he did so much wrong to our people. I cringe at his misdeeds, yet memories of better times with him still cling inside my heart."

"Was he special to you?" Mary Beth asked.

"When I was six winters of age and he was eight, we stole many kisses from one another," Dancing Butterfly murmured, a sudden sweet light appearing in her eyes. "Those stolen moments continued until I was ten and he was twelve. It was then that we realized the danger of such kisses."

She lowered her eyes. Her face grew flushed. "Those kisses started creating other feelings that felt too wonderful . . . that . . . we knew were wrong," Dancing Butterfly murmured.

She lifted her eyes and gazed again into Mary Beth's. "We knew we were in love," she said. "We grew up only tepees apart. We both knew that our hearts were bound to each other." She laughed softly, then gave Mary Beth a shy smile. "When we grew older, Night Horse told me how he had watched my shadow through the walls of my family's tepee."

Mary Beth was saddened to think that two people could love as Dancing Butterfly and Night Horse had obviously loved and yet be parted. She found it incredible that Night Horse could walk away from such a love.

She hoped that Brave Wolf was different from his brother in that respect. She would die if he ever turned his back on their love, a love that had come so quickly and wonderfully.

"We vowed to wait for one another until we were of marrying age," Dancing Butterfly continued.

"But he seemed to forget. He . . . he . . . left one day and never returned."

"When he left to join Custer and the others as a scout?" Mary Beth asked softly.

Dancing Butterfly only nodded, then wiped tears from her eyes and sat up straighter.

Just then several warriors walked into the circle of people. They were beautifully dressed in ceremonial clothes decorated with ornaments of feathers and seeds and brightly dyed porcupine quills. Some carried drums while others carried tomahawks adorned with eagle feathers; others carried nothing at all.

They sat on one side of the cleared area and began singing the bear's song as they beat their drums in a rhythmic fashion.

Dancing Butterfly's confession was temporarily forgotten as Mary Beth gazed at those warriors a moment longer, then looked over her shoulder. She strained her neck as she watched for Brave Wolf, but instead of seeing him she spotted another warrior dancing through the seated crowd.

"That is Many Wings," Dancing Butterfly whispered to Mary Beth. "He is the dance leader. Follow my lead, Mary Beth—when I stand, you stand. When I clap my hand to my mouth, you do the same. In that way you will prove that you are a willing participant in our customs, and someone who is worthy of our chief."

Mary Beth's eyes widened. What Dancing Butterfly had just said about her being worthy surely meant that he had confided in his people about his plans to marry her.

She blushed and smiled and nodded at Dancing Butterfly. "I shall do my best," she whispered back.

Then her eyes followed Many Wings. His forehead was painted red and two red stripes were drawn from the corners of his eyes down his cheeks. He wore a buffalo robe with the fur side out.

Four warriors and a boy followed him, all painted and dressed in the same manner. They began dancing in the east, came around the pole to the west, and then turned back to the east. They imitated a bear's movements, holding their hands in front of them with their fingertips pressed against their palms, shaking their heads, and stepping like bears on their hind legs.

Dancing Butterfly leaned closer to Mary Beth. "Now is the time to stand," she said, gently taking Mary Beth by the hand and urging her to her feet. "Remember to do as I do."

Flushed with excitement, Mary Beth nodded, but realized she couldn't do everything that was asked of her. The people were shouting things in their Crow language. And she knew not one word of it.

She didn't want to disappoint Dancing Butterfly, and especially Brave Wolf, yet how could she fully participate if she didn't know their language?

She saw the way Dancing Butterfly and the others clapped a hand over their mouths; that at least, was something she could imitate.

She was watching Dancing Butterfly and the others so closely, she did not see a young woman dance slowly up to the center pole. Mary Beth's attention was drawn there when everyone stopped shouting and clapping their mouths and gazed silently toward the center pole.

Mary Beth looked quickly toward it. She gasped when she saw the woman, who was dressed in a long, white fur robe with red paint in her hair, start rubbing her face against the bearskin on the pole. Then she began dancing rhythmically around it.

Soon she left and the male dancers moved around the pole, their bare feet pounding the earth in time with the beating of the drums.

Then everything stopped. All faces turned toward their chief's tepee.

Mary Beth's eyes followed. Her heart skipped a beat when she saw Brave Wolf come from his lodge wearing only a breechcloth and an otterskin headband, with a broad red stripe across his face.

As he sang the Bear Dance Song, he danced toward the pole. When he arrived there, he stopped and rubbed his face against the skin, then turned as a dish of prepared pemmican meatballs and a cup of water were taken to him. After he had consumed them, a young brave went to Brave Wolf with a bearskin robe.

Brave Wolf leaned down.

The lad placed the bearskin over Brave Wolf's head, then led him through the crowd toward a pole corral that had been only this morning erected at the far right of the central fire.

In it stood a lone, coal black stallion, blindfolded and without a saddle, its hind legs tied.

Warriors were on each side of the steed, struggling to hold it still.

The people clambered to their feet and hurried to stand around the corral.

Dancing Butterfly led Mary Beth to where she could see, then held her hand.

"What is Brave Wolf going to do?" Mary Beth asked.

Her voice, though low, carried into the crowd. Several people turned and glared at her. The rest watched their chief, their eyes wide in anticipation.

"Our warriors often capture fine and spirited wild horses. This steed was captured only this morning just for our chief's performance tonight," Dancing Butterfly explained. "It is unbroken and wild. Our chief will prove his skill today with horses. After he is with the horse for only a short while, the steed will be as tame as a newborn foal."

"But why is he doing this tonight?" Mary Beth asked. "Is this a part of the Bear Song Dance?"

"No. The dance is over," Dancing Butterfly said. "Taming the horse is just an added attraction. Watch. Enjoy."

Brave Wolf stepped up to the pole corral.

The bearskin robe slid away from him.

The young brave grabbed it up from the ground, then stepped back and was lost in the crowd.

Brave Wolf's eyes never left the animal as he

leaned down and pushed his way between the poles.

Once inside the corral, he straightened his back and continued to stare at the horse. His muscles flexed, his jaw tight, Brave Wolf stepped up to the snorting horse.

Brave Wolf itched to run his hands along the steed's jet silk skin and huge withers. He would enjoy stroking the horse's muscled flanks, for he had perhaps never seen such a beautiful stallion in his entire life.

He was anxious to call it his!

As chief, he already owned many horses. A man who had many horses was not only a rich man, but also a warrior to be admired, for how could he acquire so many steeds without being brave?

He swung himself onto the stallion's back.

When a warrior handed Brave Wolf the reins, the horse stood still, its muscles trembling.

Then one of the men removed the horse's blindfold and hurried with the other warrior from the corral. The animal snorted, bit at Brave Wolf's legs, then reared, only now becoming aware that its hind legs were tied.

All that it could do was spin quickly around. That was enough to throw Brave Wolf from its back.

As Brave Wolf slowly rose to his feet, his dark eyes holding the horse's, two warriors came quickly back into the corral, roped the horse and held it steady again for Brave Wolf.

"Untie its legs," Brave Wolf said tightly.

The warriors questioned him with their eyes, then did as they were told when Brave Wolf glared at them for even a moment questioning his command.

The warriors stepped quickly away as Brave Wolf grabbed the reins and leapt onto the stallion's back.

Brave Wolf held on to the reins tightly, using his knees to hold himself solidly in place. The horse reared again, then ran wildly toward the corral poles and leapt over them.

The crowd ran screaming as they hastened out of the horse's way. Mary Beth and Dancing Butterfly ran with them, then turned and watched again.

Mary Beth's pride in Brave Wolf grew as her eyes followed his every move.

She gasped when she thought he was going to be thrown again, then sighed when he managed to stay on. She knew he was fighting the horse's will as much as its strength.

Making a valiant effort, Brave Wolf headed the steed away from his people and the tepees. In moments he found himself riding along a wide open stretch of land.

Too stubborn to give in to the animal's meanness as it bucked again, then nipped at Brave Wolf's bare legs with its large, yellowed teeth, Brave Wolf winced in pain. But he knew horses well and knew that this animal was nearing the breaking point. He must withstand the pain it had inflicted on him.

He held tightly to the reins. He kept his knees pressed hard against the stallion's sides.

He smiled when the horse stopped rearing and began running at a slower pace. It no longer snorted. Its whinnying became low and tentative.

Brave Wolf smiled, ran a hand across the steed's muscled neck, then leaned low and whispered words of encouragement and friendship in the horse's ear.

Suddenly the horse stopped, hanging its head and breathing hard.

"You are now mine," Brave Wolf said, leaning low to put his arms around the animal's neck. "We will be devoted friends forever. Together we will be as one."

The horse nodded as though it understood.

"Let us go home," Brave Wolf said, straightening his back.

He wheeled the horse around and headed back in the direction of his village, where he saw everyone standing at the edge of the camp, their eyes anxious.

He heard the cheers and claps as he grew closer.

Mary Beth smiled and waved, the pride she saw in Brave Wolf's eyes matching the emotion in her heart.

When he got closer, she ran out and met him.

She was not at all surprised when he reached down and swept her up from the ground and onto his lap.

"Thank God the moon was so bright tonight," Mary Beth said, gazing lovingly into his eyes. "It enabled us all to watch you. It was so beautiful, Brave Wolf, how you and the horse came to peace with one another."

"We *are* as one now," he said. "Midnight, the name I have just given him, will be my main steed now. The one I have ridden so proudly for so long is now yours . . . if you will have it."

"Truly?" she gasped. "You truly want me to have it?"

"*Hecitu-yelo,* yes," he said huskily. "It will be my first gift to the woman who will soon be my wife."

"Thank you," she murmured, beaming. "I accept the gift with much pride."

She hadn't even thought about how it must have looked to his people when she had run to meet him. Now he held her tightly against him as he rode up to them.

Mary Beth scarcely breathed as she looked from person to person, the moon's glow white on their copper faces.

She couldn't believe the lack of resentment they showed toward her. They seemed mostly interested in their chief, who had once again proved his worth to them . . . his masterful ways.

He dismounted, then reached up for Mary Beth, who went willingly into his arms as she slid off the horse. "We shall now eat, sing, and be thankful to the First Maker," Brave Wolf said as Mary Beth stepped away from him.

He gazed at her violet eyes, her lovely face framed by long, reddish-gold hair; then he looked around at his people.

"My woman will leave tomorrow. She goes to Fort Henry, to seek the pony soldiers' help in finding her lost son," he said. "My warriors, those of you who searched for the child before, I ask you to leave again tomorrow and resume the search while I see to Mary Beth's safe arrival at the fort."

He gave her a soft smile, then looked at his people again. "She will return soon, for there will be a wedding celebration . . . *ours*," he announced.

He had hoped to see understanding in his people's eyes. He found it, and even approval in some. He had explained himself well in council and asked the warriors to take the message of his love for this white woman back to their lodges.

If anyone resented his decision, his choice, it did not show tonight in anyone's eyes.

Breaking the horse had been a deliberate move. He'd wanted to give his people something more to think about than their chief's announcement that he wanted a white woman to be his wife.

"Go now, my people," he said. "The night is new. I shall join you soon to share in the feasting and singing."

They all went back into the village.

Brave Wolf placed his hands at Mary Beth's waist and drew her closer. "You have been accepted," he said proudly. "Soon we *will* be man and wife."

He lowered his lips to hers.

She twined her arms around his neck and returned his kiss.

If David was with her, safe, ah, life would have been beautiful and perfect.

As they stepped away from each other, Brave Wolf laughed huskily. He reached a hand to her face and used his thumb to brush away some red paint that had smeared from his face to hers.

She saw the paint on his thumb, laughed, then placed a finger on his painted face. "No paint could ever hide your handsomeness," she murmured.

If he asked whether she was ready to make love with him, she was more than ready. Her whole soul ached for it.

Suddenly Mary Beth was startled out of Brave Wolf's arms by a chorus of coyote yelps from a nearby butte.

Brave Wolf sensed her fear and drew her close again. "You must learn to accept the coyote as a part of our lives," he said. "You see, the coyote is more intelligent than man. Coyotes will still be around when men have killed off all the other animals. They might even outlive man. They are everywhere."

"Do they ever come into the village?" Mary Beth asked warily.

"Very rarely do they venture too close," Brave Wolf said, again listening to the coyotes' songs. "They fear man even more than man fears them."

The song and laughter of his people wafted through the air, touching Mary Beth's soul.

"Let us talk no more about coyotes," she said. "I would love to join your people's fun. I feel so comfortable with them now."

"As they do you," Brave Wolf said, taking Midnight's reins and leading him toward the village. "Tomorrow is not far away, so let us fully enjoy the night."

The huskiness in his voice made Mary Beth blush, for she knew that he was not only talking of fun with his people. He had read her well—he knew what was in her heart.

Yes, soon they would be floating amid the stars as they found a wondrous love in each other's arms.

When they reached the huge outdoor fire where the crowd was now assembled on blankets, eating, talking, and laughing, a young brave took Midnight to Brave Wolf's corral.

Dancing Butterfly ran up to Mary Beth. All smiles, she gave Mary Beth a tray of food, which included the pemmican meatballs Mary Beth had helped prepare.

"It is such a wonderful night," Dancing Butterfly said, her gaze darting to Pure Heart's lodge.

Mary Beth saw why Dancing Butterfly was so radiantly happy. Night Horse lay just outside the tepee, his eyes no longer glazed with fever. He was on his way to a full recovery, and his gaze was on Dancing Butterfly.

Brave Wolf noticed the two looking at each other. He was not happy about that.

When he made Night Horse leave, what would happen to Dancing Butterfly? He knew that she loved Night Horse.

He feared for her now, feared that her love for

Night Horse might lead her into making the wrong decision, one that she would regret for the rest of her life. She was too sweet to allow someone like Night Horse to dictate her future.

Chapter Fifteen

> Out of the Indian approach to life
> came a great freedom, an intense and
> absorbing love for nature; a respect
> for life.
>
> —Luther Standing Bear,
> Oglala Sioux Chief

"I truly enjoyed the evening," Mary Beth said as she went into Brave Wolf's tepee with him. "And I never felt as though I were an intruder. I felt that most everyone accepted me."

Brave Wolf took her by the hand and pulled her down onto the thick pelts beside the slow-burning lodge fire. "They see you as their chief's woman. That is why they did nothing to make you feel uncomfortable," he said. "Can you feel it, as well? Can you feel our connection?"

"I do, and I felt it even before I would admit to myself that I could trust you and the goodness I saw in you," Mary Beth murmured. "What had just happened in my life was so horrible. How could I immediately trust a man who resembled those who took so much from me?"

"I cannot restore your losses, except perhaps, your son," Brave Wolf said thickly. "I am sorry that my warriors' search for David has not been successful." He placed his hands at her waist and drew her closer. "If the pony soldiers can do what my warriors have not been able to do, that will be good. I want nothing but your happiness."

"I do not look forward to going to Fort Henry," Mary Beth said. "At first, that was all I could think about . . . going to be with my own people. Now I cannot see any future that does not include you."

She placed a hand on his cheek. "How can love come so quickly between a man and a woman?" she asked softly. "Since I have never truly loved before, it all seems like such a miracle. I can hardly believe that I found it now . . . that I fell in love with you so quickly, a stranger until only a few days ago . . . a man who is not of my own people . . . a man most white women would fear."

She sighed. "I never feared you," she said. "Never. You did not put fear into my heart . . . only sweetness."

"You did not feel anything like sweetness at first," he said, chuckling. "If you did, you were good at pretending you hated me."

"Hate was not the emotion that I felt," she said,

smiling almost shyly. "Frustration that I could not get you to do as I asked . . . but not hate. I felt something special for you very soon after you rescued me, but I would not admit it, even to myself."

"That was then, this is now, and all is good between us," Brave Wolf said thickly. "I am a man in love. You are a woman who loves. Let us not wonder why. Let us just accept our good fortune with warmth in our hearts. Let us enjoy it."

"And by enjoy, you do mean something more than hugging one another," Mary Beth said, blushing.

No man had ever awakened this new side of herself. She actually felt sensual . . . seductive. Her body cried out for something from this man.

She wanted to experience true lovemaking.

When she had made love with her husband, she had pretended that she had received pleasure from it, when in truth her body had never been awakened to the miracle of love . . . of sensuality.

Just being with Brave Wolf had aroused these feelings in her. To think that she might experience the complete fulfillment that came with lovemaking made her whole insides tremble with anticipation.

Brave Wolf did not respond verbally. His answer was in the dark, deep passion in his eyes, and in the way his fingers trembled as he placed them at the hem of her doeskin dress and slowly began lifting it.

The mere touch of the dress moving along her flesh caused Mary Beth to melt. With each inch as more and more of her body was revealed to Brave Wolf's watchful eyes.

Her heart pounded and she blushed anew when Brave Wolf slid the dress past her breasts, their dark tips tight as the air touched their bareness.

Then she sucked in a wild breath of ecstasy when he dipped his head low and flicked his tongue across one of her nipples. He continued to slide the dress slowly upward, and then over her head, tossing it to the floor behind him.

He brought his hands to her breasts and filled them with their heaviness, his lips now sucking on a nipple.

Mary Beth threw her head back in total ecstasy as Brave Wolf showered both breasts with electrifying kisses, then brought his lips to hers and gave her a deep, long, passionate kiss. At the same time, he pressed his body against hers, until she was on her back on the pelts.

Brave Wolf kissed her for a moment longer, then rose over her and removed his own clothes. When he was as naked as she, Mary Beth saw just how gifted a man he was.

She gazed at his maleness, then brazenly reached a hand to him and touched him. His eyes glazed over with rapture as she ran her fingers slowly up and down the full length of his shaft.

She remembered well how her husband had enjoyed such touches. He had seemed to enjoy her stroking more than the actual lovemaking.

She had been happy about that, since she had never looked forward to the bedtime duties of a wife. She had been glad when her touch had satisfied him enough that he asked no more of her once his seed splashed out into her hand. That was another reason why they had never had a second child.

Now she wanted to make babies with this wonderful man. She wanted to share the sensual side of making babies with him.

"*Mitawin*, my woman, I want more than touches from you," Brave Wolf said, taking her hand away, and seeming to have read her thoughts. "I want you . . . *all* of you. I want to fill you. I want you to feel me fill you."

"I have never wanted a man like I want . . . like I *need* you," Mary Beth said, then sucked in another wild breath when he ran his hand down the front of her, then touched that part of her between her thighs that had never responded to a man before.

She closed her eyes in ecstasy when he began slowly caressing her there.

"It . . . is . . . so heavenly . . ." she murmured breathlessly.

He smiled, lowered his lips to hers, and kissed her with fierce, possessive heat. His knee eased her legs apart.

With his hand he guided himself to where his fingers had just been, and without hesitation, entered her in one deep thrust.

Feeling her inner folds enwrapping his heat, Brave Wolf groaned with pleasure.

He laid his cheek against hers, closed his eyes, and began rhythmically moving within her.

Mary Beth wrapped her arms around his neck

and clung to him, her body seeming to know how to move with his.

Oh, Lord, this time she didn't have to pretend to feel the bliss that came with lovemaking.

It was real, so very, very intensely, beautifully real.

She smiled and moved with him, giving all that she could.

It came so easily to her, as though she was practiced at it, but in truth, she was learning everything tonight.

And she was so glad that she *was* feeling these wonderful things. Had she never known such bliss, she would have felt cheated when she grew into an old woman looking back on her life.

Now, ah, now she would never feel cheated.

As Brave Wolf's lean, sinewy buttocks moved, his heat filling her magnificently, Mary Beth was flooded with more wondrous rushes of bliss.

"I never knew it could be this way," she whispered against his cheek, her voice catching when he went deeper into her, touching a place that aroused an even more delicious sensation within her.

He puzzled over what she had said.

More than once she had mentioned having not known such pleasure before.

She had had a husband!

Had her husband only selfishly satisfied his own needs, ignoring hers?

He would not question her about this. It could be humiliating for her to have to say it.

"My goal is to give you more pleasure than I take for myself," he whispered huskily, his thrusts continuing.

"But I want you to feel it, too," Mary Beth said, as he leaned up away from her to look into her eyes. "How can you not? Aren't I desirable enough to make you feel the pleasure that I am feeling?"

"Desirable?" he said, his eyes dancing. "My woman, you are so desirable I can take pleasure just by looking at you." He smiled almost devilishly. "My woman, do not think I am not feeling all the wonder of how your body responds to mine. My body is alive with you."

He pressed his lips against hers and gave her a sweet kiss as he swept a hand between them and cupped one of her breasts. "You fill my very soul with your sweetness," he whispered against her lips.

"You are sweeter," she whispered back, then melted as they came to that place where they both soared in passion's embrace . . . then lay together, still clinging, their hearts now beating as one.

"Never, oh, never will I forget this night, these special moments with you," Mary Beth said, her cheeks flushed from the heat of their lovemaking. She turned over onto her belly and gazed into his eyes. "I shall love you always, my wonderful, handsome Crow chief."

"For as long as there is breath in my lungs, I shall love you," he said, reaching out for her, drawing her down beside him again.

Sighing contentedly, she cuddled against him as

she gazed at the dancing flames of the fire. "I wish there was nothing else but now, forever and ever," she murmured.

Then she winced when she realized what she had just said.

Her son.

She could not want only moments like this forever, for that would mean she would not be with her son ever again.

She hurried to a sitting position. She was not even uneasy about sitting there naked as his eyes roamed slowly over her.

"You are thinking again of your son?" Brave Wolf said, sitting up, himself. He reached for her, placed his hands at her waist, then lifted her onto his lap, facing him. "Tomorrow comes soon, my woman. I know what tomorrow brings. We must be separated for a while, and I understand why. Your son. You must then focus only on him."

"Yes, on finding him," she said. She swallowed hard. Her eyes wavered. "What if he isn't . . . ?"

She couldn't say it.

She just couldn't think it.

She *must* find her son, or a piece of her heart would be gone forever.

"Do not think about the bad when reality may eventually be all good," he encouraged. He drew her into his arms. "My woman, as the pony soldiers are searching, so will my warriors be out looking again. Everything within my power will be done."

"Yes, I must think all things positive," Mary Beth said, smiling weakly up at him.

Then she cuddled close to him again. "Just hold me," she murmured. "Please . . . just . . . hold me."

"Then you must sleep, for tomorrow is almost upon us," he said softly. "You must get what rest you can."

"I shall hate leaving you," she said, her voice breaking. "After having found you, and loving you so much, being parted from you for even one day will be hard."

"Days pass quickly," Brave Wolf said. "Sometimes it seems that I only blink my eyes and it is another tomorrow."

"Yes, I have felt that way, myself," she said, laughing softly.

Then she eased from him and stretched out on the pelts. She reached her arms out for him. "But this is now, and we are together," she murmured. "It will be wonderful snuggling against you as I sleep."

He smiled, then moved down next to her.

He reached out for her and drew her close, their bodies melding together as though they were one.

"*Istima,* sleep, my pretty one, my woman," he said, then brushed soft kisses across her brow.

She smiled as her eyes slowly closed.

Chapter Sixteen

Let those love now
Who never loved before;
Let those who always loved
Now love the more.
—Thomas Parnell

It had taken a good part of the day to arrive at Fort Henry. The sun was lowering behind the distant mountains, but it was still light enough to see the huge fort that loomed ahead of her on the flat land surrounding it.

Mary Beth's insides quavered as she stared at the fort. It was only a short distance away from where she sat on the lovely dark sorrel that Brave Wolf had given her.

She looked at Brave Wolf. "I don't know why, but I am suddenly afraid to go on to the fort," she murmured. "When the sentries first see me alone, they will wonder why. It is unusual for a woman to be alone in this wilderness."

"I would accompany you there, but that would raise more suspicion than curiosity," Brave Wolf explained. "It is best not to let them see you and me together. Go, my woman. I shall stay hidden here among the trees, watching you, until you are taken safely inside the fort's walls. Only then will I feel that you can fend for yourself."

Mary Beth laughed nervously. "My teeth are actually chattering," she said. "I don't know what I am expecting from them to make me so . . . so . . . afraid."

"I should never have told you my opinion of Colonel Downing," Brave Wolf said ruefully. "I am sure that is why you are apprehensive about going to his fort. It is not too late to change your mind. I can take you to Fort Hope."

"No, I truly believe I have come to the right fort even though I do not look forward to meeting Colonel Downing," Mary Beth murmured.

"Just remember that those at the fort are your people, so expect understanding and kindness," Brave Wolf said, reaching a hand to her cheek. "You are a brave, courageous woman. Now is the time to use that courage."

"I believe I know what is truly causing my hesitation," she said, searching his eyes. "It is because I have to leave you. I'm so afraid that something might happen and I may never see you again."

"When you are ready to return to me, I will be

there, waiting," he promised. "I have not survived these twenty-five winters of my life to allow something to happen to me now that I have found you. True love only comes once in a lifetime. Never shall I let anything jeopardize it."

"Then I shall go on my way with a much lighter heart," Mary Beth said. She took his hand, kissed its palm, then slowly released it. "I shall go on now. Perhaps I shall find my son already safe in the hands of the soldiers."

"Had you thought that possible, nothing would have kept you from coming to this fort before now," Brave Wolf said, his voice drawn. "No, my woman, do not expect to find your son at the fort. But do expect to find people who are willing to search for him."

"Yes, I know they will, for who would not want to assure the safety and well-being of a child . . . except for people like those who stole him from me," Mary Beth said.

She inhaled a deep, shaky breath, gazed at the fort again, then smiled at Brave Wolf. "Goodbye, my love," she said. "I shall return to your arms as soon as I find something out about David."

"Faith . . . hope . . . love . . ." Brave Wolf said. "They will get you through these next hours."

He reached over and placed a hand at the nape of her neck. He drew her close and gave her a long, deep kiss, then dropped his hand away and watched her ride from him.

He dismounted, tied his reins to a low limb, then went and knelt behind a stand of bushes. He parted their branches to get a better look at the fort, and those who would open the gate to his woman.

Then he suddenly noticed something that Mary Beth surely had forgotten. The clothes she wore were not clothes ordinarily worn by a white woman. She was still wearing the doeskin dress his mother had given her.

He wanted to cry out to warn her, but he knew that the wind would carry his voice to the soldiers. They would have double cause to be alarmed if they saw a woman dressed in doeskin and heard the cry of a red man calling her name!

"Tread softly and warily, my woman," he whispered, his spine stiffening as she drew closer and closer to the fort on the steed that had been his for so long but was now hers. His jaw tightened when he saw the tall, wide gate slowly opening.

He watched with bated breath as a soldier came from the gate, brandishing a rifle. Brave Wolf's hand went to his bow as Mary Beth stopped beside the soldier, then dismounted while he took her reins in one hand, still holding his rifle in the other.

When Brave Wolf saw that she was not going to be harmed, he slid his hand away from the bow and watched until she and her horse disappeared inside the fort with the soldier.

He was unnerved about the whole situation. He felt so bad about forgetting how she was dressed, but even if he had remembered, nothing could have been different. There were none of the clothes worn by white women at his village. She would still have arrived in Indian attire.

He could not leave just yet. His eyes remained locked on the gate. His ears remained alert to any noise coming from inside the walls.

If he heard a woman scream, his heart would be turned inside out, for surely it would be Mary Beth!

Mary Beth scarcely breathed as she walked into the fort. The soldier had taken her horse and tied it to a hitching rail, while another soldier had stepped up and was now escorting her to the large cabin in the center of the courtyard.

She knew forts well enough to know that it was the colonel's dwelling and main office.

Out of the corner of her eye she saw that all activity at the fort had stopped. She could feel eyes on her, watching her every move.

When she looked at one soldier at length, she saw a strange expression of disgust in his eyes.

And she had not even been questioned by the soldier who had met her at the gate. She had just been told that he would take her immediately to Colonel Downing. The cold look in his eyes as he had looked her slowly up and down still made her uneasy.

Then it came to her like a bolt of lightning. The dress. The moccasins. Her hair, which she had worn in braids these past two days. Everything about her, except her skin and hair color, looked Indian.

A sudden flush heated her face as she looked

guardedly from man to man. She could not help wondering if they could tell she had made love with an Indian.

To all white men, a woman was no longer worth anything if a red man had "soiled" her. They couldn't know that she had made love to Brave Wolf, but it was obvious that she *had* been among Indians.

Would the colonel even be willing to help her find David? Would he condemn her for how she was dressed and dismiss her as an Indian lover?

Except for what Brave Wolf had said about this colonel, she didn't know anything about him. But from what Brave Wolf had told her, she knew that he was not a compassionate man and that he despised Indians.

Did he hate them enough to make her pay for wearing the clothes of an Indian maiden?

She felt her knees go weak at the thought of facing the colonel. Yet she could not allow herself to think that she should not have came to the fort. It was for David that she was there.

She had to hope the colonel would understand about her having been taken captive, that she'd had no choice about what to wear.

"In here, ma'am," the soldier said as he opened the door to the cabin. "Our commander is Colonel William Downing."

Mary Beth nodded a quiet thank you and walked past him and into the cabin. He followed her in.

As she entered, she became aware of a thick

smell of cigar smoke that hung in the air like fog all around the room.

Through the smoke she saw a husky, clean-shaven man sitting in full uniform, with resplendent gold epaulets, at a huge oak desk at the far side of the room. He had a thick crop of sandy-colored hair, and he appeared to be around forty years of age.

A lone kerosene lamp sat at one side of the colonel's desk, which was littered with papers, journals, and folders. Scarce light filtered through the haze of dust on the two windows in the room.

"What have we here?" Colonel Downing asked, slowly rising from his chair.

He took a thick cigar from his mouth and rested it on the edge of an ashtray. His gaze swept quickly over Mary Beth as she stood rigidly just inside the door.

"Sir, she came on horseback, alone," the soldier said after saluting the colonel. He now stood with his arms stiffly at his sides.

"Alright," the colonel growled out. "Dismissed."

The soldier saluted, then swung around and hurried from the cabin.

"Who in the hell are you and what in the hell are you doin' in those clothes?" Colonel Downing asked as he came from behind the desk.

His hands clasped behind him, he made a slow turn around Mary Beth, his eyes raking slowly over her. "Injun attire, eh?" he grumbled. "That surely means you've been with Injuns."

He stepped in front of her and looked her directly in the eye. "So, ma'am, the next question is . . . why are you dressed like that? And where are those you were with *now*?"

"My name is Mary Beth Wilson," she gulped out. "My husband was Major Lloyd Wilson. He was killed in the Battle of the Little Big Horn along with so many who were stationed at Fort Kitt. I was among those who were on their way to your fort when . . . the wagon train . . . was . . . attacked. Surely you know about that already, especially the results of the Indian ambush. I have no idea how many were killed that day, for . . . for . . . I was taken captive by a renegade, and so was my son David."

"Yes, I know about those who died," Colonel Downing said, his voice drawn. "All of them died. All of them."

His eyebrows rose. "Yet you say you survived, as did your son," he said, kneading his chin. "Mighty lucky, wouldn't you say?"

Mary Beth was first horrified by the news that everyone she had known on the wagon train was dead, then offended, for the colonel seemed to be implying something quite nasty.

"Lucky?" she squeezed out. "Do you call being abducted by renegades lucky? Do you call seeing my son stolen by a renegade lucky? Sir, I have died a thousand deaths inside my heart since I saw my son abducted."

"Renegades, eh?" he said. "So it was renegades who did the killing and who lent you Injun attire, huh?"

"Yes, it was renegades who did the ghastly deed, but no, it was not a renegade who brought me safely to the fort," Mary Beth said, lifting her chin defiantly. "I was rescued by a friendly Crow chief and his warriors. You know of him. Chief Brave Wolf. He took me in. His women gave me clothes to wear. They were generous in all ways to me. It was Chief Brave Wolf who escorted me close enough to the fort today so that I'd be safe. He has left to return to his village."

She hoped that the colonel wouldn't see the blush she felt on her cheeks, for she could not help thinking about those wondrous, precious moments alone with Brave Wolf.

She had to make certain this colonel and his soldiers never discovered her true feelings for Brave Wolf, not until she had achieved her goal here. Then she would return to Brave Wolf and become his wife.

Then the whole world could know. She would be proud to say that he was her husband, although she knew how the white community would feel about it.

To her own people she would be worse than whores that sold their bodies to men.

Yes, she must make certain no one guessed her secret while she was trying to get help in finding David.

"And so it was Chief Brave Wolf who escorted you here, eh?" the colonel said, going back to his chair and sitting down. He gestured with a hand toward a chair beside his desk. "Sit."

She moved almost defiantly into the chair, her back stiff as she sat facing the colonel.

"Sir, my son is the reason I am here," she said, her voice as tight as before. "As I told you, he was abducted, but by a different renegade than I was."

She felt the same ache in her heart as she had since that moment her son had been ripped from her side. "I have not seen David since," she said, her voice breaking. "Chief Brave Wolf sent out a search party, but he couldn't find any signs of my son. It is as though he has disappeared from the face of the earth."

"So you asked Injuns to search for your son before coming here to ask our assistance?" Colonel Downing said, again lighting his cigar and taking slow, deep drags from it. He then took it from his mouth again. "Why is that, young lady? Why didn't you ask to be brought immediately to the fort?"

"There were circumstances that made that difficult," she said, her voice catching.

"What sort of . . . eh . . . circumstances?" Colonel Downing demanded.

She was beginning to feel trapped. She couldn't tell the colonel about the time that had been taken to search for Night Horse, or about the time since his rescue, when Brave Wolf needed to stay close at hand in case he worsened.

No one could know about Night Horse. Especially not this prejudiced colonel and his soldiers. They might try to reclaim Custer's Indian scout.

"His mother was ill," was all she could say, and it wasn't a lie. When she had first arrived at the village, Brave Wolf was concerned about Pure Heart's health. It had turned out that her illness was mainly worry about her younger son.

"What did that have to do with anything?" Colonel Downing said, then shrugged. "Never mind. The fact is you are here. You are asking for our help. And, young lady, I think you've been through enough. I'll give you my support the best I can. I will send several men out soon to search for your son. Tomorrow. Describe him to me."

"He is only five. He has blond hair and blue eyes, and he is the sweetest young man you'd ever want to meet," she blurted out. She leaned forward. "Sir, please find him for me. Please?"

"We here at the fort will give it our best shot," he said. He rose from the chair. "I'd best get you to a cabin. You can relax there. And I'd stay out of view of the men. What you're wearing makes for not only conversation, but accusations you might not want to know about."

Mary Beth could feel the heat of a blush rush to her cheeks.

Did he know more than he was saying? Could he tell that she had been intimate with an Indian?

"Come with me," he said, rising from his chair. He rested his cigar on the ashtray and reached a hand out for Mary Beth. "I wish I could offer you a dress, but there are no women here. We've learned that it is not good to have women on the fort premises. I don't like having them to worry about should Indians decide to attack."

"I understand," Mary Beth said softly. "And I appreciate your kindness in offering me a place to stay. I am so grateful you will send out a search party for David."

Mary Beth was again aware of eyes following her as she stepped out into the open courtyard. She couldn't get to the privacy of the cabin soon enough.

"This is used for any overnight visitors who happen along," the colonel said when they reached the cabin. He opened the door and stepped aside, gesturing with a hand for her to go on in ahead of him.

She stepped past him and looked slowly around her. The room was nice. It was clean. It was sparsely furnished with a chair, bed, and table, but it was adequate. She didn't plan to be there for very long.

"I'll leave you now," he said. "I hope you find the room comfortable enough."

He gave her a half salute, then left her alone.

She closed the door and leaned against it. The colonel's attitude made her feel as though she had just been put through a torture chamber.

But at least the colonel had agreed to search for David. She could withstand anything for any amount of time if in the end she had her son again in her arms.

Yet she couldn't forget the men's eyes as they'd stared almost accusingly at her. She now felt afraid, for she remembered tales of how white women who were rescued by the cavalry after they had been with Indians were treated like dirt.

She stared at the bed. She was almost afraid to fall asleep.

She wanted to leave, to go where she felt safe . . . with Brave Wolf.

But she couldn't. She had no choice but to stay, for at least long enough to see if the cavalry could find her son.

Now that she knew the fate of the wagon train, she knew how lucky she was to be alive. She prayed that David was also still alive.

Keeping her clothes on, even the moccasins, she climbed onto the bed. She curled up and cried again over her son, and for those who had needlessly died.

She cried until her eyelids became heavy and she welcomed the peace that came with sleep.

She was awakened by hands around her throat.

She had slept until it had grown dark outside, yet there was enough light from the full moon shining through the window beside her bed to make out the features of her assailant and discover that he was one of the older soldiers at the fort.

She kicked him in the groin. Groaning and holding himself, he fell beside her on the bed.

Mary Beth grabbed a knife from a sheath at his right side, then leapt from the bed and held the knife between herself and the man.

"Get out of here!" she screamed, her heart thumping wildly within her chest.

He held on to his groin as he climbed slowly from the bed and backed away from her, stopping when he came to the opened door.

"You're a no-good Injun lover," he growled. "Just look at you and the way you're dressed. You're no better than a savage. You won't live long, I can promise you that."

He groaned as he staggered from the cabin, leaving Mary Beth, stunned and afraid.

Chapter Seventeen

> From their eyelids as they
> glanced dripped love.
> —Hesiod

Still holding the knife for protection, and hoping that her assailant wouldn't pounce on her in the dark, Mary Beth ran from the cabin.

She searched the spots where sentries were usually posted and saw none.

She saw no one!

She had wanted to cry out for help, hoping some soldier would come to her defense. But none were anywhere to be seen.

In the light of the moon, she looked desperately around as she walked guardedly onward. But still she saw no one to assist her. Even the barracks where the soldiers slept were all dark.

The night was as still as death, except for the sudden frightening yelp of a coyote from somewhere outside the fort's walls.

She recalled what Brave Wolf had said about coyotes . . . that they would still be on earth when man was gone.

It seemed that was true tonight. She imagined a coyote lurking near by, perhaps sniffing out her fear, wanting to be a part of the terror that had her in its grip.

"Brave Wolf," she whispered as sudden tears fell from her eyes. "If only he were here. I . . . am . . . so alone. I'm so scared."

When she heard a movement close by in the darkness, she stopped and turned, the knife poised to strike. She imagined that horrible man, whose hands were like a vise squeezing her neck, standing in the shadows, ready to finish what he had started. The skin of her neck burned and ached even now from the man trying to choke the breath from her. Surely his hands had left an imprint that would never go away.

She breathed more easily when a pretty calico cat suddenly ran up to her, purring, then rubbed against her leg as her cat had done at home in Kentucky.

She missed her cat.

She missed Kentucky.

She missed the innocence of the life she had left behind.

"Pretty kitty," Mary Beth whispered as she bent

and lifted it into her arms. "You'll keep me company, won't you?"

The cat meowed and rubbed up against Mary Beth's cheek as she gave it a gentle hug.

Then still holding the knife, Mary Beth stood up again and looked slowly around her as she walked slowly onward.

She was going to tell the colonel about tonight's incident. Surely he would find the man responsible and throw him in the guardhouse.

Only a coward would assault a woman!

She hurried now with determined steps toward the colonel's cabin. She saw no lamplight at the windows, which meant that he was surely sound asleep. But that mattered not to Mary Beth. She had to get his help.

She was so relieved that he had treated her decently even though she had seen the doubt in his eyes about what she wore.

Still her explanation seemed to have satisfied him. He had offered her kindness and a place to stay . . . even offered to search for her son.

Breathlessly, she knocked hard on the colonel's front door, the cat still purring contentedly in her arms. The purring gave Mary Beth a sense of comfort.

It was the quiet contentedness of her cat's purring that had always made Mary Beth feel warm inside when something troubled her back home, especially during those first weeks when her husband was gone to a distant land to be placed in harm's way.

Then her cat had helped get her through the tearful moments while she tried to find the courage to join her husband and tell him news that she knew would greatly disturb him.

"And, Lord, it did, oh, how it did," she whispered, tears hot again on her cheeks.

As she waited for the colonel Mary Beth looked around the fort's grounds.

It seemed strange that no wives or children were at this fort, yet perhaps it was a wise decision on the colonel's part. If Indians did successfully attack the fort, the children and wives would be at their mercy.

The door swung open so quickly, the cat jumped from Mary Beth's arms with alarm.

She saw it scurrying into the cabin between the colonel's legs; more than likely it was the colonel's pet.

"Ma'am?" Colonel Downing asked as he absently ran one hand through his thick, sandy hair; the other held a lighted kerosene lamp. "What are you doing here in the middle of the night?" The moon reflected on the blade of the knife, catching the colonel's eyes. He stared at it, then looked quickly at Mary Beth again. "Why do you have that knife? Has something happened?"

Mary Beth looked anxiously over her shoulder, then again into the colonel's questioning blue eyes. "Can I come in?" she asked, fear obvious in her voice.

Colonel Downing stepped aside. "Why, yes," he said, motioning her inside with his free hand. "Do come in and tell me what has brought you to me at this ungodly hour."

She brushed past him, glad when he had the door closed, putting a barrier between her and the horrible assailant.

"You are trembling," Colonel Downing said, holding the lamp farther out so that he could see her better. "Something terrible must have happened to you."

"Yes, it did," Mary Beth said. She wiped tears from her eyes with her free hand as she held the knife at her side with the other. She had never had the need to defend herself before coming to this wilderness. She was beginning to feel foreign to herself in many ways, because her life had taken such a different turn.

From now on, it would be different, for she would be living among a different people, learning their ways, being a chief's wife. It all seemed like a dream.

The best part of that dream was Brave Wolf.

She rushed into telling the colonel what had happened and described her assailant as best she could. She thanked the good Lord that the moon had lit the cabin, or she would never have seen her assailant.

"His voice was filled with such loathing," she said, her own voice breaking.

"Let me see your throat," Colonel Downing said, stepping closer and holding the lamp so that he could see her better.

His eyes narrowed angrily when he saw the red

imprint of the man's hand there. The skin was already bruising.

"The damn idiot," he cursed. "The cowardly sonofabitch. What was he thinking?"

"He was not thinking, he was doing," Mary Beth said as the colonel took her gently by the arm and led her into the living quarters of the cabin. "He wanted to kill me. If I hadn't thought fast enough and hurt him where no man wants to be hurt, then grabbed his knife from its sheath, I would even now be dead."

"Thank God you were able to react so effectively during such an assault," Colonel Downing said, setting the lamp on a table.

Mary Beth looked slowly around herself at the grandeur of the room. The walls provided a stunning backdrop for a Regency mirror over the mantel and a gilt-and-bronze chandelier.

Most striking of all was the elaborate French wallpaper and the carved side chairs upholstered in gilded leather.

Large neoclassical friezes and chunky molding added height to the windows, making Mary Beth momentarily forget that this was a cabin. The interior could have graced a mansion in France or England.

She was suddenly certain that a woman had lived here, even though the rules forbade it. There were lacy doilies on the arms and backs of the plushly upholstered chairs. Pretty, delicately painted ceramic figurines sat on tables and shelves.

Colonel Downing nodded toward one of the

most beautiful of the overstuffed chairs. "Sit," he said. "I'll make some tea after I build up the fire. Let's get you warmed through and through, and then I'll tell you what I'm going to do about what happened to you tonight."

Relieved that he was at this moment showing his honorable side, Mary Beth sighed as she eased down into the chair.

"Let me have the knife," Colonel Downing said, gently taking it from her hand. He placed it on the table beside the lamp, then after throwing a log on the flames, left Mary Beth alone as he went to the kitchen.

While she waited, the terrible attack came back to her, making her wince as she reached up and touched her neck. It was painful to the touch. How lucky she was to have gotten the better of the man. Surely only seconds had remained of her life!

She gazed into the flames and thought then of Brave Wolf. Oh, how she wished she was there with him now.

How she wished all of this terrible ordeal was behind her and David was with her again!

She knew that her son and the man she loved would become fast friends. David would look to Brave Wolf as a father figure, and Brave Wolf would take David under his wing, proud to call the young man his son.

"He will one day be called a warrior, too," Mary Beth found herself whispering as she envisioned David grown and muscled, riding a horse alongside the Crow warriors his same age.

There would be such camaraderie between her son and the others. She knew that he would be proud to say he was one with them!

"Here we are," Colonel Downing said as he came into the room carrying a tray on which sat a silver teapot and two cups and saucers. "This should hit the spot, don't you think?"

"I hope so," Mary Beth said. Trying to respond to his kindness, she smiled up at him.

He placed the tray on the table next to Mary Beth, then poured tea into the cups. "I'm going to have a cup, myself," he said, smiling at her, then frowning. "I might need it more than you, knowing what I soon must do."

She nodded a thank-you to him as he handed her the tea. The cup rattled against the saucer, and she realized her hands were trembling so much she could not steady them.

He poured himself a cup, then sat down across from Mary Beth in a matching chair.

The pleasant warmth of the tea eased Mary Beth's achy throat. She sipped it slowly. The colonel did likewise, looking at her in a studious fashion that was beginning to unnerve her.

She felt as though she were on display. More disturbing, she saw something in his eyes that she had seen countless times before . . . an interest men felt when they were attracted to a woman.

"Sir, you heard the assailant's description," she murmured, trying to distract him. "Do you recognize it?"

"Yes, I'm positive I know who it is," Colonel

Downing said, setting his tea aside. "It's Blackjack Tom."

"Blackjack Tom?" Mary Beth said, her eyes widening.

"Of course that is not his true name," Colonel Downing said, relaxing into the deep cushions of the chair. "His name is Lieutenant Thomas Sloan. He gets his nickname from his love of playing blackjack."

He paused, placed his fingertips together before him, and frowned. "Yep, he's a gambling man, but it seems he took one gamble too many tonight. His luck has just run out."

"Then you are going to arrest him?" Mary Beth asked, leaning forward. "You . . . are . . . going to do it tonight, aren't you?"

"I'll escort you safely to your cabin, and then I'll go and do my duty as colonel," he said tightly. "But first, young lady, we've got to get you into some different clothes. Those clothes probably caused Thomas to hate you the first time he laid eyes on you. When he looked at you, he saw an Indian squaw, not a white lady."

"But why would seeing me as an Indian . . . maiden . . . cause him to be *that* angry?" she murmured.

"I can't speak for him or look into his mind and know exactly what he was thinking, but I think I know something else that might have set him off," Colonel Downing said. He rested his hands on his knees as he continued gazing at Mary Beth. "You see, the rules here at Fort Henry weren't always as strict as they are now. Before an ambush of a wagon of wives one day, wives and children were allowed to live on the base. You see, Thomas's wife perished on the day of the Indian ambush." He lowered his eyes and cleared his throat.

He looked slowly up at Mary Beth. "So did mine," he said thickly. "So did these soldiers who were escorting the women on the outing."

"Your . . . wife . . . ?" Mary Beth gasped. "I'm so sorry."

"You are one of a very few who have escaped death after being attacked by these savages," Colonel Downing said.

"For a while I thought I would die," Mary Beth gulped out. "Had it not been for Chief Brave Wolf, I would be dead."

She noticed that the mention of Brave Wolf caused Downing to frown darkly. "You do not seem to think highly of Brave Wolf," she said guardedly. "Why is that? He has shown me nothing but kindness."

"Ma'am, after my wife was murdered by savages, I suspected every damn Indian that lived in the area," he said tightly. "Even though I had always been told that Chief Brave Wolf was peaceful toward whites, I could not rest until I checked him out personally. I went to his village. We clashed immediately."

"How?" Mary Beth gasped. "Was there a fight?"

"Not the kind you mean," he said. "It was instant dislike between us. Even though I came away knowing he was innocent of the crime, I still did not like the man. He is, and always will be, a savage just like all of the others."

"Was it something he said that riled you so much?" Mary Beth persisted, for she could not see how anyone could dislike Brave Wolf.

"Ma'am, sometimes a person doesn't have to have any reason for disliking someone," he said flatly. "It's just something that flows between them. I don't like Brave Wolf. He doesn't like me."

She understood why Brave Wolf had hesitated to bring her to Fort Henry. He not only didn't like this colonel, he didn't trust him.

"I see," was all that she replied.

"As for Blackjack Tom," he said. "When he saw you dressed like the very people he loathes, he must've snapped."

His eyes roamed slowly over her again. "And as for that dress," he said. "We'd best do something about it right now. We don't want you as a reminder of the killing of innocent women every time my men look at you."

She ran her hands slowly down the skirt of the doeskin dress. She had fallen in love with this dress the moment it had been given to her. Yet she could see how it represented all the wrong things to the soldiers.

"Come into my bedroom with me," Colonel Downing said, reaching a hand out for Mary Beth. "I've kept my wife's personal belongings in a trunk. She had many beautiful dresses. Earlier, when I mentioned your needing a dress, and said there were none here at the fort, I did not think

I could lend you one of my wife's dresses, but things have changed. It has been proven how my men feel about you, so I'd best forget my own feelings for the time being. And I don't believe my wife would mind if you wore one of her dresses, especially if it means protecting you from harm."

Although Mary Beth knew that she didn't plan to stay at the fort after David was found, she saw no choice but to accept the dress. Still, she didn't relish the thought of accompanying this man into his bedroom.

What if his intentions were illicit? What if he was just pretending to be a friend when all along he wanted what any lonely man wants from a woman?

"Sir, I'll wait here while you get the dress," Mary Beth said, standing her ground.

"You don't trust me?" he said. Then he chuckled. "Don't guess I'd blame you much, especially after what you've just been through at the hands of a stranger."

He nodded. "I'll be back in a jiffy," he said, walking from the room.

Mary Beth looked around the room again, at all the lovely trinkets that must have been acquired by his wife. They were pretty things only a woman would desire. Back in Kentucky, her trinkets were simple, yet loved no less than this lady's possessions.

"Here we are," Colonel Downing said, carrying a dress across his outstretched arm as though it were a delicate treasure. "My wife was a tiny thing like you. I'm sure the dress will fit well enough."

Mary Beth nodded and took the dress, then winced when she caught the smell of perfume on it. When she wore it, she would smell like the colonel's wife.

"I'm not sure . . ." she said, trying to hand the dress back to him.

"As I see it, you don't have any choice," he said, his eyes suddenly cold. Perhaps he was angry that she did not want to wear a dress his wife had adored.

"Come now," he said, gesturing toward the door. "I'll escort you safely to the cabin and then go and arrest Blackjack Tom. He's had it coming for some time. He's always in some kind of trouble or another, usually gambling. He's been accused of cheating more than once."

As he turned to open the door, Mary Beth looked quickly at the knife that he had placed on the table. When he wasn't looking, she grabbed it, then slid it among the folds of the dress.

When he turned and again gestured toward the door with a hand, she smiled and went past him, then walked with him across the courtyard toward her cabin.

She looked cautiously from side to side. Could Blackjack Tom be hiding somewhere nearby?

She followed the colonel, then stepped into the cabin as he opened the door for her.

"I'm sorry there are no locks on the door," he said. "But you can feel safe enough. The bastard'll be locked away real soon."

"Thank you for your kindness," she murmured.

He gave her a strange, lopsided smile, then walked away.

She hurried inside the cabin, closed the door, then leaned her back against it. Her heart was throbbing. What had made her agree to stay in a place where she knew she was in danger? For no matter what the colonel said, she *was* at risk.

She didn't know what to do. Leave? Or stay?

Disturbed by the perfume wafting from the dress, she dropped it to the floor.

Then knowing the colonel would be insulted if he saw the dress on the floor when he returned, she grabbed it quickly up again. For now, he was her only ally at the fort. She must make certain she didn't lose his support, strained as it was.

Sighing, she draped the dress over the back of a chair. She lit a kerosene lamp and slowly unbraided her hair.

When it was hanging long and loose over her shoulders, she sighed again. Just as she was ready to climb onto the bed, she was startled by a knock at the door. She went cold inside as she stared at it.

"Don't be frightened," Colonel Downing said through the door. "It is I. It's Colonel Downing."

Heaving a sigh of relief, yet wondering what would bring him back to the cabin so quickly, she went to the door and cautiously opened it.

The moonlight revealed his dark frown.

"I came to tell you that Blackjack Tom can't be arrested," he said.

"Why not?" Mary Beth asked, her eyes searching

his. "Have you changed your mind? Do you no longer see him as guilty? Look at my throat. He did this. I tell you . . . he did this to me."

"Yes, I believe you," Colonel Downing said heavily.

"Then why didn't you arrest him?" Mary Beth demanded.

"Because he's gone," Colonel Downing said. "He's nowhere to be found. I assume he expected you to tell what happened."

"Gone?" Mary Beth repeated, suddenly feeling icy cold all over. "But what about your sentries? Surely they saw him leave the fort."

"Mary Beth, he *was* tonight's sentry," he explained softly.

Now she recalled the absence of a sentry when she had needed someone to come to her rescue.

The sentry was Blackjack Tom!

Now she felt trapped. She couldn't flee into the night to go to Brave Wolf because that evil man could be out there anywhere, just waiting for the opportunity to finish what he had started tonight.

Suddenly she was aware that many soldiers were leaving their barracks, dressed and carrying firearms.

She questioned the colonel with her eyes.

"I'm sending men out to look for Thomas," he said, reaching a gentle hand to her arm. "I will post a guard outside your door. Go to bed. You can feel safe enough."

She nodded, turned, and went back inside the cabin, yet she didn't feel at all safe knowing that a soldier would be standing outside the cabin. What if that soldier had the same dark feelings about her as Blackjack Tom had had?

And . . . what about the window at the back of the cabin? Someone could break the glass and climb inside.

Truly feeling trapped, and so frightened that her knees were trembling, she didn't go to bed. Instead she positioned the chair so that it faced the window and sat down and watched . . . and waited.

She eyed the knife that she had placed on the table. She scurried to it and grabbed it.

Then she eyed the lamp and the flame burning in it. She felt much safer with the fire in the lamp blown out. She had the light of the moon to help her see whoever might come to the window.

But no one could see her.

She would be sitting in the dark, ready to kill, if necessary!

"Brave Wolf, if you only knew what I'm going through. . . ." she whispered.

Chapter Eighteen

For in my mind, of all mankind,
I love but you alone.
—Anonymous

Brave Wolf rode proudly on his new steed, the morning sun gleaming off Midnight's black coat. He looked over his shoulder at the others who rode with him. He saw their eyes moving constantly as they prepared themselves for anything that might happen.

But today their eyes searched mainly for a child who had been stolen by renegades.

Brave Wolf rode with the warriors he had assigned to search for David. He had needed something to keep his mind off Mary Beth, especially since she was with a man Brave Wolf did not like, and most definitely did not trust.

The day Colonel Downing had come to the village, Brave Wolf had been kind enough to invite him into his council house. He had even invited the white pony soldier to share a smoke with him since Brave Wolf always saw the importance of keeping the soldier leaders as allies instead of enemies. Nonetheless he had soon felt deep dislike for Colonel Downing.

Whenever the colonel had talked to Brave Wolf, it was with an air of superiority, as though the white man held himself above even a mighty Crow chief.

If the white man had even hinted that he suspected Brave Wolf or his warriors of killing his wife and those who had been with her, Brave Wolf would have ordered him from his lodge.

But as it was, it was just dislike that came between them.

Brave Wolf had not gone into council again with the colonel. He kept his distance from him and was glad that the colonel kept away from the Whistling Water Clan of Crow.

But knowing that Mary Beth was with the pony soldiers under this colonel's command even now, and had been put in the position of seeking his help, made Brave Wolf uneasy. He knew that the colonel had lost his wife in that ambush and had not taken another.

He also knew that no women resided at Fort Henry any longer and that Mary Beth was the only one there. If the white pony soldiers were lonely, would they forget their respect for a lone woman and try to take advantage of her?

He knew of Mary Beth's courage, but would it be strong enough to fend off a possible attempted rape in the middle of the night when the world was quiet and dark and only those with evil on their minds roamed?

Suddenly Brave Wolf's thoughts were averted elsewhere. A large herd of elk had become excited when they caught the scent of Brave Wolf and his warriors riding so close to them. Their sharp hooves stirred a swirling cloud of dust as they raced away.

Brave Wolf looked over his shoulder at his men and saw that they were watching the departing animals regretfully. He knew they longed to give chase and send arrows into at least one of the elk for the meat it would bring to their cooking pots.

A moment later the men looked away, for they had a mission today and it had nothing to do with hunting for food. They were hunting for a young child who had been taken by renegades.

Although his warriors had already searched for the boy, Brave Wolf continued to hope they might find the child for his mother.

He knew that the pony soldiers might also be out searching this morning. He might even come across them. He would ignore them and go on his own way, for he did not ever wish to align himself with soldiers under Colonel Downing's command.

The elk were no longer in sight. All that was left were swirling clouds of dust, and soon even they were gone. It was a beautiful morning with an azure sky overhead. It was the sort of day on which he would enjoy taking a ride with Mary Beth. He could see her smile even now, radiant and beautiful. He could see her lovely reddish-gold hair blowing in the gentle breeze.

Brave Wolf looked quickly to his left when a movement in the brush caught his eye, then watched a deer bound away on its stiff, springy legs.

He saw that this second temptation to have food for their dinner pots could not be ignored by his warriors. He saw one of them notch an arrow to his bowstring and aim, but he lowered his bow and arrow when a lovely spotted fawn came into view, following its mother from hiding.

He smiled at Brown Fox as his warrior took the arrow from his bow and slid it back in place in his quiver. Neither Brave Wolf nor his warriors ever took a mother from its baby, and most certainly no fawn was ever killed. The fawns were the promise of future hunts.

They rode onward for a while; then Brave Wolf saw a lone bull buffalo, a straggler from a herd that had moved through the area late last night.

He saw its fatness, and although he and his men had not gone in pursuit of the elk, or downed the deer, Brave Wolf could not let this animal go.

It would mean many things to his people. The *pte*, or buffalo, would provide fresh meat for immediate cooking, fat and dried flesh for pemmican, robes for beds and winter apparel, tanned hides for leggings and women's garments, as well as tepees.

But it was the meat of this bull that made stopping and killing it worthwhile. It was one of the fattest bulls he had seen in many sleeps!

He looked over his shoulder at his warriors and saw the eagerness in their eyes. He knew they did not want to ride on past, either.

He knew they understood the importance of this animal to their people. Due to the whites killing off buffalo, the herds had been thinned out. When one did have the opportunity to hunt one, it must not be ignored.

"My warriors, this one is mine," Brave Wolf said, only loud enough for them to hear. He did not want it to travel on the wind to the bull.

"It is mine to kill, but everything about it will be equally divided among us all," Brave Wolf was quick to say.

He needed this hunt to help take away some of his uneasy thoughts about Mary Beth.

He would shoot the animal himself, but leave two warriors behind to take from it what they could as he rode on with the others to continue their search for the child.

His warriors nodded, but they still notched their own bows with arrows in case they were needed to protect their chief if the bull happened to corner him.

Brave Wolf notched his own bow with an arrow from his quiver.

He rode in a slow lope toward the bull, and just

as he came close enough to shoot, the creature lifted its head, snorted, and turned to run in the opposite direction.

Brave Wolf gave chase.

He placed the reins in his mouth, holding them between his teeth, and anchored himself solidly on his steed as he thrust his knees tightly into its sides, then rode with his bow and notched arrow ready for shooting.

When he got close enough, and he could see through the cloud of dust that the bull's hooves were kicking up, he leaned toward the animal.

He carefully aimed and then loosed the arrow from his bow. The bowstring twanged in the early morning air.

He smiled when the arrow flew true and struck its mark in the bull's side. The bull fell quickly to the ground, then, snorting, managed to get to its feet again and began running through some spruce trees down to the edge of a creek.

Brave Wolf followed. He slung his bow over his shoulder and took the reins in his hands. The bull stopped, slumped to the ground again, then surprised Brave Wolf by getting to its feet again and lumbering onward.

This continued over and over again until finally it fell still beside a tree.

By then all of Brave Wolf's warriors had come up behind him. They stayed on their steeds as Brave Wolf dismounted.

He hung his bow over the pommel of his saddle, then slowly, carefully, stepping clear of the hip-deep ferns, inched his way over to the bull.

He was careful because he could see that the bull was still breathing, its sides heaving, its life's blood pooling on the ground beneath it.

Just when Brave Wolf thought that the bull was dead, and he had stepped up to it, he saw its tail move, and before Brave Wolf could draw his knife to finish the kill, the bull had leapt to its feet and slammed into his chest, throwing Brave Wolf onto his back on the ground.

The bull stood there, staring at Brave Wolf and shaking its head.

Red froth dripped from its mouth and its eyes had turned red with blood, yet it still lived.

Before any of the warriors could ready their bows with arrows, the bull pawed the ground and switched its tail, then leaned down and with its nose turned Brave Wolf over onto his stomach.

Just as it was ready to stomp on him, a warrior dragged Brave Wolf out of harm's way as four others sent a volley of arrows into the bull's side, downing it, this time, forever.

Brave Wolf leaned up and saw the arrow-riddled animal.

His heart pounded as he thought how close he had come to being mauled by the bull. From now on, he had to keep his mind clear of everything but the hunt.

He had been thinking about Mary Beth when he went to stand over the bull, thinking that some of the meat would feed not only her, but also her son, because he was determined to find David today.

That moment of distraction had almost been his last.

"You are alright?" asked Blue Thunder, a favored warrior, as he helped Brave Wolf to his feet. "My chief, you were not as careful as usual. What if you had been alone?"

"*Hecitu-yelo*, yes, what if I had been alone?" Brave Wolf said thickly.

He wiped beads of perspiration from his brow. He looked at those who had saved him.

"My warriors, all of the bull's meat, and everything you can take from it, is yours," Brave Wolf said. "Stay behind and take what you can, then return safely home to your families."

"But you downed it first," Blue Thunder said. "It is rightfully yours, not ours."

"It is yours, take it," Brave Wolf said, then hugged each of the four who had again proved their worth to their chief.

Saying nothing more, Brave Wolf went to his horse, swung himself into the saddle, then rode off with the remaining warriors.

Brave Wolf glanced down at the blood that had spattered on him from the bull as the animal had turned him over as though he were nothing more than a leaf. Today he had cheated death once again.

Chapter Nineteen

> If with me you'd fondly stray,
> Over the hills and far away.
> —Gay

It was a quiet morning. Two days had passed, and the soldiers had not been able to find David.

Feeling so many things, Mary Beth stood at the back window of the cabin, peering at the stark, tall walls of the fort.

She was glad that no one had tried to accost her again, yet she still didn't feel safe.

In fact, she felt like a prisoner.

The only time she had any contact with anyone was when food and fresh water were brought to her. Colonel Downing was always the one who came with those things.

She could not help feeling uneasy with him. She

could tell that he was motivated by something other than kindness. It was in his eyes as he slowly raked them over her. It was in the husky thickness of his voice when he spoke to her.

She had just been waiting for one move that would prove her right . . . that he was going to try to seduce her.

"I must get out of here," Mary Beth said, nervously pacing.

She gazed at the doeskin dress that she had laid out on the bed today, with every intention of leaving the fort and returning to the Crow village.

But she just didn't know how to break that particular news to the colonel.

When he discovered that she was not just a person who had been rescued by Chief Brave Wolf, but a woman who wanted to go to him and live with his people, she was afraid he would be furious.

Especially if he knew her plans to marry Brave Wolf.

She had no idea what his reaction would be.

And she couldn't just leave the fort without telling anyone. The sentries would see her and report it to the colonel.

Yet for many reasons she no longer had any faith that the soldiers would find David. They hadn't even found Blackjack Tom.

She shivered when she recalled that evil man's fingers on her throat. She reached a hand up and slowly, softly rubbed her throat, where bruises still gave evidence of the man's assault on her.

She was afraid for Brave Wolf to see the bruises. Who could say what his reaction might be?

She didn't want to cause him to confront the soldiers on her behalf, when it had only been one of them who had taken advantage of her.

She went to the doeskin dress and picked it up, holding its softness to her cheek. Yes, she wanted to wear this dress . . . not the one with the perfume of a dead woman on it.

She glanced over at the chair where two more dresses lay folded neatly. Colonel Downing had brought those to her so that she could have a change of clothes.

He had even brought some nightgowns, but she had not gone near them.

It gave her a sick feeling in the pit of her stomach just to imagine wearing them since she knew who had worn them, and with whom.

Yes. She must go now and tell the colonel her decision. No matter what he said or did, she would get on her horse and ride away from the fort and those who resided in it.

She had begun to feel more ill at ease by the minute. She was longing to go back to the Crow village, where she felt safe.

She just prayed that Brave Wolf and his warriors would somehow find her son.

Tears sprang to her eyes at the thought of never seeing David again, or holding him.

No. She *must* keep hoping that he was alive, and unharmed. She had heard how young white boys were adopted into Indian tribes and raised as one of them.

She had heard of those who were called "white warriors."

They were white men raised from childhood as Indians.

She shuddered at the thought of David ever becoming an unwilling "white warrior" for a renegade tribe, forced to ride against his own people.

Determined to stop thinking such things, and to get on with what she must do, she placed the doeskin dress back on the bed, then took a deep breath and left the cabin.

She always felt eyes following her when she was out in the open courtyard. She knew that the men still resented her presence, especially since they could not have their own wives there.

She lifted the hem of the dress and coughed when the dust stirred beneath her feet as she walked toward Colonel Downing's office. When she noticed the men staring at her feet, she dropped the dress again quickly. She was still wearing Indian moccasins.

When the colonel had tried to change Mary Beth's appearance, he had offered her his wife's shoes. She was glad that they hadn't fit, for she would have refused to wear them. It was enough to be wearing his wife's clothes.

She rushed onward and hurried into the colonel's office. Once inside, she stared through the cloud of cigar smoke and saw that the colonel wasn't at his desk. He had surely been there only moments ago, for a cigar was still smoking away in an ashtray on his desk.

Then she became aware of voices carrying down the corridor from the direction of the colonel's private quarters.

She walked quietly into the corridor, then went and stood just outside the door that led to the colonel's lovely parlor. She leaned closer to the door when she heard the colonel say something, and then someone responding. It was obvious there were several men having a meeting with the colonel in his private quarters.

She was disgruntled to realize that she must postpone her own discussion with him. She started to turn and leave, then stopped abruptly when she heard the colonel speak Chief Brave Wolf's name. He laughed almost wickedly as he continued talking.

Trembling, she eased closer to the door and pressed her ear against it, then grew more upset by the minute as she listened to the plans being made against Brave Wolf and his people. The colonel made mention of his brother and cousin, who had died at the Battle of the Little Big Horn, saying he had waited long enough to act on his anger over these deaths.

It was apparent to Mary Beth that the colonel was out for vengeance as he vowed to kill as many redskins as he could.

Then he again mentioned one warrior in particular . . . a chief . . . that he wanted to kill, the one that had brought Mary Beth to the fort. He said it made his skin crawl to know that such a lovely woman had been anywhere near Injuns. But it infuriated him to think that she had been with Brave Wolf.

He had come away from Chief Brave Wolf's village hating the bastard. The chief seemed to have such an air of superiority about him. It had been hard not to reach over and strangle him even then, but the colonel knew he'd never leave the village alive if he did.

So he had waited for the right opportunity to go after Chief Brave Wolf, who would be the first of those he would kill as he achieved his vengeance for those who had been slain during the Battle of the Little Big Horn. Seeing Mary Beth in the Injun attire had been a reminder of what he had been putting off until he came up with just the right scheme that would finally show the redskins a thing or two about slaughtering white people.

Mary Beth's mind was reeling from all that she heard this man say. She could hear the venomous hate in his voice, the loathing!

What am I to do? she wondered as she stepped slowly away from the door.

She had been so anxious to leave this place and return to the loving arms of Brave Wolf, yet now she didn't think that was what she should do. She must find a way to stop the colonel and his men from harming Brave Wolf.

"There is only one way," she whispered as she glared at the closed door.

She smiled wickedly when she recalled the lust

in the colonel's eyes when he looked at her. There was such a hunger there for her, she knew that soon he would have to act on his feelings.

She would use this weakness of the colonel's in order to find out all the plans that were being made against Brave Wolf.

She would play up to the colonel and make him believe that she cared . . . that she even hated Indians because she now blamed all of them for the loss of her son, not only the renegades.

She knew that it would be hard to play such a role when she wanted nothing more than to leave and be with Brave Wolf.

But she would do anything to save him.

She would use the old tricks that women had used for thousands of years when they wanted something from a man.

When she heard the men talking as if they were ready to leave, Mary Beth hurried back to the colonel's office and sat down on a chair beside his desk. As the men filed out and saw her there, she gave them each a soft smile.

"Well, what have we here?" Colonel Downing said as he came and stood over Mary Beth. "Lonely, eh? You are getting tired of being in that cabin all alone?"

"Yes, something like that," Mary Beth said, rising from the chair. She forced herself to reach a hand out, then twined her fingers through his. "I've been doing a lot of thinking."

"You have?" Colonel Downing said, raising an

eyebrow when he gazed down at their joined hands.

The fires in his loins flared hotter. It had been way too long since a woman had touched him. It had been way too long since a woman had gone to bed with him.

He smelled the familiar scent of his wife's perfume on the dress and ached even now to hold her. But today there was a new lady in his life, and she was actually flirting with him.

"Yes, I've had a lot of time to think about things," she murmured, playfully squeezing his hand. "As you know, I'm very upset about my son still being missing." She forced a frown. "Because of that, I can't help hating Indians. *All* of them, Colonel Downing. Every last one of them. I'd like nothing more than to forget about them and think only of you and what we can have together."

She smiled at him. "I hope I haven't mistaken your behavior toward me?" she murmured. "You do want to know me better, don't you?"

"Yes, and please, call me William," he said huskily, his eyes gleaming. "And what you just said? That pleases me a lot, for you see, I am quite smitten with you. I would definitely like to get to know you better."

His words, his flirting gaze, disgusted Mary Beth, but she continued pretending just the opposite. "Then why aren't you kissing me?" she murmured, everything within her hating the very thought of it.

But she must continue with this farce if she was

to discover the full plot that was being mapped out against Brave Wolf.

"I'm so lonely," she murmured. "I'm so sad that I may never see my David again. Will you help me? I need someone to console me."

He whisked his arms around her and brought her hard against him. "Will I ever," he said huskily, then kissed her as his body gyrated seductively against hers.

Realizing now just how hungry this man was for a woman, Mary Beth felt panic rising within her. What if she had started something that she could not stop? What if he forced himself on her now?

Mary Beth pressed her hands hard against his chest and managed to get him away from her.

"Sir, you are moving much too quickly for me," she said, knowing that her face was red with a hot blush. "I am a decent woman. I'm sorry that I made you think otherwise."

"I'm sorry," he said, coughing nervously into his hand. "I got carried away. It's just that you are so beautiful and you seemed to want what I want."

"I do, but not all that quickly," Mary Beth said. She took slow steps away from him. "Please realize that I was only recently widowed. I must show some respect for my late husband, must I not? Please understand that I do not want to rush into anything just yet. But I would so much enjoy your company until I feel it is alright to go farther than a kiss."

"Then you shall have it," Colonel Downing said, smiling from ear to ear. He stepped toward her, took one of her hands, then slightly bowed and gave her a gentlemanly kiss on her hand.

"I so admire you for being the lady that you have just presented yourself to be," he said.

"You did not think I was too brazen as I flirted with you?" Mary Beth asked, easing her hand from his. "I am not used to such things as this. I . . . I . . . was married to my husband for so long. I never knew any man before him."

"I shall honor your wishes," Colonel Downing said. "May I request your presence tonight at my dining table? I am certain you are tired of eating alone in that cabin, am I right?"

"Yes, very," Mary Beth said, forcing a soft laugh. "And, sir . . . I mean, William, I gladly accept your invitation. I shall wear one of the dresses that you brought me this morning."

"That would please me so much," he said, walking her to the door. He grabbed her by one hand and turned her to face him. "Something else. Why not move in to the spare bedroom here at my home? I have worried so much about you being out there all alone. I promise not to force the issue of . . . of . . . going farther with me until you say that you are ready. Then, Mary Beth, might you even consider marrying me? I can give you the world. I have a mansion in Boston. When I retire, I shall take you there. You will never want for a thing."

Mary Beth was stunned by all that he was offering her.

But although most women would die for such

an opportunity to live the life he described, the thought sickened her.

She could not get this man's words from her mind about how much he hated Indians and how he hoped to kill as many as he could before he died . . . especially Brave Wolf!

"That sounds wonderful," she said, hating being caught up in more and more lies.

But for Brave Wolf, she would do anything . . . except go to bed with Colonel Downing. She would have to achieve her goal before Colonel Downing—no, *William*—caught on to her plan, for he would surely expect her to share his bed before too long.

"You don't need to return to the cabin," he said thickly. "Everything you will ever need is right here for you. Let me show you to your room, and then I shall bring my wife's trunk of clothes there for your perusal. You can choose from her dresses and diamonds."

He glanced down and saw her moccasins peeking out from beneath the hem of the dress. He smiled at her. "Surely you can find at least one pair of my wife's shoes that will fit your lovely feet," he said. "We just didn't try hard enough the other time. We must get those buckskin things off your feet."

Mary Beth had to force a smile, while inside she was dying a slow death. She hoped she had not started something she could not stop.

"Come, my sweet," Colonel Downing said, placing an arm around her waist and leading her down the corridor. When he opened the door to a bedroom, she gasped at its opulence. She could hardly believe her eyes. If this was a spare room, she was surprised. The smell of the colonel's wife's perfume was much stronger here.

Had the colonel and his wife slept in separate quarters? She gave him a sideways glance. Perhaps this man was not as successful in bed as he would wish to be. If so, he might be even more anxious for a woman than a normal man.

Mary Beth hoped she had not started something she could not control. A man's hungers could go so deep, there might be no stopping him once he had even a tiny taste of a woman's sweetness.

Mary Beth had to make sure he did not get *any* taste of *her* "sweetness."

She was afraid that her life depended on it!

Chapter Twenty

Give me a kiss,
Add to that kiss a score;
Then to that twenty
Add a hundred more.
—Herrick

A bugle had just blared, sounding officers' call. As the morning sun streamed through the bedroom window, Mary Beth brushed her hair with a gold-plated hairbrush that had belonged to another woman . . . the colonel's wife.

She gazed at her reflection in the mirror that hung above a lovely oak table. Today, even dressed in an expensive silk dress, she felt out of place.

It was apparent that the colonel's wife had been a much different breed of women from Mary Beth. She had been a society woman, whereas Mary Beth had lived a much simpler life on a farm.

She knew that many women would welcome the chance to enter such a glamorous world. But all Mary Beth wanted was to be with Brave Wolf.

She even looked forward to living in a tepee, keeping it clean and neat for her husband once she became Brave Wolf's wife.

A knock on the door made her flinch, for she knew whom to expect when she opened it.

No doubt the colonel had came to invite her to breakfast in the dining room, for surely he would not ask her to join the soldiers in their dining hall. She knew that he would not want to flaunt her there for all of them to see.

"Mary Beth?" Colonel Downing asked from outside the door. "Are you awake?"

"Yes, I'm awake and dressed," she said. She sighed, for she dreaded being with him again.

But she had to see her plan through to fruition. Somehow she must find a way to discover his complete plan against the Crow so that she could warn Brave Wolf beforehand.

She placed the brush on the table, then went to the door and opened it.

Colonel Downing was freshly shaved and smelled of aftershave lotion. His uniform was neatly pressed and his hair was combed.

He was not an ugly man. This morning he was smiling with an expression that might catch any woman's fancy, except hers.

Mary Beth just wanted all of this behind her. She knew the danger she was putting herself in each day she remained at the fort, especially if anyone suspected what she was up to.

"Well, good morning to *you*," Colonel Downing said, his eyes brightening as he looked admiringly at her. He clasped his hands behind him. "You look quite fetching this morning, my dear. Quite pretty, indeed."

"Thank you," Mary Beth said, uncomfortable beneath his close scrutiny, and wanting anything but compliments from him.

"I've made plans this morning that I hope you will agree to," he said. He took his hands from behind him, now clasping them before him. "Usually I eat with my men, but this morning I am taking breakfast in my private parlor with only a few officers. Will you join us?"

"Sir, I don't think I would feel comfortable with the others," Mary Beth said, truly concerned about their attitude toward her. "Can you just bring my breakfast to me? I don't mind eating alone, honest, I don't."

"I must make a point to my men," he said, suddenly frowning. "I want no more grumbling from them about you being here, when they cannot have their own wives with them at the fort. It's imperative that they understand you are my intended."

His . . . "intended" . . . ?

That truly rankled Mary Beth, but she had no choice but to play along with him now. She had begun this game. She must finish it.

"And," he further stated, "these are my choice

men. I want them to be the first to hear about our upcoming nuptials, and also the first to know that you won't be here for long. I plan to send you on to Boston where I will join you later. I have already wired ahead and made arrangements. Even now my mansion is being readied for the new woman of the house."

Mary Beth's head was spinning with all that he had just said. This man didn't waste any time. He truly thought that she was going to marry him!

Now she felt trapped as never before. Oh, Lord, she was not sure how long she could play this role before he caught on to her.

If he did realize what she was up to, what might he do with her? Would he throw her in the guardhouse, or take her out into the middle of the wilderness and leave her?

Might he even shoot . . . or . . . hang her?

"You are so kind," she said with difficulty, finding it even harder to pretend to smile shyly. "You have actually sent word to your home that I will arrive as your wife?"

"Most certainly," he said. He reached a hand out for her. "Now will you please join me this morning? But I must confess something to you before we go. There is yet another purpose for this breakfast meeting."

"And that is?" she said, reaching out and allowing him to take her hand. She tried not to grimace, for she loathed his touch.

"I don't like wasting time over anything," he said, walking her down the corridor. "While we are eating breakfast, and my men are getting used to you being among them as my future bride, we will be discussing our plans to take care of a few Indians in this area. Thus far, I've not gone against any of them Indians unless I was forced to. I have tried to keep peace for those settlers who want to come and live in this lovely land. But after hearing from you about renegades running loose massacring people, I've decided it's time for me to do more to protect whites."

He ushered her to the door of the parlor, then stopped. "My dear, I'm going to make those savages pay for what they did to you and your son," he said thickly. "I'm sorry for how you've been treated."

She wanted to speak up and defend Brave Wolf, to say that he was anything but an evil Indian. He was everything good, and had even worked to keep peace with whites.

But she had to keep quiet, at least for now. She had to be able to sit among the men and hear, firsthand, just what their plans were.

"My dear, I know that you said Chief Brave Wolf rescued you from renegades and escorted you safely here, but he is no less a savage than any other redskin, and he must be dealt with and made to know who's the boss in these parts," Colonel Downing said. "He will be the first to know our wrath."

Shaken to the core by this man's hatred for all Indians, and especially Brave Wolf, Mary Beth fought hard to show no emotion.

"I understand," she murmured. "And, yes, Brave Wolf did assist me, but I do not know of any atrocities he is guilty of against whites. He may have pretended to be peaceful only to please me. You see, I believe he was infatuated with me. Had I not insisted on being brought to this fort, I imagine he would have tried to get me to marry him."

She absolutely hated playing this game, but she had to find a way to make the colonel open up to her.

"Why, the thought!" Colonel Downing gasped, shuddering. "It sickens me! Well, I'm here to see that he never gets such a ludicrous idea again."

She forced another smile, then went into the parlor, where several soldiers were waiting, already enjoying sweet breads and coffee.

She felt uneasy when they all turned and stared at her. She saw in them the same resentment the soldiers had shown when she first arrived in Indian attire. The beautiful dress she wore seemed to make no difference in their thinking about her.

She smiled a silent thank you to the colonel as he escorted her to a chair, then as she sat, sat down beside her.

She waited stiffly, trying to ignore the continued glares. For the moment, everything in the room was quiet. Mary Beth could hardly even hear anyone breathing.

No one said anything except the colonel. He first gave her a plate of sweet breads, a cup of coffee on a beautiful saucer, then smiled at her as he spoke.

"I have brought Mary Beth to join us today for two reasons," Colonel Downing said, looking from soldier to soldier. "First let me say that she has agreed to be my wife."

Mary Beth flinched when she heard the gasps of shock on each side of her.

"The wedding will be as soon as our resident preacher can prepare things," Colonel Downing said, smiling at Mary Beth. His smile waned when he saw her flushed face and the uneasiness in her eyes. He understood. More than one of his soldiers was giving her angry glares.

He directed his eyes back at his soldiers. "Mary Beth will spend only a few more days here among us. Then she will go to Boston, where she will make her residence at my home until I can join her when I retire, which I plan to do very soon," he blurted out. "The recent massacres have awakened me to how short life can be. Now that I have found a woman like Mary Beth who has promised to marry me, I want no more of the military life. I'll be retiring soon. I am anxious to become a mere citizen of Boston, a *husband*."

There were fresh gasps, and Mary Beth was the center of attention again.

She, too, was stunned, that the colonel was ready to give up everything for her. She began to wonder if she would be able to get away from him as planned. She knew that he would be out for blood once he discovered the truth behind her promises.

He would hate her with a passion, for she would be responsible for making a fool of him in the eyes of all who knew him. No man liked to be made a fool of, especially by a woman . . . and not just any woman . . . one who loved an Indian.

"But first, men, I want to make one last splash as a colonel," he went on. He leaned forward in his chair. "Today we finalize our plans against Chief Brave Wolf. He is to be the first of many who will pay for our losses at the Battle of the Little Big Horn. And as I have told you, I have a bone to pick with that particular savage, anyhow. No Injun looks down at Colonel Downing as though he is my superior. Well, he will regret ever putting himself above me. Let us talk now and agree to a plan to erase that savage from the face of the earth . . . and then onward, to others."

Immediately all attention was averted from Mary Beth. The soldiers got a look of greed in their eyes, like a man gets before winning a hand of poker.

Mary Beth stiffened and eyed the men, one by one, as each offered his suggestions as to how this surprise attack should be carried out.

They all agreed to the final plan, then left the room one by one, leaving Mary Beth and the colonel alone.

"I saw how uncomfortable that talk made you," Colonel Downing said as he took Mary Beth's hands and urged her to her feet. "I understand. You're a woman. No woman wants to hear about death and destruction, not even if it is against the very people who stole her son from her."

"It does sound so . . . so . . . bloodthirsty," she managed to say in a soft voice.

"What happened to your husband in that dreadful battle was bloodthirsty," he growled out. "And your son? Who is to say what the heathens have done to him?"

That made Mary Beth lower her eyes. She hated thinking about what might be happening to her son at the hands of the renegades.

She was reminded again, though, of how fortunate she had been. She had been rescued by a wonderful Crow chief.

She had to find her way back to Brave Wolf's village and tell him all that she had heard today. She might be saving more than him and his Crow people. The plans were to annihilate all of the Indians within reach of Fort Henry.

"I'm sorry," the colonel said, gently placing a finger under her chin. He lifted it so that his eyes and Mary Beth's met. "I sometimes speak before I think. I did not mean to imply the worst about your son."

She hoped that he wouldn't see the hate in her eyes, for at this moment she hated this man worse than Blackjack Tom, who had still not been found. Hearing the plans against Brave Wolf had been even worse than feeling fingers around her throat, tightening, tightening.

Right now it seemed as though a vise was around her heart, doing the same.

"It's alright," she lied. "I understand how you feel. It's just terrible that life has to be this way . . . that there should be any more deaths."

"Better they than we," Colonel Downing said,

chuckling. "Now let's get on with talk about a wedding," he said, smiling broadly. "I believe we'll have the ceremony before I ride out with my soldiers for the killing."

She cringed at the thought.

Her mind was desperately planning how she was going to manage to get free of not only this fort, but also this man . . . especially before wedding vows were spoken between them!

Chapter Twenty-one

For thee the wonder-working earth
puts forth sweet flowers.
—Lucretius

Brave Wolf pushed his half-eaten tray of breakfast foods away from him. He stared blankly into his lodge fire as he again became lost in troubling thoughts. Now that Mary Beth was no longer with him, he was not sleeping well, nor had he wanted to eat.

He even found it hard to perform his duties to his clan.

He only hoped that his people did not notice. He had tried hard to put up a good front.

But in his eyes, if anyone looked closely enough, was a quiet torment. He knew the sort of man Colonel Downing was. He was cold-hearted, calculating, and had a deep-seated hatred for all Indians.

It had taken all the willpower that Brave Wolf could muster to tolerate the insolent colonel that day he had came to have council with Brave Wolf after renegades had ambushed and killed the army wives.

"I must at least try to see her," he whispered to himself.

That was what he must do. He would hide close to Fort Henry and try to catch a glimpse of Mary Beth from afar. If he did see her and saw that she was alright, he would rest much easier at night. He would dream better dreams.

He wondered when she planned to return to him. How much longer would she feel that she must stay to know whether or not her son could be found by the soldiers?

And when she did decide to leave, how could she explain her departure to the colonel? If he knew that she wanted to return to the Crow village, to live among the Crow, he might not allow it.

Filled with so many doubts and questions, Brave Wolf decided that today was the day he would try to find some answers. He would go and watch for Mary Beth. But if he did not see her, what then?

How could he return to his village without knowing how she was? Might not the torment be twofold if he went and did not see her?

No matter what, he had to at least give it a try. If luck was on his side, she might even today ride from the fort on the beloved steed that was now hers. She might be ready to put her old life behind her and forge ahead with the new.

But if she had not received any word yet about her son, would she be ready to look forward and let the past die as it should die?

They had such a wonderful future together.

They would have many children to replace the one she had lost, if indeed David was gone. They would have sons *and* daughters.

That made him smile despite the misery of missing her.

He had no duties to tend to today for his people. His brother was faring well enough—so well, in fact, that soon a decision must be made about his future.

His people had begun to tolerate his presence among them, had even begun to forgive the error of his ways. Night Horse seemed to have changed back to the warrior he had been before being lured away by greed. His future was in his own hands.

Shaking his head, Brave Wolf went back to thinking of his own future. He had begun making himself a new medicine bundle, which he hoped would not only busy his hands and mind while Mary Beth was gone, but also bring him good luck.

The new medicine bundle was made now and before he left the village today, he would uncover it and get it blessed by his people's shaman, Many Clouds.

Having it with him today would almost ensure that he would see Mary Beth, for all the while he was making the new medicine, she had been in his heart and mind.

He went to the back of his tepee, knelt, and began slowly, almost meditatively, unfolding the thin piece of doeskin in which he had kept his new medicine.

He unfolded the last corner of the doeskin and smiled as he gazed down. He had made a hoop from a red willow branch. He had wrapped it in buckskin, then painted it half blue and half black and tied a hawkskin and some red feathers to it. It had taken a good portion of one day to complete it.

"My chief?"

The voice of Many Clouds made Brave Wolf turn toward the lowered buckskin flap at his doorway. Even before the sun had risen fully along the mountaintops, he had gone to Many Cloud's lodge and told him that today was the day for him to bless his new medicine. He was there now, at his chief's request, to do so.

Brave Wolf gazed at his medicine once again, then rose from his haunches and went to the doorway. He held open the buckskin flap.

"Welcome," he said, stepping aside so Many Clouds could enter.

Many Clouds returned Brave Wolf's smile, embraced him, then walked with the younger man to where the new medicine lay awaiting his blessing.

"I see that your new medicine has been properly made," Many Clouds said, moving to his haunches before it. "The black paint represents night and the blue the earth. The red feathers represent the clouds and the hawkskin, your vision."

"*Hecitu-yelo*, yes, you have read my new medicine well," Brave Wolf replied. "I have already smudged it and sung to it in order to make it powerful."

Many Clouds turned his eyes toward Brave Wolf. "All it needs now is my blessing . . . then use it well, my chief."

"I will have use of it today," Brave Wolf said. "I will carry it with me on my quest."

"I do not even have to ask what that quest is," Many Clouds said, placing a gentle hand on Brave Wolf's shoulder. "I have seen your restlessness since the woman rode out of our village. I see in your eyes how you ache to hold her again."

"You are the wisest of wise," Brave Wolf said, nodding. "I *do* plan to ride today to try to get a glimpse of my woman. I must see that she is not harmed by the pony soldiers. I am glad that you understand the needs of a man who has fallen in love with a woman different from himself. When I look at her I see no color. I see my heart."

"A man cannot choose which woman his heart leads him to, it is his heart that does the leading and choosing," Many Clouds said, lowering his hand. "I trust your heart's judgment, my chief. It has never led you wrong."

Brave Wolf gave Many Clouds a warm hug, then sat down beside him as the shaman began singing and chanting over the new medicine.

"It is now blessed," Many Clouds said, slowly rising. "Guard it well, my chief. You will be guarding your future."

Brave Wolf embraced Many Clouds again, then led him to the door.

When the shaman had left the lodge, Brave Wolf knelt before his medicine again, then slowly folded it back into the doeskin.

He left it there until he had his stallion readied for travel, then went for it and carefully placed it in his travel bag at one side of his horse.

When he returned to his lodge he bypassed his bow and quiver of arrows. Instead, he fastened a sheath that held his large knife at his right side, then carried his prized rifle to his horse. After sliding it into his gunboot, and making certain he had enough ammunition, he mounted his steed and rode from the village.

When he reached open land, with the mountains behind him, he rode at a hard gallop. He hoped that before the moon replaced the sun in the sky he would have seen his woman. If she looked as though she had been mistreated at the hands of the whites, he would go to war without hesitation!

Chapter Twenty-two

But true love is a durable fire;
In the mind ever burning,
Never sick, never old, never dead,
From itself, never turning.
—Sir Walter Raleigh

Mary Beth had had no idea how quickly the colonel's marriage plans would evolve. The wedding was actually set for tomorrow!

Although she now knew what the soldiers had planned against Brave Wolf, she had not been able to find a way to leave the fort to go and warn him.

With the soldiers often being lax about their sentry duties, especially at night, Mary Beth had thought it would be easy to get her horse and leave under cover of darkness.

Shc had observed the gate being opened and

closed enough times to know how to get it open without making any noise. But the problem had been finding it unguarded.

Now she had only one more night left, and then she would have no choice but to tell the colonel the truth . . . that she didn't want to marry him.

It was critical that she find a way to escape.

She smiled. Her eyes lit up with an idea that surely would work. She was thinking it through when a knock on the bedroom door startled her.

Her pulse raced because she knew who it was. Colonel Downing.

She had not had enough time to flesh out her plan, but she knew enough to get it in motion, and pray that God was on her side today.

Her knees strangely weak from fear of what she was about to do, Mary Beth went to the door and opened it.

She forced a smile for Colonel Downing, who was grinning from ear to ear.

"It is all set," he said, brushing past her. "Tomorrow is the big day. It's all arranged. We shall be saying our vows this time tomorrow."

He grabbed her by the hand. "You are making me so happy," he said. "I have never been as lonely as I have been since my wife's passing. My one regret is that I must send you on to Boston so soon. But I must, for it was I who set up the rules that no women would be allowed to live at the fort. I must not be the one to break my own rules."

"I'm so looking forward to going to Boston," she

murmured, wondering about how good she was getting at lying. She had never been one to lie. She had always been straightforward and honest. But circumstances had made her do what she must in order to survive.

"Your home sounds like something from a storybook," she said. "Thank you, William."

Oh, how she hated calling him by his first name. It made it seem as if she cared for the arrogant, cruel man, when in truth she loathed him so much she could hardly stand being in the same room with him.

"My house and everything about it is even better than I have described," he said, chuckling. "My dear, you will not want for a thing. I will have servants, maids, and anyone else you ask for, at your convenience. You won't even have to brush your own hair any longer. It will be done for you."

"It does sound like heaven," she said, lying through her teeth with every word she spoke. "Tomorrow, you say? We'll be wed tomorrow?"

"I hope you can put from your mind any guilt about marrying so soon after your husband's death," he said huskily. "I can hardly wait to—"

He stopped before saying anything about making love. He had seen her stiffen and realized that it still might be too soon for her.

But nevertheless, she *would* marry him tomorrow. He could not wait any longer.

"There is one thing that I want in order to make our marriage ceremony perfect," Mary Beth said, putting her plan in motion.

"And, my dear, what is that?" he asked, clasping his hands behind him. "Anything you want will be yours."

"I want flowers," she said breathlessly.

She watched him to see if he thought there was anything odd about her request.

"I want a lot of flowers," she quickly added.

"But there is no way to have flowers here, so far from any city with florists," he said.

"I see something in your eyes—perhaps a way to have flowers?" He chuckled. "Alright, tell me what you have cooked up in that pretty head of yours. Where do you plan to get those flowers?"

"On my way here, not far from the fort, I saw a field of wildflowers," she said. "I could go and pick many of them. They would suffice, don't you think, for a wedding bouquet for me to carry, and for one huge vase to sit amid the candles during the ceremony?"

His eyes widened. He smiled. "Why, my dear, you *are* looking forward to our nuptials, aren't you?" he said, taking one of her hands and kissing its palm. He held it to his heart. "Yes, flowers. We shall go and pick many, many flowers."

"We?" she said, feeling her hope waning. "I don't need an escort just to pick flowers. In fact, I look forward to doing it all by myself. I don't want you to see the flowers until after I have arranged them prettily for our ceremony."

She stepped closer to him and placed a gentle hand on his cheek. "William, dear, I am doing this for us, for our wedding," she murmured. "Allow me to do this. I want to make the flower arrangement so beautiful. I want to surprise you."

He quietly took her hand away. "I would never allow you to ride through those gates alone and risk losing you to a renegade," he said thickly. "I, myself, will escort you. Then if you need some private moments alone to pick what you want, to be a surprise for me, I will turn my back."

Mary Beth's hopes of getting a chance to escape fell apart even as her heart felt like it was breaking.

She was beginning to realize that she couldn't tell Colonel Downing she wouldn't marry him. He was dead set on marrying her, *tomorrow*, and if she suddenly refused, who was to say what he would do with her? He most certainly would not allow her to leave for any reason, except to go to Boston after their marriage.

"William, do you promise to let me have some moments alone to pick the flowers?" she asked, hoping that perhaps she could ride off on the powerful steed Brave Wolf had given her.

If she could just get far away enough to hide, so that Colonel Downing couldn't find her, then she might find a way out of this nightmare.

"Absolutely," he said, smiling. "And we shall leave on our little outing soon, my dear. First I have to attend to some business. I shall send one of my soldiers with a large gunny sack from the kitchen to transport the flowers to the fort."

"Thank you," she murmured as she walked him to the door. "I can hardly wait to start picking."

He gave her a soft kiss on her cheek, then

walked away with light steps, his mood obviously buoyant.

Sighing, Mary Beth went back into the bedroom, closed the door, then leaned her back against it. "What am I to do?" she whispered, tears filling her eyes.

"Where will this lead?" she wondered, throwing herself on the bed.

She pummeled her fists on the mattress, cursing the day she had decided to come to Fort Henry. She had not achieved anything but a sentence worse than death, marrying Colonel Downing.

Chapter Twenty-three

> If ever those shalt love
> In the sweet pangs of it, remember me.
> —Shakespeare

Brave Wolf took some dried elk jerky from the parfleche bag he kept on his horse, then reached into his other travel bag and touched his new medicine. He gazed heavenward and said a soft prayer to the First Maker. Then he sat down on the bluff, where he was protected from view by a stand of brush.

When Brave Wolf had first arrived in the late afternoon yesterday, he had secured his steed back from the bluff in the shade of a cottonwood tree, then had taken his knife and cut through the leaves and limbs of the brush just enough to give him a clear view of the fort down below, yet not enough to reveal his presence there.

He felt great relief knowing that Mary Beth was safe and alive at the fort. He had seen her step from the large cabin in the center of the courtyard to get a breath of fresh air.

He had not seen any signs of a young white brave at the fort, which he thought he would if David was there; it was not normal for a child his age to stay cooped up inside.

He assumed the pony soldiers had had no more success at finding David than Brave Wolf's warriors.

His hair still wet from a morning dip in a nearby stream, Brave Wolf got comfortable on a blanket that he had spread there yesterday for his comfort. He sat directly before the open space in the brush and yanked a big piece of jerky off with his teeth.

His eyes darted from here to there as he saw much activity down below in the fort.

It was morning. The pony soldiers were apparently doing their daily chores.

But he wasn't there to look at soldiers. He wanted to see Mary Beth again. He wanted to go and get her and take her home with him. He wanted to tell her how much he needed to feel the throb of her throat against his lips as he kissed her there. In the naked dark of night he wanted to feel her smooth, sweet skin and warm breasts with his hands. . . .

His thoughts stilled and his eyes widened when he saw Mary Beth step from the colonel's cabin, followed by the colonel himself. His gaze raked over Mary Beth. She no longer wore the doeskin dress. She was dressed in white woman's attire.

She looked beautiful today with her hair hanging long and loose in the sun, the soft breeze making it ripple down her back. The dress she wore was one that seemed to be made of a much lighter fabric than doeskin. The breeze caused the full skirt to flutter around her legs, revealing her slender ankles.

His pulse raced when he saw where Mary Beth and the colonel were headed. The horse corral!

When they stopped at the corral, Brave Wolf's heart skipped an anxious beat at the possibility that Mary Beth might soon be riding out of the fort.

He searched among the steeds with his eyes and soon found the sorrel he had given to Mary Beth. It was already saddled.

He watched as Mary Beth went to the dark sorrel and slowly ran her hands over its withers. His eyes narrowed when the colonel placed his hands at Mary Beth's waist and lifted her into the saddle.

Brave Wolf pushed the limbs of the brush farther apart so that he could get a better look. The colonel mounted another steed, then rode with Mary Beth through the gate that had been opened for them.

Curious about where the colonel might be taking Mary Beth, Brave Wolf yanked his blanket off the ground, stuffed it in the travel bag, then leapt into his saddle and began making his way down the steep slope of land.

When he reached level ground, he made his way

through a thick stand of cottonwood trees that blocked his view of Mary Beth and the colonel. He was moving blindly now through the trees, not sure if he was going in the right direction. He wanted to get free of the trees so that he could look in all directions and follow Mary Beth and the colonel.

When he heard Mary Beth's voice, his heart skipped a beat and he stopped quickly. He dismounted and tethered his horse's reins to a tree, then crept stealthily onward on foot, his rifle clutched hard in his right hand.

Chapter Twenty-four

A woman's whole life
is a history of the affections.
—Washington Irving

"If it wasn't for President Grant's stubborn insistence on a humane policy toward Indians, we'd have gotten the advantage of the savages way before now," Colonel Downing said as he rode beside Mary Beth. "As it is, many innocent soldiers died alongside Custer."

He realized what he had just said and looked quickly toward Mary Beth. "I'm sorry," he said. "That was careless of me. I did not mean to remind you all over again of your husband's death. Again I spoke before I thought."

"I understand," Mary Beth said, controlling her temper, for it was not the reminder of Lloyd's death that bothered her as much as the Colonel's hatred of Indians.

"I'm glad you understand," he said. Then he smiled as they continued onward. "Ah, that Custer. Did you know they called him the Boy General? He was hoping to gain the Democratic nomination for President. A stunning victory over hostile Indians could have made him a national hero overnight. Yep, he'd have been our next President." He frowned. "As it is, more than likely Grant will be elected again."

Mary Beth didn't hear what he had just said. She could hardly believe her eyes. She *had* recalled a field of flowers, but what she now saw spread out before her wasn't the same. This was twice the size. It was a wildflower delight.

Everywhere she looked she saw a different sort of flower. There were carpets of purple, white, yellow, pink, and blue.

She drew rein and quickly dismounted.

She stood in the midst of the flowers, still in awe of the loveliness that surrounded her. For the moment she was able to forget the ugliness of life that she now knew so well.

"They are so beautiful!" she said, sighing. She turned and smiled at Colonel Downing. "Thank you for allowing me to come here. I am not only enjoying the opportunity to collect flowers for our marriage, but also just being here where it is so lovely."

"You are a delight," Colonel Downing said, dismounting. He took the large gunny sack to Mary

Beth and held it open for her. "Pick to your heart's content. I shall hold the bag for you."

Mary Beth smiled, then began plucking away. While she was picking the flowers, she caught a movement in the trees where a thick stand of cottonwood stood only a few feet away from her.

Her heart skipped a beat when she saw another movement, but she dismissed it, thinking it must be a deer out on its morning search for food.

Then the movement stopped. If it was a deer, perhaps it had stopped to eat some autumn berries.

She resumed picking flowers, then saw a scattering of small purple asters that grew on into the forest.

She stretched her neck and saw that they went far along the ground beneath the trees. She had always adored asters. They grew along the riverbank behind her cabin in Kentucky.

She turned quickly toward Colonel Downing. "I have collected enough of the larger flowers," she said, carefully placing the last of them in the bag. "I have spied a favorite flower of mine which I would love to use for my hand bouquet at the wedding."

"Asters are your favorite, eh?" Colonel Downing said, a haunted look in his eyes. "They were my wife's favorite as well. She, too, carried a bouquet of asters on our wedding day. She chose white over purple."

For a moment Mary Beth almost saw the human side of this man as he spoke about a time in his life that had been so precious to him. She felt empathy for him, then quickly reminded herself the sort of man he was.

He was an Indian hater. He was planning to kill Brave Wolf.

"I'm sorry I reminded you of your wife and . . . and . . . your wedding day," she murmured. "Would you rather I not gather asters for our nuptials? If not, I will understand."

"No, I would like you to carry them," he said, resting the bag on the ground. "I shall wait here while you pick them. But do not go so far that I cannot see you. I do not have to remind you of the dangers."

"Yes, I understand," she murmured. "I shall be quick about it."

She sighed when she moved among the starry little flowers growing in the forest. They reminded her of her home and David, who always picked a bouquet for her when they were sitting on the riverbank, fishing for an evening meal.

She fell to her knees and carefully picked one after another. Then a movement a few feet away from her made her heart skip a beat. If it was a deer, surely it would have bolted by now.

But instead, whatever it was had moved closer.

Hoping it was not a renegade, Mary Beth started to cry out for the colonel, then stopped and gasped. Relief flooded her senses when she saw who it was.

Brave Wolf!

He was standing in the shadows where only she, not the colonel, could see him.

Excited, yet troubled at the same time as to how she could go to Brave Wolf without alerting the colonel, Mary Beth rose slowly to her feet. Her knees were trembling as she gave Brave Wolf a quivering smile.

Then she thought of a plan. She turned to Colonel Downing, who was still watching her, and who, fortunately, had not seen Brave Wolf yet.

"William, I have a problem," she said, frowning.

"What sort?" he asked, raising an eyebrow.

"I need to answer a call of nature," she said, forcing a grimace on her face to make her suffering look real. "Can you please turn your eyes away while . . . while I . . . well, you know."

She could see how uneasy that made the colonel, and how his face flushed.

He laughed nervously, then nodded. "Do not be long about it," he said. "Remember the dangers."

"I will not feel right doing it . . . here . . . so close to you," Mary Beth said, again forcing a grimace so that he would believe she was desperate for relief. "William, please understand that I will only feel right if I step farther into the trees. Please, oh, please understand that I am a shy woman."

"I have not spied anything suspicious, so I believe it will be safe. Yes, my dear, go as far as you must to feel comfortable with your . . . er . . . chore," he said, his face reddening even more.

"But please turn your back," she said, ducking her head to pretend shyness. "I have never been in such a predicament before. I am . . . oh, so . . . embarrassed."

"Don't be," the colonel said. He quickly turned his back to her. "Hurry on, Mary Beth. Please get it done as quickly as possible. I shall worry about you every moment my eyes are not on you."

"Yes, I understand, and I appreciate your concern," Mary Beth said.

She dropped her handful of flowers and nodded toward Brave Wolf as a way to tell him to meet her halfway.

She ran into the woods then and flung herself into his arms.

"I can't believe you are here," she said, only loud enough for him to hear. "Why did you come? It is like a miracle sent directly from heaven."

"I was concerned," he said thickly. "I had to make sure you were safe."

"Thank God you did."

"What about David? Did the colonel and his soldiers find your son?" he asked.

She hung her head. "No," she said, her voice breaking.

He lifted her chin with a finger. "But you are safe now," he said. "You are here for me to touch, for me to hold."

She framed his face between her hands. "I have something I must tell you," she murmured.

She explained about the colonel's plans, her own scheme to learn the details of the attack, and how the colonel had a wedding planned.

Mary Beth saw the hatred in Brave Wolf's eyes and was not surprised.

"But nothing he has planned for me will happen now," she said, reaching up and hugging Brave Wolf.

"We have to get the colonel to come into the forest," she said. "We must make sure that no one from the fort sees what we are going to do. When he gets here, you can tie him up, and then we can leave! By the time the soldiers find him, we will be safely at your village. You can get your warriors ready for the attack."

Then her smile faded. "As soon as the colonel is found, he will bring his soldiers to your village," she said, her voice drawn.

"No one will find him for a while," Brave Wolf said. "We will have time to prepare ourselves to stop the slaughter that he has planned."

"Call for him," Brave Wolf then said. "Pretend that your skirt is caught on briars. He will come to help you."

While Brave Wolf readied his rifle, she shouted at Colonel Downing.

"William, oh, William, I am afraid that I am in trouble in another way!" she cried. "My skirt is caught on dreadful briars. I . . . I . . . can't get it freed. Can you come and help me?"

She held her breath when he shouted back that he was coming.

Brave Wolf hid behind a tree. A moment later Colonel Downing appeared with a rifle in his left hand, a questioning look on his face when he saw that she was not even near briars, much less caught in them.

"What . . . ?" he said, then gasped and dropped his rifle as Brave Wolf stepped from hiding, his rifle aimed at the colonel's chest.

"What the hell is going on here?" Colonel Downing growled as he raised his hands in submission. He glared from Mary Beth to Brave Wolf. "There is no way in hell you could've planned this. It's just my damn luck that this savage happened along at the right time for him to take advantage of the situation."

"Mary Beth, rip off the hem of that dress you are wearing so that we can use it to tie him," Brave Wolf said, his rifle still poised, his jaw tight, his eyes lit with fire as he glared at the colonel. "And *wash-echu,* white man, while she is doing that, start walking ahead of me."

"You won't get away with this," Colonel Downing growled as he walked onward, stopping for only a moment to give Mary Beth a cold glare. "You are nothing but a whore, an Injun-loving whore."

Mary Beth ignored him as she ripped big lengths of the bottom of the dress away. The colonel gasped and went pale at the way she was treating his late wife's dress.

"Move onward," Brave Wolf growled at the colonel. "We have some distance to cover before I tie you and leave you bound to a tree. I have to make certain that it will be a while before you are found."

Mary Beth came up beside Brave Wolf with several strips of the dress. "Our horses are back there," she said, nodding toward another section of trees, where she and the colonel had left their steeds tethered in the shade.

"We will get him secured, then retrieve both horses," Brave Wolf said, still following the colonel. "We will take the colonel's horse with us to the village."

"No one will know where to look for me," the colonel said, his voice a low whine.

"That's the general idea," Mary Beth said. "And there obviously will be no wedding tomorrow. Even if Brave Wolf hadn't arrived today, I still wouldn't have married you. I had planned to escape from the fort tonight. It sickens me how you are planning to attack Brave Wolf and his people."

"You'd not have gotten far," Colonel Downing said, his voice filled with rage. He looked over his shoulder at Brave Wolf. "You will pay dearly for your mistake today."

Brave Wolf only smiled, for he would be prepared for the soldiers' arrival. Thanks to Mary Beth, he knew there would be a war between them.

The colonel glared at Mary Beth. "Everything you promised, everything you said, was a lie?" he demanded, still stunned at her role in what was happening. "You purposely lied to me so that you could learn my plans? You never meant to marry me?"

"I'm surprised you ever thought I would," Mary Beth said. "How could you not see the loathing in my eyes when I looked at you?"

"You will die alongside the savage heathens," Colonel Downing growled out. "You . . . will . . . regret ever having humiliated me. I will enjoy killing you myself."

"Those are foolish threats for a man who is at the mercy of a savage Crow chief," Brave Wolf said, his voice filled with sarcasm. "I could kill you now and no one would ever find your body. The animals that roam this forest would see to that."

"You wouldn't kill a bound man," Colonel Downing said, his voice breaking.

"You see me as a heathen savage, so why would you not believe me capable of doing that to you?" Brave Wolf said, his voice tight.

Colonel Downing's eyes wavered; then he looked away from them and walked on.

"It is not much farther now," Brave Wolf said, glancing at Mary Beth. "I know a perfect place to leave him."

She sighed heavily, glad that things had worked out for her and Brave Wolf, but worried about the colonel's wrath when he was found and rescued.

She only hoped that Brave Wolf had a lot of allies who would stand beside him, for she thought there were more soldiers stationed at Fort Henry than the Crow in Brave Wolf's village.

Chapter Twenty-five

Every lover is a warrior,
and Cupid has his
camps.
—Ovid

"At this moment I feel so many different things," Mary Beth said as she cuddled against Brave Wolf before the fire in his lodge. "I feel thankful for having met you, relief that I am here again with you, and sadness over my son not being safe with us. And I cannot help being afraid over what is to come . . ."

She couldn't finish what she was going to say. She hated even thinking about what might transpire after the colonel was found. She knew that the anger Colonel Downing felt would motivate an attack even more vicious than he had previously planned against Brave Wolf's people.

"I feel many things myself," Brave Wolf said. He softly stroked her arm as he gazed down at her nakedness. He was always in awe of her beauty, the sweet curves of her body, and the lusciousness of her breasts which would one day nourish their children.

"None of those emotions include fear," he said. "I am confident that when the colonel does manage to get free and come for vengeance, we will be ready."

"There are so many of them," Mary Beth gulped out. "And . . . and . . . there was such hate in their eyes when they saw me dressed in Indian attire. If the colonel would have allowed it, I believe they'd have killed me."

She reached a hand to her throat and softly stroked the spot where the bruise was now yellowing. "I have proof of their hate . . . of their loathing," she said. She had told Brave Wolf of the attack on her. "Had I not thought quickly enough, I would be dead now."

He bent low and brushed kisses across her neck, then rose over her and blanketed her with his body. "My woman, no man will ever touch you wrongly again," he said, his body pressed softly against hers. "I will never allow you to be put in that position again."

"The evil man is . . . is . . . still out there somewhere with the same hate in his heart for me," she murmured, sighing with pleasure when Brave Wolf slowly slid his shaft into her warm wetness, her folds opening to him as though they were the petals of a flower opening to the beckoning of the sun.

"Let me repeat, my sunshine . . . you are safe," Brave Wolf whispered against her lips as he withdrew again. "Close your eyes. Think of only good things. Think of where our bodies take us when they are intertwined. We have time to share these precious moments. Even as I speak I hear more and more friends coming into my village to join with my warriors. Together they will stand up against the Fort Henry soldiers and make certain they never again make the mistake of coming to my village. My warriors are meeting at the council house. I shall join them soon. But for now, you are the center of my attention. I ached for you so while you were gone."

"As I ached for you," Mary Beth said, smiling into his eyes. Then her smile faded. "Brave Wolf, the United States Government might see what you are planning to do as wrong. What if they do? The whole United States cavalry could come down on your people."

He brushed a gentle kiss across her lips, then smiled into her eyes. "I am in the right, and the United States Government will see that I am when a report is sent to them about what has happened," he said. "I know the President well, and he will understand that I have been *pushed* into such an action as this. He knows my love of peace."

He placed a gentle hand on her cheek. "When

the President receives word about how Colonel Downing has broken our treaty, it will be the colonel who will be reprimanded, not me," he said. "He will be stripped of his command."

"But things might have changed since the Battle of the Little Big Horn," Mary Beth said, closing her eyes in ecstasy as he once again thrust into her, then withdrew. "The President might see all Indians as responsible."

"He is a smart, just man and he will only send the cavalry to punish those who killed the whites on the battlefield," Brave Wolf said, wanting to feel the wonders of their bodies locked together, and how it made a sweet peace throughout him. "It was General Custer who went for the fight and caused it. Not the warriors who downed him."

"Let us talk of it no longer, at least not now," Mary Beth whispered. She twined her arms around his neck, bringing his lips to hers, giving him a long, deep kiss as he entered her and their bodies moved rhythmically together.

She drew her lips away for a moment and said, "Do you not know? We are the only two people in the universe." She closed her eyes in total ecstasy as he kissed her again, this time with an almost desperate, hungry need.

She was overwhelmed with the joyous bliss of the moment.

They clung.

They rocked.

They kissed, their mouths urgent and eager as she moved her body sinuously against his.

Brave Wolf felt a rapturous spinning sensation rising up within him, flooding his whole body with the warmth and beauty that making love with her created.

He swept his arms around her and drew her even closer to him. The softness of her folds was warm against him as he thrust more deeply within her.

Unable to hold back any longer, he gave one last thrust, then clung to her as their bodies quivered and their sighs of total pleasure blended against each other's lips.

"I do not want to let you go," he whispered against her cheek as they lay breathless together. "I want to believe that the only thing that is real is what we have together. I do not want to leave this lodge and be reminded of what lies ahead. I pray to the First Maker above that I will have the ability to win my fight for the rights of my people. I wish that I could blink my eyes and the fight would be over and you and I were able to resume a life that is sweet and good and filled with peace."

"That is the way it shall be as soon as that evil man is taken care of," Mary Beth said, stroking his cheek with a gentle hand. "My love, soon it will be over. We will go to bed each night not having to worry about what Colonel Downing might have in mind for us next. He will have no men to command. He will no longer be a colonel."

"He will be found, you know," Brave Wolf said, easing away from her. He sat up, reached a hand to her, and drew her next to him. As they faced the fire, he pulled a soft pelt around both their shoulders, so that they sat, their shoulders touching beneath it. "He might even now be safe at the fort and making plans against us."

"I doubt they shall find him this quickly," Mary Beth said, shuddering at the thought of his fury when he was discovered tied against the tree, his mouth gagged. "But, yes, he will be found. The soldiers will not leave a stone unturned until he is found.

"I am amazed at you," Mary Beth went on, gazing into his midnight-dark eyes. "How can you be so calm when you know that the colonel *will* be found and that he will waste no time coming here to seek vengeance against you and me. He must hate me with a passion."

"The colonel will be too blinded by his anger and humiliation to even think about the time I have had to round up help to fight against him," Brave Wolf said. He smiled slowly. "He will not consider just how many might now be here to make a stand against him."

"I hope your calculation is accurate about how many men you need to make a solid stand against Colonel Downing," Mary Beth said.

"Word has been sent by my scouts about the colonel's plans, and many Crow clans are coming together even as we speak. We will form a united front against the enemy," he said, smiling slowly. "And there are others arriving soon that might surprise you."

"Who?" she asked.

"Do you not recall me making mention of a Colonel Anderson from another fort that I urged you to go to instead of Fort Henry?" Brave Wolf said.

"Yes, I remember. He is in command at Fort Hope," Mary Beth said. Her eyes widened as he told her that Colonel Anderson would also join the fight against Colonel Downing.

"I am not certain whether or not I told you everything, how I knew this colonel from another time, another raid on innocent Indians," Brave Wolf said, his voice tight. "We became fast friends when we met one day to defend a weakened band of Crow, who were in the midst of a massacre from a renegade group of Cheyenne. At that time, we discovered that soldiers from another fort were fighting alongside the renegades. The colonel in command was none other than Colonel William Downing."

"Truly?" Mary Beth gasped.

"Colonel Downing retreated under fire and later paid for his misdeeds by being ordered to the guardhouse for a month," Brave Wolf said, sighing heavily. "But he soon was assigned a new post, Fort Henry, where he seemed to walk a straight line, until now."

"So you sent for Colonel Anderson to help fight the evil colonel," Mary Beth said, nodding.

"Yes, I knew that Colonel Anderson would want to help with this fight," Brave Wolf said, his eyes narrowed. "I anxiously await his arrival. We will embracc once again as friends."

"You do seem to have worked it all out," Mary Beth said, sighing with relief.

"Colonel Anderson and his soldiers have been spotted!" a voice said from outside the tepee. "I have sent a warrior to greet them."

"That is good," Brave Wolf said, suddenly standing. "I shall join you all soon in the council house."

He reached down and grabbed his fringed breeches and stepped quickly into them, then drew a fringed shirt over his head. His fingers went through his long, jet-black hair, straightening it.

He turned to Mary Beth and reached a hand out for her. "Come with me," he said thickly. "Be a part of the council."

"Truly?" she asked, rushing to her feet. "You truly want me to?"

"You are a part of me, so, yes, I wish for you to sit at my side in council, for soon you will also be a part of my people," he said. He bent low and picked up a doeskin dress that she had been given as soon as she arrived at the village; the silk dress had been burned in his lodge fire.

She slid the dress over her head, then stopped and gazed into Brave Wolf's eyes. "What about Night Horse?" she blurted out. "What if he is discovered here by Colonel Anderson?"

Brave Wolf's eyes wavered, for he had temporarily forgotten the dangers of his brother being there and what Colonel Anderson might think about it.

Chapter Twenty-six

He clothes himself in the skin
of animals and decorates himself
with the plumage of birds.
—Anonymous

As the sun was lowering in the sky, casting shades of orange and pink on the tepees in the Crow village, Brave Wolf and Mary Beth stepped from Brave Wolf's lodge just in time to see Colonel James Anderson and his blue-coated soldiers ride up. Mary Beth gazed up at a slender man dressed in full uniform, whose hair was as red as the poppies she grew in her flower garden in Kentucky. His eyes were a shade of golden brown as they smiled down at Brave Wolf, then turned to Mary Beth.

She immediately liked him. She could see the

difference between him and Colonel Downing. There was not even an ounce of prejudice in this man's eyes and behavior.

"*Hohahe,* welcome to my village, *kola,*" Brave Wolf said, stepping up to the colonel's horse and reaching a hand of friendship up to him. "It is always good to see my friend and ally."

He clasped hands with Colonel Anderson for a moment, then dropped his hand as he gazed at the huge contingent of soldiers the colonel had brought with him.

Brave Wolf looked past them and saw how many Crow friends who had arrived to join the fight.

There was no doubt in his mind that he would best Colonel Downing and his soldiers.

"So this is Mary Beth Wilson," Colonel Anderson said, dismounting. He held out a hand to her. "Ma'am, Swift Lightning, one of Chief Brave Wolf's warriors, who brought the message that I was needed here, explained about your presence in his village."

She could tell by his gentle smile and his handshake, which she quickly accepted, that he held no resentment of her, even though she was wearing an Indian dress. She did not look past him to see the other soldiers' reactions. Having this colonel's acceptance was all that was important.

"I've heard much about you, too," Mary Beth said. "It is so good to know that some white soldiers understand the plight of the red man. Thank you for coming."

"I knew of your husband," Colonel Anderson

said, his smile waning as he eased his hand from hers. He clasped his hands together behind him as he stood tall and slim in his immaculate blue uniform. "He had recently been given orders to join my soldiers at Fort Hope. It is a shame that General Custer chose that day to attack, for your husband was to leave for my fort on that very date."

Mary Beth paled. "Lloyd did not confide that in me," she murmured.

"I am sure he thought he would have time to tell you later, after the battle at the Little Big Horn," he said, his voice drawn.

"Yes, I'm sure he thought he would be able to tell me later," she murmured. Then she gazed up at the tall colonel again. "It would have been nice to know he was under your command, not Colonel Downing's. He . . . he . . . is a mean, manipulative, cunning man. He has planned a massacre. He was going to start here, at Brave Wolf's village."

"I am here to see that his plans are foiled before they even begin," Colonel Anderson said, gently patting her on the shoulder. "Ma'am, please accept my condolences about your husband. I'm sure he was a fine man . . . a brave soldier."

"Yes, he was both of those, and . . . and . . . more," Mary Beth said, her voice breaking. "I knew him since we were children."

"Come with me to the council house," Brave Wolf said to the colonel, then looked past him at all the soldiers who remained dutifully on their steeds. "Please bring as many of your soldiers into the council as you please."

Brave Wolf smiled as he looked past the colonel at all the Crow warriors, who were also anxious to join the council. He was glad that when he had ordered a new council house built, he had seen that it was double the size of most normal council houses. This lodge was large enough for eighty men to sit in. It was twenty feet high, with the First Maker painted on one side of the room, the evil spirit on the other.

"I believe we might be more crowded than usual, but comfortable enough," he said, then turned to Mary Beth. "I want you to join us. What we will be discussing has much to do with you. You suffered at the hand of a soldier at Fort Henry."

"Ma'am, what happened to you at Fort Henry?" Colonel Anderson asked as he handed his reins to a small brave.

"She was attacked," Brave Wolf said when he saw that the question made Mary Beth uncomfortable. "If you will look at her neck, you will see signs of that attack. A soldier came into her room in the dark and started choking her. Fortunately, she was able to save herself."

"I am sorry to hear of such atrocious behavior," Colonel Anderson said, frowning. "Was the man reprimanded?"

"Like the coward he was, he fled before anyone could get the chance to reprimand him," Brave Wolf said, nodding toward the entranceway of the council house as he made a turn toward it.

"And so he was never dealt with, eh?" Colonel

Anderson said, going into the council house with Brave Wolf and Mary Beth.

"He is paying for his crime now by having to hide," Brave Wolf said, stunned noting that many of his people were already inside the council house. Brave Wolf nodded and smiled to them as he passed by, stopping with Mary Beth and Colonel Anderson when they came to a thick cushion of pelts that had been spread beside the fire for their chief.

He nodded to the colonel to sit first, and then he and Mary Beth sat down with Brave Wolf beside the colonel.

The evening was cool, the fire in the council house warm and welcome. Everyone became quiet as those outside filed in.

Where there was no room to sit, they stood.

Brave Wolf stood and smiled from person to person, then motioned with a hand for Colonel Anderson to stand beside him.

"Our friend and ally Colonel Anderson has come to join our fight against those who wish to see us dead," Brave Wolf said. "Welcome him, my people. Welcome him."

His people made grunts of welcome.

Then Brave Wolf turned to the chiefs of the other Crow tribes. "Now let us welcome our Crow neighbors who have come to form a united front against the enemy."

There were more grunts, and then Brave Wolf and the colonel sat back down.

A young brave brought a pipe wrapped in a red cloth to Brave Wolf.

He nodded and accepted it, then laid it before him and slowly unwrapped it. The bowl was of red stone, which represented the earth. The stem of the pipe was wood, representing all that grew upon the earth. Twelve feathers hung from the stem, representing all winged things of the air.

An Indian believed that to smoke was to pray. By mingling his breath with sacred tobacco and fire, the smoker was put in tune with the universe.

Another young brave brought a tiny bag of tobacco. Brave Wolf took the bag and sprinkled the tobacco into the pipe, then gave the empty bag back to the child.

Another boy brought a flaming stick to Brave Wolf. He also took this, then held the fire to the tobacco and sucked until the pipe was lit.

Then he shook out the fire at the end of the stick, handed it back to the child, and held the bowl of the long, flat-stemmed pipe in his right hand. He took three puffs from it, then handed it to his left to Colonel Anderson.

Brave Wolf was proud that Colonel Anderson had shared the pipe in council many times and knew the procedure well. Smoking was strictly ritualized. No one was ever to take more than three puffs at a time. Each man always handed the pipe with a ceremonious sweep to his left-hand neighbor, until it made its way around the room.

Tobacco was one of the three holiest objects of worship to the Crow. All children wore a small packet of tobacco as an amulet necklace. The two other holy objects were the sun and the moon. To the sun a man always offered an albino buffalo cow if he had succeeded in killing one. The dead cow was placed on a scaffold set up in the prairie.

Sharing the pipe took quite some time this evening, for there were many more present than usual.

Finally it was done, and the pipe was laid on a stone before Brave Wolf, the smoke still slowly spiraling from the bowl. Brave Wolf sat with his back straight and his legs crossed, his hands on his knees, as he looked slowly around the room.

"We are gathered here today to defend our rights as a people," he said solemnly. "It is known now that there are those who are scheming to take not only our freedom from us, but also our lives. I have sent messengers out far and wide and spread the word to our friends about the planned massacre. It is good to see all of my friends today who have come to help defeat the enemy."

He turned his eyes to Colonel Anderson. "Although Colonel Downing is white, he is your enemy as well, and I am glad you realize that and have come to help fight him," he said. "Thank you, my friend. We are honored today by your presence. It is good to have allies such as you."

He paused, looked away from the colonel, and momentarily smiled at Mary Beth, who was sitting quietly listening and watching. His pride in her made his heart swell; then he gazed into the crowd again.

"The First Maker made the mountains, rivers, and land for all of us to share in a peaceful manner," he said. "In those mountains are plenty of elk and black-tailed deer. White-tailed deer dwell at the foot of the mountains, and the streams are full of beaver. There used to be herds of buffalo, but they are not as plentiful now because of those whites who needlessly kill them. We must protect what buffalo are left."

He stopped, cleared his throat, then again looked slowly around him. "Above all else, it is our lives that we must preserve, and today we are gathered to talk about how that can be done, so that those who wish for our destruction will not be victorious over us," he said forcefully. "When I sent word for our allies' help, I had thought it would be to stand up against those who came to attack. But I have thought better of that. Why should we wait for the fight to come to us? Let us take it to them, so that if there is bloodshed, it will not be on our soil!"

The listeners smiled, nodded, then grunted in approval.

"We shall have a vote," Brave Wolf said, standing. "Those who are in favor of going to Fort Henry, stand. Those who do not approve, remain seated."

Immediately everyone stood, women and children and warriors, as well as those soldiers who had found a place inside.

Feeling pleased that everyone agreed with his

plan, Brave Wolf motioned for everyone to sit again.

"We will leave before dawn tomorrow. Our warriors have scouted the enemy. They see no unusual activity at Fort Henry yet, which means the soldiers are not ready to attack."

He smiled down at Mary Beth, then turned to his people again. "It might also mean that their colonel has not yet rejoined them," he said, his eyes dancing.

"Let us all leave the council house and eat and dance and sing," Brave Wolf said, nodding toward the doorway. "After the women heard I was planning a council, they busied themselves making a variety of food for us to eat afterward. I believe I can smell it over the cookfires even now. There is buffalo tongue, roasted buffalo hump, and much more to share."

The women laughed softly and were the first to leave.

Mary Beth saw Dancing Butterfly looking toward her, and hurried away from Brave Wolf to join her.

"I am so excited about everything," Dancing Butterfly said as she rushed inside her tepee with Mary Beth at her side. "Night Horse has remained hidden, but after the feast he is going to ask Brave Wolf if he can stay with his people. We can finally get married!"

"I don't believe Brave Wolf will ask him to leave, but what of the council?" Mary Beth asked as she helped wrap hot bread in big rolls of buckskin to take out for the feasting. "Will the rest of your people agree to let him stay?"

"Why would they not?" Dancing Butterfly asked, lifting a heavy pot of rabbit stew from her fire. "They have seen how humble he has become since he has returned home. Surely they no longer see him as part of the enemy."

"I hope you are right," Mary Beth said, but she did not believe that many had yet forgiven Night Horse for what he had done. She had heard too many wondering why he was still in the village now that he was well enough to leave.

"I know I am right," Dancing Butterfly said, beaming. "Perhaps when you say your vows with Brave Wolf, Night Horse and I can say ours at the same time."

Mary Beth gave Dancing Butterfly a quick look, then glanced away when Dancing Butterfly questioned her with her eyes.

"Let us go and join the others," Mary Beth murmured. "I am so happy that Brave Wolf has decided to take the battle away from the village."

"It is good to know that we will not have to fear being killed as we sleep in our lodges," Dancing Butterfly said, shivering. "No one knew when the soldiers were planning to come. Now the warring is going to them. That is a much better plan."

"I plan to go with them," Mary Beth blurted out. "I want to be a part of what happens at Fort Henry."

"You cannot do that," Dancing Butterfly gasped out. "Fighting is for men only."

"I do not believe there will be an actual fight," Mary Beth said, walking from the tepee with an armful of wrapped bread while Dancing Butterfly walked beside her carrying the heavy pot of stew. "When the soldiers at Fort Henry see how many are approaching them, and especially see that among them are white soldiers with Colonel Anderson at their head, they will not even attempt to fight. They will surrender immediately."

"You do not know that for certain," Dancing Butterfly said, giving Mary Beth a worried frown.

Mary Beth swallowed hard, for it was true that she was not certain of anything, except that she would not stay behind. After all, she was part of the reason behind this fight.

Only tomorrow would tell whether or not she had made the right decision.

Chapter Twenty-seven

Love knows nothing of order.
—Saint Jerome

The morning air was filled with a hazy fog, making it almost impossible to see a foot ahead of them as the soldiers and Crow warriors rode toward Fort Henry.

Mary Beth felt proud to be a part of the group. She had feared that when it came down to the final decision, Brave Wolf would not allow it.

But he had seen the pleading in her eyes and had heard the longing in her voice when she explained how she wanted a role in the demise of Colonel Downing.

It was not because of anything he had done to her personally, because he had actually wanted what was best for her. But it was the venom she had heard in his voice when he was plotting against Brave Wolf. The colonel wanted to kill as many Indians as he could with the manpower of his soldiers.

At heart, he was a vicious, prejudiced man.

She still could not understand how he had been given back his command after being arrested for attacking an innocent Crow village.

Only last night she had learned from Colonel Anderson that Colonel Downing had been reinstated because he had relatives in Washington who had spoken up for him.

As the morning sun broke through the fog, Mary Beth jumped with alarm when far to her left a large herd of elk were startled, their sharp hooves stirring a swirling cloud of dust, their white rumps looking like war bonnets.

Then Mary Beth looked behind her and saw the many soldiers who rode side by side with the warriors. She felt goosebumps rising on her arms to see their camaraderie . . . to see the soldiers and the warriors together in such force . . . as allies. She could not help wondering why it couldn't be that way with all whites and Indians. Then there would be no more bloodshed between them.

She gazed ahead again, and sighed when she saw what seemed to be a dreamland. The sun slanted through the trees at her left side, where the meadow reached into a forest of mixed aspens and cottonwoods. Growing there were the same wildflowers that she had been plucking when Brave Wolf rescued her from Colonel Downing.

She glanced over at Brave Wolf, who was just now telling Colonel Anderson about where he had left Colonel Downing.

She drew a tight rein when Brave Wolf and Colonel Anderson stopped, a command being sent behind them which stopped all the warriors and soldiers.

"We shall go and see if he is still there. If so, our chore will be much easier," Brave Wolf said, dismounting. He gazed at Colonel Anderson as he swung himself out of his saddle, then looked over at Mary Beth. "Come. I know you also want to see what Colonel Downing's fate is."

"Thank you," Mary Beth said, sliding into his hands as he reached up to help her from the saddle. She glanced nervously into the thickness of the forest, then into Brave Wolf's eyes. "Do you think he is still there, or do you think he's been rescued and is even now at Fort Henry plotting against you?"

Brave Wolf dropped to his haunches and studied the ground around him, then looked ahead at the grass that grew up to the lovely meadow of flowers.

He ran a hand over the grass and ground, then glanced up at Mary Beth, and then at Colonel Anderson. "I see no sign of many horses coming through here, which there would be if a search party had come this way," he said. "It is my guess that he is still there."

"What a surprise he will get when he sees us returning, and not alone, but with Colonel Anderson," Mary Beth said, smiling. She turned to Colonel Anderson. "I'm so glad that you realize the depth of this man's prejudices and are ready to see that he is relieved of his duties forever, not only for a short while."

"Yes, it will delight me to do this," Colonel Anderson said, his jaw tight. His eyes narrowed angrily. "Just let this sonofabitch's relatives in Washington try and save him this time. I shall go to Washington myself if need be, to speak against him *and* his relatives."

"Come. Let us go now and get the man," Brave Wolf said, standing and resting his hand on his sheathed knife. "I am the one who tied him. I shall be the one to set him free."

"But not to true freedom," Mary Beth said, wading through the tall grass and knee-high ferns. "He deserves what he will get, and perhaps even worse."

They walked silently onward, and when they came to a break in the trees, where they could see the tree to which they had tied the colonel, Mary Beth gasped and went pale.

"He is gone," she said, her voice breaking. "Someone *did* come and find him. Oh, Lord, how long has he been gone? Is it enough time that he has gotten his soldiers ready to attack?"

She turned to Brave Wolf and grabbed him by the arm. "Could he have gone a different route and already arrived at your village, Brave Wolf?" she gasped out.

Brave Wolf saw the fear in her eyes.

He placed a gentle hand on her cheek. "Do not

let fear of the unknown do this to you," he said quietly. "Let us go and see if we can discover how he escaped. Then we can decide our next step."

Mary Beth nodded.

She gazed over at the colonel, whose eyes were filled with the same fire she saw in Brave Wolf's, then walked on between them until they reached the tree where they had last seen Colonel Downing.

All that was left of his captivity were the pieces of his wife's dress that had been used to tie him to the tree.

Brave Wolf bent to his haunches and picked up one of the strips. He studied it, then handed it up to Colonel Anderson. "No knife was used to cut these. It is not a clean cut," he said, reaching for a sharp rock that lay close to the trunk of the tree. "No. He did not use a knife, nor did anyone else use one to release him. He somehow managed to get this sharp rock close enough to cut the cloth in two."

"I wonder when," Mary Beth said, looking guardedly from side to side. "He might still be near, watching us."

Brave Wolf studied the ground. "Blood," he said. "There is blood here."

"What could it mean?" Mary Beth gasped, paling at the sight of the blood.

Brave Wolf gave her a quiet look, then studied everything around him again. He noticed crushed leaves and bent grass which had not been damaged by him, Mary Beth, or Colonel Anderson. He could tell that whoever had stepped there was going away from the tree, not toward it.

He stood and looked at the trail the colonel had left. He began stealthily following it and saw more drops of blood.

Mary Beth hurried up next to him, with Colonel Anderson soon at her other side. "What do you see?" she asked, trying to see what Brave Wolf was following. She shivered at the sight of more blood.

"I have always been skilled at tracking," he said, glancing up at Mary Beth for a moment, then studying the path again. "Colonel Downing walked where we are now walking. But do you see? He did not walk in a straight line. He seemed to be staggering."

"From weakness? Or from having been harmed by an animal?" Mary Beth asked, shivering.

"From weakness would be my guess," Brave Wolf said, then walked to the edge of the forest, where the trail of blood led out into the beautiful wildflowers. There he lost it because the flowers were too thick to see through to the ground. But he did see in which direction some were bent. That was where the colonel had surely walked.

"We shall make better time on horses," Brave Wolf said, turning to hurry to his steed.

Mary Beth ran to keep up with him and was soon on her horse, riding between Brave Wolf and Colonel Anderson, with the contingent of soldiers and warriors following close at hand.

"There he is!" Mary Beth cried, catching sight of someone just pushing himself up from the covering of flowers. "He surely fell there and was resting before moving onward. He had to have heard the approaching horses. See how he teeters even now as he tries to stumble back away from us? He is trying to run. Now he is falling again!"

They hurried onward and when they reached the colonel, found a pitiful sight. He lay where he'd fallen, his clothes in shreds, his eyes swollen and red. He cowered as Brave Wolf and Colonel Anderson dismounted and went to stand over him.

"Don't hurt me," Colonel Downing cried. "Just help me. Please . . . help . . . me."

Mary Beth dismounted and went to stand beside Colonel Anderson as Brave Wolf knelt down beside Colonel Downing. She gasped and covered her mouth with a hand when she saw his bloody leg, where it was obvious that he'd been bitten.

"Coyotes came," Colonel Downing sobbed as he gazed down at his swollen leg. "They surrounded me. They attacked. But thank God, only one actually bit me. Then they left."

Colonel Anderson went and knelt down beside the ailing colonel. Together, he and Brave Wolf got Colonel Downing to his feet, then helped him to Mary Beth's horse and into the saddle.

After he was there, he leaned low and clung to the pommel. "Thank you," he breathed out. "Thank you, thank you . . ."

Brave Wolf handed the man the reins, then went back to Mary Beth. "You can ride with me," he said. "I could not make him walk to the fort. Not in his condition."

"I understand," Mary Beth said, already knowing the depth of his goodness, even toward an avowed enemy.

She went with him. He lifted her onto his horse, then positioned himself behind her as Colonel Anderson mounted and edged his horse closer to Brave Wolf's. "Now what should the plan be?" he asked. "Finding him like this changes things somewhat."

"You have trusted soldiers who work as scouts, do you not?" Brave Wolf asked, looking over his shoulder at the soldiers.

"Yes. What are you suggesting?" Colonel Anderson asked.

"As I see it, Colonel Downing is the only one who is at fault here," Brave Wolf said tightly. "The soldiers under his command only did as he told them. If they plotted to attack us Crow, it was under his orders."

"Yes, Brave Wolf, from what I heard, Colonel Downing was the main one who wanted to attack you and your people," Mary Beth said solemnly. "The others joined, but none sounded as eager as the colonel. They were being egged on. What else could they do but agree?"

"Knowing that, Colonel Anderson, I would suggest you send two of your most trusted soldiers on to Fort Henry and tell them what has transpired. Let us alert them that we are coming with their colonel, and that he is wounded," Brave Wolf said.

Colonel Anderson nodded. "That is a very good plan and I will do as you suggest," he said. He wheeled his horse around and moved among his soldiers, as Brave Wolf moved among his warriors, each telling his men of the new plan.

Mary Beth stared at Colonel Downing, who still sat slumped over in the saddle, sliding an occasional downcast look her way. She didn't trust him at all.

Brave Wolf came back to Mary Beth. He watched the two soldier scouts ride off at a hard gallop toward the fort, then reached over and took Mary Beth's hands. "We will wait for the soldiers' return," he said. "Then it will be safe to go on. We will stay at the fort for only as long as it takes to see that Washington is informed of the colonel's plans to attack Indians, contrary to his orders. Then we will return home and begin another search for your son, for it would make everything perfect if he could be there to join us for the wedding celebration."

"It would be wonderful," Mary Beth said, trying to make out the fort in the distance. She wondered if the sentries had noticed the large contingent of soldiers and warriors so close at hand.

Her heart pounded as she sat there, her eyes watching for the return of the two soldiers. When she finally saw them riding back, her eyes grew wide when she saw how many soldiers from the fort were accompanying the two scouts. For a moment fear squeezed her heart, but it left again when the soldier scouts under Colonel Anderson's command arrived with the good news that everyone was welcome at the fort, and that Colonel

Downing would be detained in the infirmary until orders came from Washington.

Colonel Anderson complimented the soldiers, then rode on ahead to meet those others who were still coming toward them.

Mary Beth watched, wide-eyed, when he reached the soldiers. He was warmly greeted by each soldier.

"He must know them," Mary Beth said, giving Brave Wolf a questioning look.

"Many of them were at one time or another under Colonel Anderson's command," Brave Wolf said, smiling. "The colonel only confided that to me this morning. That was one reason I allowed you to come with us. I knew that once the soldiers at Fort Henry discovered Colonel Anderson was playing such a big role in today's activities, all would go well."

Colonel Anderson came back and stopped beside Brave Wolf. "Neither you nor your warriors need go any farther," he said, reaching a hand over and placing it on Brave Wolf's shoulder. "I have everything under control." He smiled at Mary Beth, then grinned at Brave Wolf again. "Go and have a lovely wedding, you two. My only regret is that I shall not be there to celebrate with you. I am going to make it my duty to see that orders come through to deliver Colonel Downing to my fort, where I will put him behind bars."

"Thank you for everything," Mary Beth said. "And . . . sir . . . if ever you run across a five-year-old white child among any Indians you meet, ask him his name. Perhaps you will be the one to find my little David."

"I shall spread word among all I know to keep a watch out for him," Colonel Anderson said, removing his hand from Brave Wolf's shoulder. He saluted them both, then rode off, his soldiers all riding with him.

Brave Wolf turned to Mary Beth. "It is done," he said, smiling broadly. "Now we can put our minds on more important things. Today I will send those warriors who are riding with us in different directions. They will once again search for your son. I shall tell them to return home tomorrow at dawn, though, for I want them to join our celebration of marriage."

"Tomorrow," Mary Beth said, blushing. "Actually? Tomorrow? We will become man and wife?"

"*Hecitu-yelo*, yes, tomorrow," he replied, smiling.

Mary Beth gazed down at the wildflowers. This time she really did want some for her wedding.

"May I take the time to pick some flowers?" she asked softly.

"You do not have to ask permission of me to do anything," Brave Wolf said, dismounting.

He held her horse's reins as she began picking these flowers she loved the most. While she was gathering blossoms, he directed his warriors about the search.

When she heard a thundering of hoofbeats, Mary Beth stopped and stared at the warriors as they rode in every direction.

She gazed heavenward and prayed a soft prayer that this time the search would be a successful one.

Chapter Twenty-eight

Here are fruits, flowers, leaves and branches.
And here is my heart which beats only for you.
—Paul Verlaine

Mary Beth lay snuggled in Brave Wolf's arms. She smiled when she thought of what this special day was—her wedding day; then she frowned sadly when she remembered what else the day might mean to her. She might again receive word that her son was nowhere to be found.

If only the warriors brought him back safe, this day would be doubly blessed.

But if they didn't, she would count her blessings for having found Brave Wolf, and let that happiness wipe away as much sorrow as possible.

She ran a slow hand over Brave Wolf's soft, copper skin; his back was so smooth and hairless, so beautiful. She was naked as well and scooted even closer to him so that she could feel the heat of his skin against hers. The lodge fire had burned down to low, glowing embers.

Each day brought cooler temperatures. Soon snow would fall, blanketing everything with its wondrous white. It seemed impossible that when that snow fell she would be wife to a powerful Crow chief, preparing his meals, sewing his moccasins, and being everything to him that he wished her to be.

She would show *him* how to make angels in the snow, lying full length in it and moving her arms so they left the impression of wings.

She would encourage snowball fights like the ones she'd shared with her son when he was old enough to walk out into the snow and make snowmen and snowballs alongside her.

"What are you thinking so hard about?" Brave Wolf asked as he turned to gaze into her eyes.

"How did you know I was thinking about anything?" she asked, always marveling at his astuteness. "I thought you were asleep."

"I was until only moments ago," he said, brushing fallen locks of hair back from her eyes. "When I awakened and felt your body against mine, I became aware that your breathing had slowed. I knew that was because you were in deep thought about something."

"Snow," Mary Beth said, running a hand over his muscled, hairless chest. "I was recalling times with my son in the snow. He loved snow. He loved helping me make snowmen."

"Snowmen?" Brave Wolf said, cocking an eyebrow. "How can men be made of snow? How would you make one?"

Mary Beth laughed softly. "Haven't your Crow children learned how to make snowmen?" she asked. "Have they not made and thrown snowballs?"

"They know very well the art of making and throwing snowballs at one another, but no, not snowmen," he said, then looked quickly toward the closed entrance flap, where Dancing Butterfly was speaking softly.

"What does she want this early in the morning?" Mary Beth asked, glancing up through the smoke hole at the top of the tepee. "Why, the sky is only now turning to morning."

"I did not tell you what is required of you today before our wedding ceremony," Brave Wolf said, moving to his feet. He hurried into fringed breeches and shirt, then stepped into moccasins.

"What *is* required of me?" Mary Beth said, quickly dressing herself.

"You must go for a while to a willow shelter that has only this morning been made for you," Brave Wolf said, waiting for her to be fully clothed before sweeping aside the entrance flap so that Dancing Butterfly could enter.

"Why would I go there?" Mary Beth asked, fully dressed and now stepping into her moccasins. She smiled at Dancing Butterfly as she came in.

"Are you telling her about the willow shelter?" Dancing Butterfly asked Brave Wolf, a buckskin parfleche bag hanging from her shoulder. "Have you instructed her as to what will be done there to prepare her for your wedding?"

"*Ka*, no, I have not told her anything except that she is to go to the willow shelter," Brave Wolf said, giving Mary Beth a soft smile. "It is time to go there now, my sunshine. When you emerge from the shelter, you will be ready for the ceremony that will make us man and wife."

Somewhat apprehensive, Mary Beth gave him a nervous smile, then left the lodge with Dancing Butterfly. She noticed that hardly anyone was up yet. Everything in the village was quiet, except for an occasional whinny from a horse in the corral, or the distant bark of a coyote.

The sound of the coyote brought back the moment when she had seen Colonel Downing and learned that a coyote had attacked him while he had been tied to a tree. She now knew to fear them and keep her distance.

Then she noticed another sound, which made her stop abruptly. "Did you hear it, Dancing Butterfly?" she asked, looking slowly around her.

"Hear what?" Dancing Butterfly asked, stopping beside her.

"A cat," Mary Beth said, still looking, and now listening again. "I heard a cat's meow."

"A cat?" Dancing Butterfly said, visibly stiffening. "Do you mean . . . you . . . heard a panther's cry or a bobcat's?" She looked guardedly all around her. "Do you think one is near?"

"No, not them," Mary Beth said, her eyes widening and brightening when she saw a cat running toward her, a cat she had seen before. It was Colonel Downing's calico cat! She had seen it at Fort Henry. It had rubbed against her legs, purring. She had even lifted it into her arms and stroked it.

The last time she had seen it was when it had run past her into his cabin.

"Poor kitty," Mary Beth murmured as she bent to her knees and gathered it in her arms. It gazed up at her. "Look at your fur. It's all matted and sticking together. Where have you been? What trouble have you been in? And why aren't you at the fort?"

Of course she knew she would never have any answers to those questions. All she knew was that she was going to keep the cat if it wanted to stay with her. She adored cats.

She had been lonely without the one she had left behind in Kentucky.

It truly saddened her that she would never see it again.

"Do you want to be mine?" Mary Beth asked, hugging the cat to her chest as she continued stroking it. She was glad when it began purring, which proved that it was content to be with her.

"Where did that cat come from?" Dancing Butterfly asked as she knelt down beside Mary Beth. "Why is it so small? Is it a baby bobcat?"

"All cats like this are small," Mary Beth murmured. "They are raised to live in houses, not out in the wild. As you can see, this cat has had some hard times since it left the fort."

"You have seen this cat before?" Dancing Butterfly asked, still gazing at the creature. "What is that noise it is making?"

"Yes, I have seen it before, and the noise is called purring," Mary Beth said, now standing and walking with Dancing Flower toward a small curved dwelling made of willow limbs. "The purring means that for the moment, while I am holding it, it is contented."

She gave Dancing Butterfly a soft smile. "I want to keep her," she said. "I hope Brave Wolf won't mind."

"He is a lover of all animals, so, yes, he will allow you to keep it," Dancing Butterfly said, stopping just outside the small hut. She gazed at the doorway, then looked at the cat. "I think it is alright that the cat accompanies you during your purification."

"Purification?" Mary Beth asked, taken aback. "What . . . sort . . . ?"

Dancing Butterfly giggled. "Do not be afraid," she murmured. "The ceremony is quick and harmless."

"Do all Crow women have such purification ceremonies before they become married?" Mary Beth asked.

"They usually go through much more than purification," Dancing Butterfly said, ducking down and entering the small structure.

"What else?" Mary Beth asked, leaning low and following her.

She sat down as Dancing Butterfly sank gracefully to the floor. The cat now rested on Mary Beth's lap, curled up and asleep, though it still purred.

It was as though the cat had sought her out just from their one meeting. She knew that cats were smart. They were known to travel for miles and miles to get back home if somehow lost. Was it possible this cat had traveled many miles to find her?

"You ask what else the Crow women do before their wedding day?" Dancing Butterfly said, holding the bag on her lap, but not yet opening it. "They stay in a special hut such as this. They abstain from meat for four days, their sustenance only being wild roots during that time. On the fourth day, they bathe, get new clothes, which they smoke over a fire of evergreen leaves, then return to their loved one for the marriage ceremony."

"Why wasn't all that required of me?" Mary Beth asked, still stroking the cat.

"Because you are not full-blood Crow, and because too many things got in the way of such preparations," Dancing Butterfly said, removing two tiny vials from her bag. "Your ritual this morning will be simple enough. Not much is required of you before you become my chief's wife."

"What is in those vials?" Mary Beth asked, eyeing them speculatively.

"Incense," Dancing Butterfly murmured. "You will be purified with incense before returning to Brave Wolf."

A familiar voice now spoke from outside the small hut. It was Brave Wolf's mother.

Mary Beth glanced toward the entranceway just as the elderly woman bent down and gazed inside. She saw that Pure Heart was holding a ceramic platter, on which were small twigs that were aflame.

"I have brought fire," Pure Heart said. "I shall leave it and go awaken Night Horse. Now that the soldiers are gone, it will be safe for him to attend the wedding."

"I wish there were to be two weddings today," Dancing Butterfly said, her voice proving her disappointment that she had not been asked by Night Horse to marry him.

"My child, when Night Horse gets over his guilt about all that has happened, and when he sees that his people have forgiven him, then he can make a true life among us again, with a wife and children he can call his own," Pure Heart said solemnly. "But this transition has begun. He has accepted a lodge that a friend of his youth built for him. He sleeps there now. Perhaps one day you will sleep beside him as his wife."

"He seemed so withdrawn last night after all the soldiers were gone," Dancing Butterfly said, nodding a thank you when she took the small platter of fire from Pure Heart. "I worry about his frame of mind. I know that when I hid away with him during the time the soldiers were here, there was much shame in his eyes. I am not sure he can ever forget that shame and start a new, good life that might include me."

"In time, my child, in time," Pure Heart said. She groaned as she stood up again. "Do not take long. I am anxious for my firstborn son to finally have a wife who will then bear me grandchildren." With that, she left the hut.

Mary Beth felt a blush rush to her cheeks at the mention of grandchildren. Then she concentrated on the matter at hand as she watched the procedure that would purify her.

Dancing Butterfly sprinkled incense from one of the vials into the flames, and then incense from the other. When smoke came up from both vials, intermingling, Dancing Butterfly held the container closer to Mary Beth, and with a hand waved the smoke so that it fully enveloped her.

Understanding that this was a serious ritual, Mary Beth tried not to sneeze when the smoke curled up into her nose. She lifted her chin, closed her eyes, then opened them again when she realized the smoke was no longer there.

She gazed questioningly at Dancing Butterfly.

"It is done," Dancing Butterfly said, smiling broadly at Mary Beth. "You have been smudged."

Mary Beth did not question the word "smudged," just accepted that it meant something special to the Crow. In time she would know everything about all of their rituals and customs.

But today?

She would just accept each as it was introduced to her, for each would surely take her closer to the moment when she would be the wife of a wonderful Crow chief!

A sudden mournful cry split the air, ending the moment of wonder.

"Pure Heart," Dancing Butterfly gasped. She hurried out of the small dwelling.

With the exhausted cat still asleep in her arms, Mary Beth left the hut and gazed ahead where she could see Dancing Butterfly running toward the tepee that had been erected only last night as Night Horse's private lodge.

Mary Beth saw Pure Heart standing outside the tepee, her eyes filled with tears, her arms stretched heavenward, wailing "Why, why?"

"Lord, no," Mary Beth murmured, paling. "Something has happened to Night Horse. He . . . is . . . surely dead."

She hurried onward along with other members of the village, toward the tepee. Just as she arrived, she saw Brave Wolf take his mother into his arms to console her.

"He is gone!" Pure Heart cried. "His bedding is not warm, which means he did not sleep there. He must have left in the middle of the night!"

Mary Beth was relieved to hear that Night Horse wasn't dead, for although she knew the worst about him, she had grown to like him the few times she'd been with him. He was a man who had surely been fun to be with as a youth, so long ago. His eyes had seemed to dance with mischief as he actually joked with Brave Wolf a time or two.

And now? She wondered why he had left?

Had his affection for his family and people all been pretense?

And what about Dancing Butterfly? This was the second time Night Horse had left her.

Soft sobs drew Mary Beth's eyes quickly to Dancing Butterfly. She was standing with slumped shoulders and crying into her hands.

Mary Beth wasn't sure what to do. Should she go and help her in her time of sorrow? Or should she stay out of it and let the woman grieve in her own way, alone?

Her heart did go out to the beautiful maiden, though. Dancing Butterfly loved Night Horse with a passion. She had truly wanted to marry him and had hoped now that he was home again, they would eventually become man and wife.

Now it seemed he had turned his back on everyone again, even the woman he loved.

"Why, Brave Wolf?" Pure Heart sobbed. "Why would your brother leave like that? It is so cruel to a mother who loves him so much. And have I not shown him in enough ways how much I care? Did I not show him that I even forgave him? I was so attentive to him, how could he not know that I love him even as much as the day when he was born into this world all tiny and defenseless?"

She looked desperately up at Brave Wolf. "Son,

Night Horse is almost as defenseless now as the day he was born," she said, her voice breaking. "Out there alone, with so many wanting him dead."

"Night Horse took a horse and a gun," a young brave said as he stepped up to be heard. "I saw him leave. He asked me not to alert anyone to his leaving. I was afraid not to do as he asked. The gun. He could have shot me as he killed so many of our kind on the battlefield."

"He is gone . . . he is gone . . ." Pure Heart said, slowly shaking her head back and forth. "I shall never see my second-born again. He is gone because he wants to be gone."

"That is not necessarily so," Brave Wolf said. He placed his hands on his mother's shoulders. "Mother, do you not see the true reason he left?"

"What true reason?" Pure Heart asked, searching his eyes.

"It is because of the cavalry being here," Brave Wolf explained. "*Ina,* I am sure the soldiers' presence made Night Horse feel vulnerable and threatened. He knows that if the cavalry ever learned he was alive, they would want him. They would want to make him pay for what they think was his role in their defeat."

"But why? He fought on *their* side," Pure Heart sobbed out.

"Because they might believe Night Horse purposely spoiled Custer's plans. He might even now be afraid that I, and our people as a whole, would be seen as enemies because we hid him from those whites who might want him. He might have left, Mother, to keep us free of such suspicion in the future. So I do not think badly of him for having left. I see him as giving and . . . courageous."

"It is good that you can see him in that respect," Dancing Butterfly said bitterly as she stepped up beside Brave Wolf. She angrily wiped tears from her eyes with the backs of her hands. "I see him as . . ."

She stopped before saying anything else. She just sighed and tried hard not to make things worse today for Pure Heart and Brave Wolf.

Mary Beth gave Dancing Butterfly a look of understanding, then gazed at Brave Wolf, whose life had also been touched today by Night Horse's sudden departure. She gently placed a hand on his arm. "I'm sorry," she murmured. "I know that you are torn in many directions. I am so sorry."

She went to Pure Heart and touched her on the cheek. "Whenever you need me, to talk, or anything, I am here for you," she murmured.

Mary Beth noticed that the sight of the cat in her arms distracted Pure Heart so much, she even stopped crying. Mary Beth saw it as a good distraction and smiled, for when Pure Heart reached over and ran her hand over the cat's soft fur, she saw a softness enter the old woman's eyes, and knew that this cat had come today for more than one reason.

It had came to help an elderly women cope with a loss that was breaking her heart.

"Where did this animal come from?" Pure Heart

asked, still stroking, sighing when the cat awakened and began softly purring. "And listen to it. It is making such a contented noise."

"The cat is purring because it *is* contented," Mary Beth said, then handed the cat to Pure Heart. "Here. Hold her. Feel her sweetness. I had a cat of my own that . . . that . . . I left in Kentucky."

Pure Heart took the cat, then cuddled it in her thin arms. "Cat . . . this is a cat," she murmured. She gazed curiously up at Mary Beth. "The only cats I know about are black and large and dangerous, and also bobcats. Is this cat related to either of them?"

"Well, I guess, in a way, but it is nothing like them," Mary Beth said, reaching over to stroke the cat. "This cat is tame. It hasn't a wicked bone in its body."

Mary Beth loved the way the cat leaned its face into her hand, as though it knew it had found a loving home.

"I would like to have a cat for myself," Pure Heart said. "It would fill my empty heart and my empty home with such love. The noise it makes, which you call purring, fills my heart with a bliss I cannot even explain."

"That's what cats are good for," Mary Beth said, then forced herself to ask. "Do you want to keep the cat for yourself?"

She badly wanted the cat, but knew that Brave Wolf's mother needed something to take away the pain of losing her second-born son all over again.

"Is it mine to keep?" Pure Heart asked, questioning Mary Beth with her eyes. "Where did it come from? How do you know it so well?"

"It belonged to . . ." Mary Beth stopped before saying the colonel's name, for she was afraid that if she told Pure Heart whom the cat had belonged to, she might not want anything to do with it. She would not want to know that evil man's hands had stroked its fur.

"I'm not certain who its owner was," Mary Beth said, hating to lie even for a good cause. "The cat just happened to find me one day . . . when . . . I was at Fort Henry. But she got frightened away by the soldiers. I hadn't seen her again until now."

"Her?" Pure Heart said, gazing at the cat again. "Is this cat a she cat? She will have babies some day?"

Mary Beth only then realized that there was something different about the cat that she had not noticed before. With its fur so matted, its shape was better revealed. There was a puffiness about its tummy. Mary Beth's cat had given birth to kittens many times. This was exactly how her cat had looked when it was pregnant.

"This cat is heavy with kittens as we speak," Mary Beth said, beaming at the thought of the cat having kittens so that she might have one for herself, perhaps even two.

"Kittens?" Pure Heart asked.

"Babies," Mary Beth said, reaching over to stroke the cat again. "She is going to have babies. Mine had eight at a time. Who is to say how many this one will have?"

"Eight babies, I mean kittens," Pure Heart said, her old eyes beaming.

Suddenly the morning that had been so filled with sorrow was now filled with hope and love.

"I shall care for her with all the love of a mother," Pure Heart said, turning to go to her own lodge with the cat.

Mary Beth turned to Dancing Butterfly. "I'm sorry for your loss," she murmured, then drew Dancing Butterfly into her embrace. "Please don't be too sad. There will come a time when you will meet someone else. You are so beautiful, there will be many who will want to court you."

"I have never wanted anyone but Night Horse, nor shall I ever," Dancing Butterfly said, a sob catching in her throat. She eased from Mary Beth's arms. "But I have done enough crying this morning. I am sorry. I shall not do anything else to ruin your special day. I shall do everything to make it a happy one."

"You have already done a lot for me," Mary Beth said. She smiled radiantly up at Brave Wolf. "I have been smudged. I am ready to become your bride."

He went to her and drew her into his embrace. "Can you be happy even though we have no good news about your son?" he asked thickly.

"How can I not be happy on my wedding day when I am marrying the most wonderful man in the world?" she murmured, clinging to him.

She closed her eyes when David came into her mind's eye.

Just as Dancing Butterfly had to move on with

her life without someone she loved, so must Mary Beth. In time the hurt would surely lessen.

But today?

Ah, yes.

She had her wedding and all the wonderful memories that would come with it to sustain her on those days when her loss weighed heavily in her heart.

And she had not given up on seeing her sweet son again. She . . . would . . . never give up!

"It is time for you to dress in your special attire, while I dress in mine," Brave Wolf said, leaning Mary Beth away from him so they could look into one another's eyes. "You will go with Dancing Butterfly to her lodge. There she has laid out the most beautiful doeskin dress for you to wear. I shall go to my . . . no, *our* lodge and prepare myself for you."

Mary Beth's heart was singing. She giggled with happiness, then looked up at Pure Heart, who was just now entering her lodge carrying the cat. She felt good about having found a way to help the elderly mother of her beloved Brave Wolf cope with the loss of a son she more than likely would never see again.

"Come now," Dancing Butterfly said, taking Mary Beth by the hand. "It is time!"

Mary Beth's heart raced with excitement. She had never thought she could love a man so much.

But she did, and he loved her in return. And they were going to become man and wife only a short while from now.

"Is this really real?" she said, drawing Dancing Butterfly's eyes to her. "Is this truly happening? I am soon to be married to Brave Wolf?"

"It is all very real," Dancing Butterfly said, her eyes no longer filled with tears, but instead, laughter. "Ah, what a wonderful man you are getting, and what a wonderful woman he is getting in you."

Mary Beth blushed. "Thank you," she murmured, then followed Dancing Butterfly into her tepee. She stopped and stared disbelievingly at the dress that was spread out for her.

She had never seen anything so beautiful!

Chapter Twenty-nine

Lo, this is she that was the
world's delight.
—Swinburne

There was still a steady throb of rawhide drums outside the lodge where the newlyweds lay on a bed of thick pelts. Delicate asters lay close by, the flowers chosen by Mary Beth to hold during the wedding ceremony.

The air was sweet with incense that Brave Wolf had tossed into their lodge fire. That fire lapped slowly now around the logs, like fingers caressing them, giving off a soft light and creating dancing shadows along the inside walls of the tepee.

"I shall never forget this day," Mary Beth said as she lay beside Brave Wolf. "It was as though I was walking on clouds as I stood beside you during the ceremony. And the dress. Ah, the dress. It was almost as white as linen and so beautifully trimmed with ermine and ornamented with porcupine quills and beads. I especially loved the necklace of rock swallow feathers that your mother gave me to wear. I felt like a princess."

She snuggled closer and giggled. "I still do," she murmured. "I am dizzy with happiness."

Mary Beth ran her fingers through Brave Wolf's loose and flowing raven-black hair. "And you," she murmured. "You were so handsome in your fringed doeskin attire, with your hair in braids bound in otter fur. I loved your hair that way, but I must confess, I like it much . . . much better loose and flowing."

She leaned her face into his hair. "I love its smell," she murmured. "I love its thickness."

He took her hand and kissed its palm, then held it over his heart. "Dancing Butterfly was making that dress for our ceremony before she knew you, and before Night Horse left to join the whites as a scout," Brave Wolf said. He released her hand and leaned on an elbow so that he could get a full look at his new bride.

She was so beautiful, the very sight and nearness of her spread fire throughout him.

"Even when Night Horse disappeared from Dancing Butterfly's life, she continued making the dress," he went on.

"Then why did she give it to me to wear?" Mary Beth asked, gazing into her husband's eyes. "Does she not have hope of one day marrying, herself?"

"She gave up that hope when Night Horse walked out of her life," Brave Wolf said, reaching a hand out to gently cup one of her breasts.

"Do you mean the first or the second time he left?" Mary Beth asked softly.

"When he left the first time, she finished the dress and stored it away, but vowed even then she would not wear it on her wedding day, if ever should there be one for her," Brave Wolf said, leaning down to brush soft kisses across her brow.

"Then even if Night Horse had stayed this time and married her, she would not have worn this beautiful dress?" Mary Beth asked.

"*Ka*, no, she wouldn't have. She had decided never to wear it at all, for when she designed it and began making it, it was for only one purpose—for her wedding day with my brother," he said. "And I do not mean a possible wedding day should he return, as he did for a while. It was made for only that one special planned wedding, one of innocence and sweetness before Night Horse became someone none of us knew anymore. To wear it after he had returned would not have been the same. His leaving to fight alongside whites had tarnished the memory of why she was making the dress in the first place."

"Yet she gave it to me to wear," Mary Beth said.

"Perhaps I should not have told you the story of the dress," Brave Wolf said, placing a finger under her chin and turning her eyes back to his. "Does it make it less special in your eyes to know why Dancing Butterfly did not plan to ever wear it?"

"It is still special to me, even more so, because I now know just how special it was to her at one time," Mary Beth murmured.

She moved so that her body was molded perfectly against his, laughed softly, then sighed with pleasure when he suddenly took her gently by the waist and swept her beneath him.

"You are such a beautiful bride," he said, his eyes filled with adoration as he gazed down at her.

The startling beauty of her nakedness caused the fires within him to build to an almost feverish pitch.

He placed a knee between her legs and parted them, her thighs opening to him as he placed his maleness perfectly within her.

"Let us not talk any more about dresses," he said huskily. "Let us just feel tonight, my sunshine. Let us just feel the wonders of our bodies joining as not only man and woman, but as husband and wife."

"I love you so," she whispered as she twined her arms around his neck and her legs around his waist. "*Mihigna*, husband, fill me with your heat. Take me with you to paradise."

"*Tawicu*, wife, I am already there," he whispered against her lips. "Being with you is paradise."

He touched her lips wonderingly with his, then swept his arms around her and held her close as he kissed her long and deep, until her lips quavered with passion against his.

Waves of liquid heat pulsed through Brave Wolf as he thrust into her over and over again.

He slid a hand between them and filled it with one of her breasts, feeling her nipple tighten against his palm.

His hand kneaded her soft fullness, his tongue now lightly brushing her lips as his body moved faster in quick, sure movements.

Mary Beth clung to him, oh, so lost in waves of ecstasy. She could feel the pleasure building and spreading within her, her passion almost cresting.

"Do you feel my hunger . . . my need?" Brave Wolf whispered against her lips as he leaned back only far enough to be able to look into her passion-clouded eyes. "Do you feel how badly I want you?"

"I feel it . . . I know it . . ." Mary Beth whispered back, her face hot with a flush of building excitement. "Do you feel my need of you? Can you feel my undying love?"

"I feel it, and I see it, and I taste it when I kiss you," he said huskily. He leaned low and swirled his tongue across one of her breasts, causing Mary Beth to cry out with rapture. She sighed deeply as he took her nipple into his mouth and began sucking.

She arched her back and untwined her arms from around his neck, now clenching her fists at her sides, for the pleasure was so overwhelmingly beautiful, she knew she could not go on much longer without letting herself go over the edge into total ecstasy.

When he moved away from her, then knelt over her, she questioned him with her eyes.

He smiled down at her, then stroked her body with his lips and tongue, descending from the taper of her neck to her breasts, where he moved from one breast to the other with soft, warm kisses.

When his tongue swept downward, across her tummy, Mary Beth groaned with pleasure and closed her eyes at the bliss of the moment.

When he touched her private place, where only he had been, and his warm tongue caressed her there, she at first thought to brush his head aside. But she could not deny that his caresses were wonderfully pleasing, and allowed them.

She licked her lips.

She sighed.

She twined her fingers through his hair to encourage even more of what she had at first thought might be wrong.

Then just before she leapt over that last barrier into the final throes of ecstasy, he blanketed her body with his again, penetrated her deeply, and began hungry, deep thrusts.

They clung to one another as they came to that place where stars seemed to explode inside their heads, and where their bodies blazed with joyful bliss.

Afterwards, when they were lying side by side again, only their hands intertwining, Mary Beth gazed over at him. "How could it ever be any more beautiful than it was for us tonight?" she murmured, her face still hot with the aftermath of love-making. "Everything within me came alive with passion. I was far beyond coherent thought when you took me over the edge into ecstasy."

"As was I," Brave Wolf said, chuckling. "At that moment I was not a chief, I was a man . . . a *mih-igna*, a husband."

"But you *are* a chief, a beloved one at that," Mary Beth said, leaning up on her elbows as she gazed admiringly at him. "As you are now a husband, also a beloved one. And soon you will be a father, as I will be a mother again."

She sighed and rolled back onto her back. "Again," she murmured. "Oh, how I wish that David could have been here to make this day one hundred percent perfect."

"My sunshine, do you not know that he *was* with you?" Brave Wolf said as he moved to his side and placed a gentle hand over her heart. "In there, my sunshine. In there. Your son is always with you in your heart."

Tears came to her eyes. Not sad tears, but happy tears that came from realizing just how wonderful a man she had found and married. "Only you would think to tell a woman that on her wedding night," she murmured. "That proves that you are unselfish in your thoughts. Tonight you could be demanding so much more of your wife. You are so sweet and special, my husband. I hope I never disappoint you."

"You could never disappoint this husband," Brave Wolf said, sitting up. He placed his hands at her waist, drew her up and arranged her on his lap, facing him. "You are so radiantly beautiful tonight. It would be so easy to make love over and over again, but I also see some weariness in your eyes. It has not been an easy time for you these past days. My wife, let us sleep. Let me watch you sleep. I doubt that I can go to sleep just yet. I am so full of you, oh, so full of you."

"As I am you," Mary Beth murmured. She leaned forward and twined her arms around his neck and gave him a sweet kiss. "My *mihigna,* I hunger for more tonight than sleep. It would please me so if you would take me on that road to paradise again."

He smiled into her eyes, then gently rolled her beneath him again.

Their bodies came together with the magic only they could create for one another.

Chapter Thirty

I'll woo her as the lion
woos his bride.
—John Home

The sound of a cat meowing outside their lodge awakened both Mary Beth and Brave Wolf.

Mary Beth sat up and listened more carefully, then hurried into a blanket-robe and went to the entranceway. She slid aside the flap when she heard the cat's soft cry again.

It was early dawn and there was just light enough for Mary Beth to see the beautiful calico cat, its green eyes gazing up at her as if to say I belong to *you*, not Pure Heart.

Then Mary Beth saw something else. A mouse, and not any ordinary mouse. It was white-footed. She saw it was dead and also saw the cat's teeth marks in its bloody side. She gasped softly when the cat gazed down at the mouse, slapped at it with a paw, then looked up at Mary Beth again.

"What is it?" Brave Wolf asked as he came to Mary Beth's side with his breechcloth on. He followed her gaze and saw the cat and then the mouse.

"The cat seems to have brought me a gift this morning," Mary Beth said, smiling at Brave Wolf.

"A mouse?" Brave Wolf said, arching an eyebrow.

"This is the way a cat shows its affection . . . its fondness for someone," Mary Beth said. She reached down and swept the cat into her arms.

When it snuggled close to her and began purring, she knew that her reasoning was correct. The cat had chosen her to be its master over Pure Heart. The mouse was its way of delivering the message of ownership to her.

Brave Wolf went outside, took the mouse by its tail and tossed it away. He washed his hands in a basin of water that was kept outside, then went back into his tepee and knelt beside Mary Beth. She was sitting beside the glimmering embers in the firepit, slowly stroking the cat.

"I'm not sure what I should do about this," Mary Beth said, glancing at Brave Wolf. "The cat is so content when she is with me. I feel that I should accept her as mine, since it is so obvious that she prefers me, yet what about your mother? The cat seemed to help take away some of the loneliness that Night Horse's departure caused."

"She is a caring, understanding woman," Brave Wolf said, reaching over to stroke the cat's soft fur. "She would not want the cat to stay with her if the animal prefers you. She would want the cat to be happy."

He ran his hand gently over the cat's tummy. "And there soon will be kittens," he said, smiling. "Mother can have her choice of . . . how did you call them?"

"The *litter,*" Mary Beth said, still stroking the beautiful animal. "Pure Heart can have her pick of the litter. Perhaps she can take more than one if that is her preference."

"Then that should settle it," Brave Wolf said. "That should make her happy enough."

"How do I tell her?" Mary Beth said.

"I shall go and explain it to her," Brave Wolf said.

"I truly hope she won't be too sad over this," Mary Beth said. "Yesterday she was so brave and courageous about accepting her loss all over again. She was even a part of our wedding ceremony, though I know that she was hurting deep inside herself."

"My brother knew that it was best for him to leave, yet I regret the hurts he caused all over again," Brave Wolf said, combing his fingers through his hair to straighten out its morning tangles. "My mother is not doing as well as Dancing Butterfly. She carries her hurts more deeply. I understood why she went back to the privacy of her lodge immediately after our wedding vows were spoken. Did you understand, as well?"

"Yes, very much so," Mary Beth said, sighing. "She has lost her son again. I lost mine only once. I would hate to think of the heartbreak if I had him back and then he suddenly disappeared again. As it is, both your mother and I carry empty spaces inside our hearts over such grievous losses."

"Brother?"

The voice brought both Mary Beth and Brave Wolf quickly to their feet. Mary Beth clung to the cat as she hurried to the entrance flap beside Brave Wolf.

Her eyes widened when she saw Night Horse standing there, and not alone!

She recognized the man who was tied up and whose eye was swollen shut and bloody.

"Blackjack Tom," Mary Beth gasped out, stunned.

"Night Horse, who is this?" Brave Wolf asked, stepping out of the tepee with Mary Beth beside him.

"My brother, when I left yesterday, I planned to stay away, but I could not," Night Horse said, his voice full of emotion. "I kept thinking about the hurts that I was again leaving behind. Yet I saw the strain I put on everybody when the soldiers came. Had they known I was here, things would have been different. The soldiers might not have helped you, but instead seen you as an enemy because you were harboring a man they now suspect. I thought everyone would be better off without me, but my heart would not allow me to stay away.

My woman . . . my mother . . . my brother . . . my *people* seemed to call to me. I had to return. I shall face all questions, either from whites or my brethren, and pay whatever price I must pay, but I am tired of causing hurts by disappearing."

He gave Blackjack Tom a shove, causing him to fall on his knees.

The man with the beady black eyes looked humbly up at Night Horse, then lowered his eyes to the ground.

"This man, whom I know as Blackjack Tom from my acquaintance with the white pony soldiers, was lurking directly behind your lodge, my brother," Night Horse said venomously. "He had a knife. Had I not come along when I did, I believe he would have entered your lodge from the back by slicing his way through the skins. I did not know why he would do this, or whom he planned to kill, until I forced answers from him."

"And what did he say?" Mary Beth asked, her voice breaking, for in her mind's eye she was reliving that night all over again, how the dark shadow of the man loomed over her as his hands tightened around her throat!

"He said nothing at first, but when I placed his own knife at his throat, he spoke loudly and clearly of wanting to kill you, Mary Beth, and then my brother Brave Wolf," Night Horse said, his voice tight. "When I heard his plan, I could not help hitting him."

"After I gave him information, he shouldn't have hit me," Blackjack Tom whined.

"He should have done worse than that," Mary Beth said angrily. "You are a filthy, cold-hearted man. You are a coward, for only a coward would enter a woman's room at night with plans to kill her. I am so glad that Night Horse found you. I hope you hang."

She looked at Brave Wolf. "You *will* take him to Fort Hope, won't you?" Mary Beth asked softly. "Colonel Anderson will see to it that he gets what he deserves. I . . . I . . . don't think you should take on the responsibility of doing anything, yourself. If word spread that you did something to a white soldier, even though he deserted his post and is wanted by all of the United States cavalry, the government would not take kindly to your handing down his punishment."

"I do plan to take him to Colonel Anderson," Brave Wolf said thickly. "And he will want to know how Blackjack Tom was captured. Night Horse, what shall I say? You are still in danger of being hunted by the white pony soldiers, for they will want to question you about your role in Yellow Hair's defeat."

"I thought all of that through and I believe it is my duty to go and tell everything to Colonel Anderson," Night Horse said, his chin lifted proudly. "I know that you think Colonel Anderson is a good, wise man. I will take the chance that he will believe my story, and if he does, I will be free to return to my people, if they still want me."

"You are wanted, my son, by all who know you and have always loved you," Pure Heart said as she came shakily toward Night Horse. "I heard your voice, my son. At first I thought your voice was coming to me in a dream. When I fully awakened and looked outside and saw you, I knew that my prayers to the First Maker had been answered."

She flung herself into Night Horse's arms. "My son, my son, please do not leave me ever again," she sobbed out. "It gets harder each time. I felt as though my life was slipping away when I saw you were gone again."

"*Ina,* I am sorry that I caused you pain again," Night Horse said, gently stroking her thin, old back through her doeskin robe. "I have returned, but I must leave again to speak with Colonel Anderson as I deliver the captive to him. If Colonel Anderson believes me when I say that I had nothing to do with the attack on General Custer, and he tells me I am a free man, I will come home again. This time I will stay. I want to join the next hunt and bring much meat home for your plate. I want to be there for you always, Mother."

He looked over his mother's shoulder at Brave Wolf. "I want to ride side by side with you on the hunt, to challenge you in games again, as we did when we were young brave," he said earnestly. "My brother, I want to be everything to you."

"Night Horse, oh, is that truly you, Night Horse?" Dancing Butterfly cried as she came running toward him.

Pure Heart stepped aside just as Dancing Butterfly reached Night Horse, tears flowing from her eyes when she saw her son reach out for the woman he had loved since they were children.

"I am sorry that I hurt you again," he said, holding her tightly. "I am here to stay, if the soldiers will allow my freedom."

"They will, oh, my love, they will," Dancing Butterfly sobbed as she clung to him.

Brave Wolf bent down, grabbed Blackjack Tom by an arm, and yanked him to his feet. "Your days of killing and maiming are over," he growled out. "Your days of accosting women in the dark are over. I will see to it that you are taken in chains to be confined in the guardhouse at Fort Hope. You will never be able to touch my wife again."

"Your wife?" Blackjack Tom gasped out, paling as he looked quickly at Mary Beth. He glowered. "I was right to try and kill you. You *are* an Injun lover. You . . . you . . . actually married one." He spat at her feet. "You whore."

Mary Beth gasped and took a shaky step away from him, then flinched when Brave Wolf slapped him hard across the face, causing his neck to make a strange snapping sound.

Mary Beth gazed disbelievingly as Blackjack Tom's head hung limply, his chin touching his chest as his knees buckled and he fell to the ground.

"Is . . . he . . . dead?" she gasped out.

"No, but he will be unconscious for a while, which is good since he has many miles to travel before Night Horse hands him over to Colonel Anderson for incarceration," Brave Wolf said. He turned to Night Horse. "I will tie him more securely, in case he does awaken. Then, my brother, you should take time to eat before heading out for Fort Hope."

"I shall fix food for him," Dancing Butterfly said. She glanced quickly at Pure Heart, who she knew would want to spend those moments with her son in case he was not allowed to return to his home again.

"Pure Heart, I shall fix breakfast for you and Night Horse," Dancing Butterfly murmured, smiling. "Go and be with your son alone. I shall join you soon with the food."

Pure Heart smiled broadly, locked an arm through Night Horse's, and walked away with him. She stopped and looked inquiringly at Mary Beth when she saw the cat in her arms.

"She came to me this morning," Mary Beth said. She held the cat out to Pure Heart.

Pure Heart didn't take the cat. "The cat has never looked as content in my arms as she does in yours. If you wish to have her as yours, I understand," she murmured. Then she smiled. "And I soon will have Night Horse to fill the empty spaces in my heart with his smile and laughter. I do not need the animal."

Mary Beth heard the hope in Pure Heart's voice. She prayed that Night Horse would be allowed to return to the village.

"Then I shall keep her," Mary Beth murmured. She ran a slow hand over the cat's tummy. "But if you wish, you can have a kitten very soon to call your own."

"I would like that," Pure Heart said, smiling radiantly.

She turned her eyes down to the unconscious man. "He may be a bad man, but he might just be the reason for my son to be set free," she said. "If Night Horse is seen as the one who is responsible for capturing the man that the pony soldiers are looking for, might not they reward him by allowing him his freedom?"

"I would hope so," Mary Beth said, giving Brave Wolf a questioning look.

"Yes, I, too, would hope so," he said. "I do hope that my brother is given his freedom and allowed a fresh start with his life, for I believe he deserves it. By capturing Blackjack Tom and saving us from what might have been a quick death, Night Horse has redeemed himself. He deserves a second chance."

Mary Beth gazed down at Blackjack Tom, again reliving what he had done to her. "Not everyone deserves a second chance," she said, shuddering. "This man . . . this Blackjack Tom . . . doesn't!"

Chapter Thirty-one

Is it, in Heav'n a crime,
to love too well?
To bear too tender or too
firm a heart?
—Alexander Pope

It was the last cicada-shell moon of old summer and the second leaf-falling season at the Crow village for Mary Beth. She was now the happy, proud wife of the chief of the Whistling Water Clan. She knew this was the season when new tepee poles were cut and the women busied themselves making certain their lodge skins were renewed and whitened.

Mother Earth's bounty had provided a rich harvest again this year. The Crow people had plenty of geese, ducks, sage hens, deer, and antelope.

Much game had been brought into camp and smoked, as well as fish from the nearby river. In the plum thickets and blueberry bushes, there had been plenty of sweetness.

The Crow people had worked hard to prepare for Mother Earth's change of dress, when the hungry moon of winter would shine down on the breathless nights, when bears slept and the small buffalo herds would be pawing through the snow for grass after the downy snow fell from the sky.

Soon Mary Beth would wear a long robe of the softest, whitest doeskin which she had proudly sewn for herself.

But today, when the air smelled of the delicious scents of autumn, reminding Mary Beth of all of her autumns in Kentucky, she was not overseeing the making of new tepee poles, nor was she concerned about making certain their lodge skins were readied for the long months of winter which lay just ahead of them.

She was with Dancing Butterfly, acting as midwife with Pure Heart, as her friend readied herself for the second child that would soon be born to her and Night Horse.

Night Horse, who had not been arrested by the United States Government, who was free to live his life now with his Crow people and wife, could not even be near the birthing lodge. Dancing Butterfly moaned and groaned in heavy labor in the lodge, which was set far back from the others of the village. It had been built of bent willow branches and was to be used only for the birthing of this one child; then it would be dismantled, its willow branches never to be be used again for anything.

"I wish my husband could be with me," Dancing Butterfly said, grabbing at her huge belly when another sharp pain caused her to bear down. "My husband. Oh, my husband. Why cannot he be here with me? I wish so badly to be held by him."

"This is your second child. You know the custom, Dancing Butterfly," Pure Heart said as she bent to her knees and planted one stake into the ground at one corner of Dancing Butterfly's pillow. Mary Beth knelt at the other corner and hammered the second stake there.

"Hurry, oh, please hurry," Dancing Butterfly said as she tossed her head from side to side, her sweat-wettened hair spraying moisture with each toss. "I feel it is time. I . . . feel . . . it. I know that the baby's head is coming down. Soon. Oh, soon my child will be in my arms."

"The stakes are planted," Pure Heart said, settling down at the foot of the bed of pelts beside Mary Beth, who would assist in the childbirth in any way she could.

Mary Beth was proud to have been chosen as one of Dancing Butterfly's midwives. It proved just how close their bonds were as friends.

She glanced over at Pure Heart, whose old eyes were filled with eagerness; she was going to be a grandmother for the second time in two years.

It made Mary Beth sad that Pure Heart's first grandchild had not been Brave Wolf's and Mary Beth's, nor even her second.

Mary Beth had not been able to conceive. It was hard for her to understand, because on her very wedding night with Lloyd, she had become pregnant.

She had always believed she never got pregnant again because of the scarcity of times they had shared in lovemaking.

But she had been with her beloved Brave Wolf every night since their marriage except for that time of month when she had her weeps, and no Indian husband even came near his wife at that time.

Mary Beth had finally grown used to spending that time of month in the village menstrual hut, where all women went and sewed or did other handiwork to pass those days and nights away from their husbands.

Yes, it just did not seem right that Mary Beth had not gotten pregnant after all those wondrous moments in her husband's arms. She could only conclude that it had to do with David not having been found, that she could not relax in the right way to become pregnant.

She didn't understand, nor could she change anything. She had learned to take the bad with the good and be content for the moment.

What would make her happiness complete was to have a child born of her and Brave Wolf's love. Although she hated to admit it, she had given up on ever seeing David again.

It had been too long now.

And after all the searches by not only Brave Wolf

and his warriors, but also his Crow allies, as well as Colonel Anderson's men, David had not been seen anywhere. Mary Beth had no choice but to accept that her son was lost to her forever.

Now if only she could get pregnant. Surely another child would fill that empty space in her heart left by David's absence.

Her thoughts returned to the present when Dancing Butterfly screamed and gripped the stakes. Mary Beth listened to Dancing Butterfly say many rapid words in the Crow tongue, smiling when she recognized them; she now knew their language as well as her own.

Dancing Butterfly had just said many unpleasant words to express her frustration over being in labor for so long and having nothing to show for it!

If it were Mary Beth, she would say a few choice words under those conditions, but they would soon be followed by a prayer. On the other hand, she would give anything to be having those labor pains.

Surely she would not be as impatient as Dancing Butterfly or speak such words of frustration. Mary Beth's frustration came from being childless.

Pure Heart sat beside Dancing Butterfly with a small vial that held a combination of ground roots and broth from a cooked horned toad.

"This will help your pain," Pure Heart said as she slowly rubbed the liquid across Dancing Butterfly's swollen abdomen. "Close your eyes. Breathe in . . . breathe out. Soon you will make me a very proud grandmother again."

"Both Night Horse and I are proud to give you another grandchild," Dancing Butterfly said. She tossed her head back and forth and gritted her teeth when another pain slammed through her.

"There is one more thing I can do for you," Pure Heart said. She reached over and grabbed a small jug. She held it to Dancing Butterfly's lips with one hand as she slowly lifted her head with the other. "Drink it slowly. This will hasten the birth."

Dancing Butterfly swallowed the liquid in small sips. When she was finished, Pure Heart set the empty jug aside and moved to Dancing Butterfly's side. She held her tightly above her swollen abdomen. "Push," she said, her eyes watching as Mary Beth moved closer to Dancing Butterfly's outspread legs. "Mary Beth, reach inside her. Help the child. Help the child now."

Mary Beth blanched at the thought, but nodded weakly. When Dancing Butterfly screamed and gave another hard push, Mary Beth reached slightly inside her just as the head of the baby slid down into her hands.

Soon the child was in Mary Beth's arms, its first cries filling the small space of the hut.

Pure Heart came to her, her eyes shining with happy tears and waited for the afterbirth to slide free, which it did in a matter of seconds.

Pure Heart placed it in a wooden basin, then gazed at length at the child.

"It is a *wiyanna*, a girl child," Pure Heart said, sighing as she slowly took the baby from Mary Beth and cradled it in her own arms.

"My granddaughter," Pure Heart said as Mary Beth measured off three fingers on the wet unbilical cord and sliced it with a knife, cutting the navel cord.

Since the child was a girl, Mary Beth rolled the cord up in a piece of cloth and put it into a beaded sack that would be fastened to her cradleboard.

When the child was old enough to wear an elk-tooth dress, this bag would be tied to its back.

Mary Beth knew of the other procedures which followed childbirth. Two days from now, Dancing Butterfly would heat a steel awl and pierce her child's earlobes with it. She would then stick a greased stick through the perforations. When the wounds healed, tiny earrings would be inserted.

Four days after the child's birth, Dancing Butterfly would cover the baby's face with a sacred red paint and lift her four times while the village shaman, Many Clouds, held smoking bear root to the child's wincing eyes. Then he would name her.

Now that Mary Beth had completed the first chores, she was able to stop and take a longer look at the tiny thing in Pure Heart's arms. Dancing Butterfly leaned up on an elbow, finally free of pain, and her eyes were filled with love as she gazed at her newborn.

Ah, the child, Mary Beth marveled to herself. She was so pure and so beautiful, it made tears come to her eyes, for she had always wanted a daughter so that David would have a sister.

Now Mary Beth didn't have a son or a daughter, but she could, she *would* enjoy her best friend's child to the fullest. She was anxious to see the newborn placed in the cradleboard that Mary Beth had made for her. She had lined it with beautiful white rabbit fur and decorated it with pretty beads for the baby to look at and play with.

She looked forward to helping feed the baby when she was old enough to be fed stew of boiled corn and crushed berries.

"She is so tiny," Mary Beth said, reaching over to take one of her hands and marveling over how little the fingers were.

Her gaze shifted to the feet. She smiled at the tiny, curled-up toes.

Then she moved her eyes slowly over the naked baby, seeing her beautiful smooth copper skin, the darkness of her eyes as she peered up at her grandmother for the first time, and the shock of black hair on her head, almost enough already to braid!

When the baby smiled that first time, it was pure heaven for all who witnessed it.

"We must cleanse her and then give her to her mother for feeding," Pure Heart said, slipping the child into Mary Beth's arms. She reached for a wooden basin of water that had been prepared what seemed to Mary Beth hours and hours ago. "Mary Beth, you hold her. I will wash her."

Mary Beth didn't take her eyes off the child as she was washed. She smiled as Pure Heart wrapped the clean child in a soft doeskin blanket and placed her in her mother's waiting arms.

Mary Beth almost turned away as the child was placed at her mother's breast for the first time. It was almost too much for Mary Beth as she recalled the first time her David had suckled from her own breast. At this moment, her longing for her son was twofold.

But she knew that she must get hold of herself. She wanted to be happy for Dancing Butterfly and Night Horse, not envious!

She watched as Pure Heart took a bowl to Dancing Butterfly. While the child suckled, Pure Heart helped Dancing Butterfly eat what was required of her after having just given birth to her child . . . a piece of broiled buffalo hump which had been dipped in fat. Dancing Butterfly would eat it just once. Then she would be made to abstain from any cooked meat for several days.

"And now it is time to get the proud *ahte*, the father," Mary Beth said, crawling toward the small entranceway. The birthing hut was not tall enough for anyone to walk within it.

She hurried outside, where both Brave Wolf and Night Horse stood, their eyes anxious.

"I heard my baby's first cry," Night Horse said, glancing from the entranceway to Mary Beth. "Tell me. Is it a *micinksi*, a son? Or a *wiyanna*, a daughter?"

"Your son has a sister, you have a beautiful daughter," Mary Beth said.

She moved into Brave Wolf's arms as he reached out for her. She wished that she was telling him she had just given *him* a child. She was afraid that just possibly she might never be able to.

She embraced Brave Wolf, then turned and

stood at his side, his arm around her waist, as they both watched Night Horse go to the hut.

"She is truly the most beautiful little girl I have ever seen," Mary Beth said as she smiled up at Brave Wolf. "One day I, too, will give you a child. I know it, Brave Wolf. I . . . just . . . know it."

"You fret too much over it," Brave Wolf said. He turned her and placed his hands on her shoulders. "My wife, my *sunshine,* do you not know that you are enough for me?"

"You are so wonderfully sweet to say that," she murmured. "I do love you so much, Brave Wolf."

"As I do you," he said, then dropped his hands and took hers. "As soon as we give my brother time enough to see and hold his child, I want to go and hold my niece."

"You will adore her," Mary Beth said, smiling at the memory of the child's tiny sweetness.

"In four days she will be named," Brave Wolf said thickly. "In four days . . ."

Mary Beth knew that although he tried to comfort her, he longed for a child as much as she did. It was in the way he gazed at the birthing hut, and in the way he talked about the child, and even in his anxiousness for her to be named. She *must* find a way to have a child for him.

If not, oh, what then?

Could he truly see her as enough forever?

She doubted it, for he was a proud chief, who would surely want to show off many children to his people. Otherwise, would he not look less virile in their eyes?

Yes, it did worry Mary Beth. How could it not?

It seemed that in the end, her marriage would depend on whether or not she was able to have a child.

Chapter Thirty-two

And this maiden,
she lived with no other thought
than to love and be loved by me.
—Poe

It was spring, in the grass-growing moon, when everything was new and smelled sweetly of flowers.

It was a time of hope and love, as the women prepared packs of extra moccasins and pemmican for their husbands to take along on the hunt.

Two days ago Mary Beth had joined the women in singing farewell songs of encouragement to Brave Wolf and his warriors as they left the village on their prancing, magnificent steeds. Each warrior had carried his own choice of weapon, some bearing guns, others bows and arrows, and others spears.

It was wonderful to see the harmony of the Crow hunters who would bring home a bounty of meat, her husband in the lead.

Mary Beth had just returned from the river with Dancing Butterfly and the other women, their baskets and pots filled with fresh water.

Mary Beth inhaled deeply and smelled the savory smoke of elk meat being roasted over a large outdoor fire. The meat had come from an earlier, briefer hunt three days ago. Each husband had brought home a supply of fresh meat to sustain his family during the long hunt.

She stood with Dancing Butterfly, watching Little Horse playing with a group of other four-year-olds.

All Crow boys, even as young as four, were subjected to vigorous training in running, swimming, wrestling, archery, racing, hunting, and riding. But on this early morning, they were enjoying a time of play and camaraderie. Some splashed in the stream, laughing, while others played tag.

"My son grows more and more into his father's image," Dancing Butterfly said, pride in both her eyes and voice. She turned and looked toward her tepee, then smiled at Mary Beth. "Night Horse tells me our newborn daughter is in *my* image." She laughed softly. "Of course he would say that, even knowing she is too young to look like anyone but herself."

"Yes, she is only two weeks old," Mary Beth said, as she looked at Dancing Butterfly. "You have two daughters and one son, yet your body shows no signs of ever having had any children. It is as voluptuous as it was before you had children."

"It will be the same for you," Dancing Butterfly said, then sucked in a quick breath and paled. "I am sorry. What I said made it sound as though you have not had a child, yet you have. How could I forget about your son David? How could I be so insensitive?"

"Many have forgotten about him," Mary Beth said, sighing. "I never shall, though. Never, never."

Then Mary Beth gave Dancing Butterfly a warm hug. "And do not feel bad about what you said," she murmured. "I know what you meant."

She stepped away from Dancing Butterfly and gazed down at her own flat belly. She placed her hands on it. "Soon, ah, soon, all will know that at long last their chief's wife is with child," she said excitedly. "For too many moons now I have seen our people's eyes watching me, filled with disappointment and sadness as they gaze at my stomach. They wish for a son in their chief's image, one that can one day be as great a leader as his *ahte*, his father. I have felt so, *so* inadequate because of those looks."

"I am sorry you have felt that way," Dancing Butterfly murmured. "Had our people known how they were making you feel, they would feel bad, too, for they love you, Mary Beth. Everyone loves you."

"And I love them," Mary Beth said, turning to go back to her lodge.

"Come inside my lodge with me," Dancing Butterfly encouraged. "Bead with me for a while. I know how concerned you are about our husbands not being home from the hunt yet. They do not usually stay away as many nights as they have this time."

Mary Beth looked toward the outer perimeters of the village as she had done so often since daybreak. She was puzzled over why it should take so long for the warriors to return. No doubt with the dwindling herds of buffalo, it was more difficult to find the animals.

She was especially eager for Brave Wolf to return home this time. She was certain now that she was finally with child.

She had not told Brave Wolf yet because she had not wanted to disappoint him in case she was not pregnant after all.

Now that she had counted off six full weeks since her monthly should have started, she was ready to tell Brave Wolf the wonderful news. She smiled when she saw a deer bounding away into the forest thicket.

"It is so wonderful to know that you are with child," Dancing Butterfly said. "Thank you for sharing this with me."

"I wanted Brave Wolf to be the first to know, but I just could not wait a moment longer to say it aloud to someone," Mary Beth said, beaming. "That person *should* be you. You are such a wonderful friend."

Dancing Butterfly giggled. "When we first met I did not treat you like a friend," she said softly. "I was so cold . . . so cruel . . . so untrusting." She sighed. "I was so *wrong*."

"You were right not to trust me," Mary Beth said. "I am white. Not many whites had given you cause to trust them." She sighed and smiled. "I am so glad that you soon saw me as no threat to your people and decided to take me into your heart as your friend."

"*Special* friend," Dancing Butterfly corrected. She dropped her hands from Mary Beth's and knelt when her son came running to her, his eyes wide with excitement.

"Mother, White Coyote opened his eyes," Little Horse cried, flinging himself into his mother's arms. "I just saw him do it. His eyes are such a pretty color." He glanced toward the sky, then smiled again as he looked at his mother. "They are the color of the sky."

He stood up and grabbed one of his mother's hands, then reached for one of Mary Beth's. "Come. See," he said eagerly.

Mary Beth took one of Little Horse's tiny hands and went with him and Dancing Butterfly to a small hut made of willow branches, where they crawled inside.

Mary Beth's heart went out to the lone white coyote that had rejoined its tiny brothers and sisters in nursing. There was a difference between him and the others, for they were not coyotes at all, but kittens.

Two days before Brave Wolf had left for the hunt, he had found an abandoned white coyote pup not far from the village. He had searched for its mother, but finally gave up on finding her.

Devoted to his nephew Little Horse, he had brought the pup home to him.

It was Little Horse who had ever so nonchalantly taken the pup and placed it amid five kittens as they nursed from their mother. The pup was soon nursing alongside them, as though it had been born with them.

The mother cat had taken the pup in and licked and groomed it as though it were her own.

Mary Beth was touched deeply by the sight of the kittens and coyote together, the kittens all black, contrasting with the white. And seeing the tiny pup, she had finally gotten over the fear of coyotes which had stayed with her from the first moment she had heard them howling in the darkness.

She smiled down at the mother cat, who seemed to smile back at her, for this was the very cat that had once belonged to Colonel Downing. Sweetness, as Mary Beth had named her, had given birth to many litters, all grown now and happily keeping the Crow people's cornfields free of white-footed mice, and the huge and ugly kangaroo rats that abounded in Montana.

"You cannot see White Coyote's eyes now," Little Horse said, sighing. "He is feeding again. But you can come back later to see or I can bring him to you when he is through feeding."

Mary Beth patted him on a cheek. "He is a beautiful puppy," she murmured. "I'm glad you love him so much."

"Uncle Brave Wolf was so nice to build this special birthing hut for the mother and her kittens," Little Horse said. He smiled from ear to ear. "I want to give one of these kittens to each of my special friends." He turned pleading eyes up to Mary Beth. "Aunt Mary Beth, can I? Can I have these kittens for my friends?"

"Yes, sweetie, you can," Mary Beth said. She laughed softly. "There are always enough kittens to go around. It seems that Sweetness has a male friend somewhere who keeps her belly filled with kittens."

The sound of horses outside the hut made Mary Beth turn. She and Dancing Butterfly exchanged big smiles.

"Finally they are home," Mary Beth said, hurrying from the small hut.

Just as they got outside and stood up, Mary Beth saw the large group of warriors entering the village, but there was someone else among them.

Her heart skipped a beat, and she grabbed Dancing Butterfly's hand. "Is that a child on a pony beside Brave Wolf?" she asked, her voice breaking. "Oh, Dancing Butterfly, am I seeing right? Is it a young boy? Is his hair golden?"

Dancing Butterfly gazed intently at the child, whose skin was sun-bronzed and whose waist-length hair was the color of wheat. He rode proudly in his small saddle and wore only a breechcloth and moccasins.

"Yes, Mary Beth, you are seeing a young brave who is surely around nine winters of age and whose hair is the color of wheat," Dancing Butterfly said, her own heart pounding at the sight, because she knew that she had just described Mary Beth's David!

"Oh, Lord, oh, Lord," Mary Beth cried, bolting toward them, her braids bouncing on her shoulders, her arms outstretched as the child came closer on his pony.

"David!" Mary Beth cried. "David! David!"

"Mama!" he cried as he leapt from his horse and began running toward her. "Mama!"

They met halfway.

Mary Beth fell to her knees and gathered him into her arms.

She clung and sobbed.

Brave Wolf dismounted and fell to his knees beside his wife and the young brave he would gladly call son. He gathered them both within his arms.

Mary Beth gazed at Brave Wolf. "I do not know how you managed this, but, oh, thank you, thank you," she said, the tears hot on her lips. "My son. He is home. He is safe. He is alive!"

David clung for a moment longer, then as Brave Wolf leaned away, the child looked into his mother's eyes. "Mama, I never let myself forget you, your love, the prettiness of your smile and eyes," he said, tears streaming down his cheeks. "Mama, I knew that I would see you again."

He lowered his eyes, then looked into hers

again. "Mama, I remembered the prayer I said each night back at our home in Kentucky and I prayed that same prayer often, hoping I would find you when I became a great warrior who could travel far and wide to search for you," he said. "But Brave Wolf, who I now know is your husband, found you for me."

"We were hunting," Brave Wolf said. He placed a gentle hand on the child's shoulder. "Two Cheyenne warriors, one a powerful chief, joined our hunt. While we were becoming acquainted, I told him about you and that you were white. The chief told me about his adopted son, who is also white. I asked how he came to have the child, and for his description. It was moments later that I knew I had found David. And just as I thought it, the warrior spoke David's name to me, as his name was before he gave him the Cheyenne name Lone Bear."

"Lone Bear . . ." Mary Beth said, framing David's tanned face between her hands. "My son . . . Lone Bear."

She slowly looked at her son, up and down, smiling at how healthy and tan he was. She could hardly believe that he was there for her to love and touch forever and ever!

Then her eyes went to a warrior who came up beside Brave Wolf.

Brave Wolf placed an arm around the warrior's shoulder. "This is Black Feather, who has fathered Lone Bear since the day he rescued him from a band of renegades," he explained. He nodded from Black Feather to Mary Beth.

"Black Feather, this is Mary Beth, my wife," he said, pride in his eyes and voice. "This is Lone Bear's mother. Is not she as beautiful as I described her to you?"

Black Feather smiled and nodded. "*Ah-hah*, yes, and even more," he said. He reached a hand out to Mary Beth. "It is good to finally meet the mother of my son Lone Bear."

Mary Beth hesitated.

Her smile waned.

She didn't like the way this warrior still spoke about David as though he were his . . . his to *keep*.

"I see that what I have said put alarm into your eyes," Black Feather said, slowly lowering his hand to his side. "Although I still refer to Lone Bear as my son, I know that in truth he is yours, and that I must say farewell to him today. It is my wife, who is barren, who will find it difficult to accept this reality. He has become everything to my wife . . . and to me."

"But you will not ask for him to leave with you?" Mary Beth asked hopefully. "You truly give him back to me although it is obvious how much you want and love him?"

"It is only right that he be with his true mother," Black Feather said. "He kept you alive inside his heart. He spoke of you often. We sent out many search parties for you but never found you."

"You were so close, yet so far?" Mary Beth said.

"No, we were never close, not until recently," Black Feather said. "My people are new to this land. We are a misplaced people now. We have been ordered onto a reservation. We were on our way there when we stopped just long enough for me and my warriors to hunt. That is when we came across Brave Wolf. He shared his meat with us. Then we shared talk."

"Which led you to mention my son?" Mary Beth softly questioned.

"It was your husband who asked if I had seen in my recent travels a white boy living among any tribes I have been with," Black Feather said. "Guessing he was referring to my white son, I hesitated to tell him, yet when he talked of a mother whose heart was hurting, I could not keep the truth about my white son to myself any longer."

Tears flooded Mary Beth's eyes. "Thank you, oh, thank you, for being honest and open with my husband," she said. She bent to her knees and drew David into her arms once again. She gazed up at Black Feather. "But I know how hard this has to be for you, and for your wife. She will surely be as heartbroken as I was when I lost my son to those renegades."

"At first she will be, but after she has had time to think about it, she will be happy that Lone Bear is finally reunited with his true mother," he said thickly. "You see, you were always in his nightly prayers. I was there at his bedside with him. I heard them."

Mary Beth was deeply touched that her son would use the Christian prayers that she had so devotedly taught him. She was touched that this Cheyenne chief would allow him to, had even joined his nightly prayers.

All of this time, when she was so worried about her son, he was with a caring, wonderful family, instead of with the renegades being taught their evil ways, which meant that God had also answered *her* prayers.

"You say that you have been ordered onto a reservation," Mary Beth said. "The Crow were also, but thus far we have been allowed to stay on land that was given to the Whistling Waters Clan by treaty. Were you not included in such a treaty?"

"We Cheyenne have signed many treaties with the white eyes, but the white eyes broke them all," Black Feather said, his voice cold and flat. "We have been ordered to the reservation. If we do not comply, we will suffer because of it. My people have suffered enough. We go to the reservation. We will make our home there."

"Stay with us," Brave Wolf quickly said. "We can make room for you. We can ride together on the hunt. We can be as one people."

Black Feather gazed over his shoulder at the many Crow people who were crowded together now, watching.

He turned his eyes back to Brave Wolf. "You are kind to offer, but that would seem to be the easy way out," he said. "But what might appear easy for us would bring hardships on you." He sighed. "My brother, I must return now to my people. I must go to my wife, who is in mourning as we speak . . .

mourning for a son whom she can no longer call hers."

David rushed to Black Feather and flung himself into his arms as Black Feather knelt and received him. David clung to him. "*Ahte*, father, I shall miss you so much," he said with a sob. "I . . . shall . . . miss *Ina*."

"I know," Black Feather said, gently stroking the boy's back. "In life, there are many things that one must face and deal with. This is just one more thing for you."

"Yes, I know," David said, slowly leaving the comfort of arms that had held him often these past winters.

He stepped away from Black Feather, then stood at Mary Beth's side. Her hand took his, their fingers intertwining. "But I am so happy to be with my true mother," he said. "Please tell my other mother that I shall always remember her and love her, but I must be with my true mother."

David gazed up at Mary Beth. "She has been without me for much too long already," he said with the voice of an adult. "She should not have to suffer such heartache any longer, or ever again."

Mary Beth was touched by how grown up her son was being. He had not only grown in inches and in years, but also in his mind and heart.

"It is good to see a new sort of happiness in your eyes," Black Feather said, reaching a gentle hand to David's shoulder. "It is your true mother who has placed it there."

Then he turned again toward Brave Wolf. "In

time, surely we will meet again," he said. "Until then, my brother, be happy with what you have, for it can be taken from you so quickly."

He turned to David again. He bent down and gave him a fierce hug, then stood again. He gazed at the boy for a moment longer, then turned and walked to his horse.

He mounted his steed, then rode away without looking back.

Suddenly Mary Beth was aware of someone else at her side. She turned and saw that it was Brave Wolf's mother, her weak, old eyes squinting as she gazed down at David.

"So this is your son," Pure Heart said in a voice that was so weak she could hardly speak. She was being held up between two warriors. She had aged and often seemed at death's door, yet stubbornly bounced back, smiling at how she had cheated death again.

"Yes, this is my David," Mary Beth said proudly, bending to pull him into her arms. She smiled into his eyes. "I'm not sure I can get used to calling you anything but David."

"Then do not," he said. "You see, Mother, I always felt like a David, not a Lone Bear."

"You are so dear," she murmured, hugging him to her heart. "You are my David. My darling, sweet David."

Then she stood. She gestured toward Brave Wolf's mother. "David, this is Pure Heart," she murmured. "She is Brave Wolf's mother. She is now your grandmother."

Then she turned to Dancing Butterfly. "And this is Dancing Butterfly, who is now your aunt and who is my very best friend in the world," she murmured.

Little Horse ran up and clung to his mother's skirt, his dark eyes slowly assessing David. In his free arm, the coyote pup lay cuddled and asleep. He smiled at his father as he came now and stood beside Brave Wolf.

"And this child is Little Horse," Mary Beth said, gesturing toward him. "He is Dancing Butterfly's son, who is now your cousin." She smiled at Night Horse. "And this is Night Horse, Brave Wolf's brother and Little Horse's father."

Mary Beth saw that her son was having trouble absorbing so much. She started to take his hand to lead him home with her and Brave Wolf, but stopped when Little Horse stepped away from his mother, toward David.

"Do you want to hold White Coyote?" Little Horse asked, smiling up at David, who was twice as tall as he.

"A coyote pup! And he is white," David cried. He held his arms out. "Yes, I would love to hold him."

Little Horse gently laid his pup in David's arms.

David beamed.

"Will you be my friend?" Little Horse asked, his eyes wide.

David smiled and nodded, then walked away with Little Horse to a crowd of children, who began asking David questions all at once.

But Mary Beth saw how David suddenly turned and looked at Black Feather who was riding from the village. She saw the shine of tears in his eyes. Then he turned his head quickly away, as though he knew it was best not to linger over the pain of parting.

She sighed with relief when she saw him talking with the children.

She turned to Brave Wolf.

"I have not only brought home our son, but also much meat for our plates," Brave Wolf said, just as horses approached, dragging travois covered with fresh slabs of meat.

"It is not so much buffalo meat as deer," Brave Wolf said. "But no matter. It is good and nourishing for all of our bellies."

Mary Beth reached for him, then drew him into her arms. "Do you know how happy you have just made me?" she murmured. "My darling, thank you from the bottom of my heart for bringing my son home to me."

"It is good to see the peace in your eyes that your son's return has put there," Brave Wolf said, holding her close as his people clamored around the meat-laden travois. He watched his mother being taken back to her lodge, then held Mary Beth away from him.

"Tonight we will have a great celebration," he said. "We will celebrate the reuniting of you and your son, and the good hunt."

He saw a sudden mischievous glint in Mary

Beth's eyes, then noticed how her hands slid down and rested across her belly.

"My darling, we have even more to celebrate than that," she said, her eyes dancing. "My adorable chieftain husband, I . . . am . . . with child."

His eyes brightened and widened. "You are pregnant?" he gasped, then laughed and lifted her into his arms. He swung her around playfully as he shouted out the news for everyone else to hear.

Mary Beth giggled and found this moment to be oh, so very, very delicious!

Chapter Thirty-three

> I am certain of nothing but of the
> holiness of the Heart's affections,
> of the truth of Imagination—what the
> imagination seizes as Beauty must be
> truth, whether it existed before, or not.
> —Keats

The skeleton trees were laced with the white of a recent snowfall. Two years had passed. Now the parents of two sons, Mary Beth and Brave Wolf were content if no more children were born to them.

Things had changed in their lives.

They had moved onto the reservation where so many were now forced to live, but they still had good enough land for gardens and were able to hunt.

Mary Beth was so glad Brave Wolf had seen that his family's tepee was large enough for all of them to be comfortable. She would never forget the day the conical lodge was finished. It was so tall . . . so round . . . so beautiful.

Just after the lodge was up, she watched in awe as Brave Wolf burned sagebrush and weeds inside the tepee, and as the smoke appeared through the hides, he had told her this process would keep out the rain. Only then did he open the vent at the top of the tepee for the smoke to escape.

Inside were spread robes for his family's comfort, and he had made four backrests of willows strung with sinew and covered with buffalo hides.

Since their move onto the reservation, Mary Beth had another good female friend besides Dancing Butterfly; and Brave Wolf had a new friend too . . . Black Feather and his wife. He and his people were assigned to the same reservation.

Now David was fortunate enough to have two sets of parents to dote over him, and Mary Beth didn't mind sharing him. She saw David as fortunate to have so many who loved him.

It was still dark-face time, the period just before dawn began to color the eastern horizon. Old Woman Moon was lowering in the star-scattered sky, the sun soon to replace her.

Mary Beth lay in Brave Wolf's arms, snuggling close. He had been up only long enough to place wood on the coals in the firepit. The flames were just catching hold, sending warmth behind a blanket-curtain, where David slept in complete privacy, and onto a small bed of pelts, where Mary Beth and Brave Wolf's other small son slept soundly and sweetly.

Mary Beth and Brave Wolf's bed was enclosed by a sort of curtain made of the skins of elk. It completely encompassed them, giving them the privacy they needed when they wanted to make love.

"Today will be fun for all the children," Mary Beth said. "With the snowfall come games and sledding."

"I have just finished making a new sled for David," Brave Wolf said.

"It's so interesting how you made the sled from buffalo ribs fastened together with rawhide," Mary Beth murmured. "I'm sure David and his friends will enjoy it so much."

"As will they enjoy the many snowball fights that the children will start," Brave Wolf said.

"And I shall again make angels in the snow for you," Mary Beth said, laughing softly.

"We have time for a different sort of fun before the children awaken, my Sunshine," Brave Wolf said, sliding his hand beneath the pelt that covered him and Mary Beth. He ran his hand over her soft curves. "We have time to make love before the children awaken."

She turned to him and molded her body against his, then he held her gently at the waist as he slid her beneath him.

"My love, before you came into my life with your sunshine, laughter, and heart-melting gazes, my lodge was a place of emptiness," Brave Wolf said, his eyes gazing into hers. "There was no heartbeat next to me. There was no hand to reach out for me in the middle of the night. There was no wondrous, sweet press of a woman's body to take me into the deep of sleep."

He smiled. "But now?" he said. "I have all those things that I had only dreamed about before you came into my heart and life. You are my *everything*."

"I was so alone . . . so afraid, until you came along and swept me away from my fears and loneliness," Mary Beth murmured. She placed a gentle hand on his cheek. "My husband, you gave me back my life, my reason for being. *You*. Oh, my darling, you were my knight in shining armor. You rescued me."

"Your knight?" Brave Wolf said, arching an eyebrow. "Shining armor?"

Mary Beth giggled. "When I was a young girl and had idle time on my hands, I read many, many books," she said. "I adored reading about damsels in distress and knights who rescued them. These knights wore armor to protect their muscled bodies, somewhat like the shield that hangs from the lodge pole, which is carried into battle to protect you."

"Books," Brave Wolf said, nodding. "When I was in Washington in council with the Great White Father, there were many talking leaves on shelves in his huge council house. When he saw my interest in them, he took a book from the shelf and showed it to me. He read passages from it to me.

It was a story about another president. His name was strange, like Lincoln."

"Yes, President Lincoln," Mary Beth said. "He was a wonderful president."

She didn't tell him that President Lincoln had been assassinated. Such a topic of conversation seemed misplaced at a time when they were speaking of pleasant things.

"Darling Brave Wolf, your body against mine speaks of other things besides knights, damsels, and presidents," Mary Beth said softly. "It speaks of needs . . . of desire."

He laughed throatily, then pressed his lips against hers, and as the stars winked down at them through the smoke hole above, they made love and whispered sweet words against each other's lips.

"*Mihigna,* husband, I could never be as content as I am now," Mary Beth whispered against his.

"*Mitawin,* my woman, you and our children are my contentment," he whispered back as they rocked, clung, and soared off together into the clouds of total bliss.

For them, life was *wasteste,* good, very good!

Author's Note

Dear Reader:

I hope you enjoyed reading *Savage Hero.* The next book in my Savage Indian Series, which I am writing exclusively for Leisure Books, is *Savage Trust,* about my own people . . . the Cheyenne Indians. The book is filled with much passion, intrigue, and adventure.

Those of you who are collecting my Indian romance novels and want to hear more about the series and my entire backlist of books, can send for my latest newsletter, bookmark, autographed photograph, and fan club information by writing to: Cassie Edwards
6709 North Country Club Road
Mattoon, Illinois 61938

For an assured response, please include a stamped, self-addressed, legal-size envelope with your letter.

You can visit my website at: www.cassieedwards.com.

Thank you for your support of my Indian series. I love researching and writing about our country's beloved Native Americans, our country's first people.

Always,
CASSIE EDWARDS

Wounded and in desperate need of help, David Walker has survived the treacherous journey to reach the blue-eyed, blond-haired girl of his memories. And in Hannah's arms he discovers Heaven. But torn between the white man's world and his Indian heritage, David wonders if he's been saved or damned.

The man who calls himself Spirit Walker bears little resemblance to the boy who comforted Hannah during her darkest hours at the orphanage. There is nothing safe about the powerful half-breed who needs her assistance. Still, the schoolteacher will risk everything to save him, for their love is strong enough to overcome any challenge.